"That's it." Ron picked up the Pug on his return and looked him squarely in the eyes. "No more stealing, understand?"

For a moment black ears drooped, tail unknotted, and the broad mouth sagged. For a moment one could almost believe he was truly sorry. Almost.

The moment Ron replaced the canine culprit on the deck, his entire body flashed back to perky exuberance. He turned on his partner in crime, who'd been dozing in the sun, and began racing around her, barking and daring her to play.

At first she ignored him, but when he dove in to pull her tail, she leaped to her feet and took off after him. Tucking his tail between his legs—he'd learned Barbie-Q could often get close enough to seize him by it when it curled over his back—he dashed away. As they made circuit after circuit of the cottage, barking and yelping, Ron asked, "When did Nancy say she'd be back?"

Praise for Gail MacMillan

"Be prepared to be hooked on the first word of the first page and go on to the next with anticipation. Her stories will live in your heart long after the last page is read."
~*Rebecca Melvin, Publisher, Double Edge Press*
~*~

"Gail MacMillan's stories delight the senses and brighten the dark days of winter like a candle glowing on a windowsill. Best enjoyed while curled up in your favorite chair...with some hot cocoa and a faithful canine companion."
~*Sue Owens Wright, author, newspaper columnist, and two-time Maxwell Medal recipient*
~*~

"Gail MacMillan's stories place you in a well-worn comforting chair. She writes of deep-rooted rural customs and traditions, of her love of dogs and horses. She shows glimpses of truth in revelatory detail."
~*Heather White, Editor, Saltscapes Magazine*

To All the Dogs I've Loved Before

Learning About Life Through Love

by

Gail MacMillan

To All the Dogs I've Loved Before: Learning About Life Through Love

COPYRIGHT © 2015 by Gail MacMillan

All rights reserved. No part of this book may be used or reproduced in any manner whatsoever without written permission of the author or The Wild Rose Press, Inc. except in the case of brief quotations embodied in critical articles or reviews.
Contact Information: info@thewildrosepress.com

Cover Art by *RJ Morris*

The Wild Rose Press, Inc.
PO Box 708
Adams Basin, NY 14410-0708
Visit us at www.thewildrosepress.com

Publishing History
First Wildflowers Edition, 2015
Print ISBN 978-1-5092-0212-6
Digital ISBN 978-1-5092-0213-3

Published in the United States of America

Dedication

Over the years, together with my husband Ron, I've been caregiver to over a dozen dogs. Every one of them has been unique and has left indelible paw prints on my heart. Moreover, every one of them has left me wiser in the ways of life and love.

The lessons I've learned from my dogs are invaluable, gems of understanding, perseverance, and acceptance I may never have discovered if I hadn't shared my life with them. This is my tribute to all the dogs I've loved before.

The Beginning

When I was eighteen months old, my father snapped a picture of me leaning against a chair in my grandparents' parlor. My beloved stuffed dog Fluffy sat comfortably ensconced between its arms. That old photo speaks volumes about my love and respect for Fluffy and all the real dogs that would come after him.

Some of my earliest memories include my mother, Fluffy, and me curled up in that chair in my grandmother's parlor (my parents and I lived with my maternal grandparents until I was six), my mother reading animal stories by author Thornton W. Burgess to her enthralled daughter. A dedicated amateur actress, my mother read with such passion and emphasis I became forever enamored with words. She never failed to honor my pleas for "just one more chapter, please, please, please, just one more chapter."

At night when I crawled into bed, Fluffy clutched beneath my arm, my father would take over. A gifted storyteller in the oral tradition, he would lull me to sleep with tales of his boyhood on the farm, of his adventures with the people and animals that lived there. All ended well, either happily or at least with a satisfying conclusion. All but one.

I'd been begging for a dog story, but he'd been reluctant to indulge me. Finally, one evening, after my most persistent begging, he drew a deep breath and told me about a dog he'd had as a boy, a husky named Jack. He and Jack shared many adventures around the farm, including the day Jack burrowed under the chicken coop to dispatch a skunk. Clutching Fluffy, I giggled over the tale. Poor, stinky Jack.

My father paused and looked away.

"Go on, what happened next?" I couldn't wait for more of Dad and Jack's adventures.

"Time for sleep." He drew the blankets over me.

"Daddy…?"

"Jack got old and died," he said. His voice sounded funny, sort of broken. He bent and kissed me on the forehead. "Real dogs do that. Good night, Fluffy." He patted my inanimate friend and went out of the room.

Although Jack's story left me startled and sad, it didn't quell my desire for my father's stories. I continued to beg, "Please, Daddy, tell me another story. A true story."

None were ever again about dogs, but he continued to oblige. While I'm not sure all his tales were the gospel truth, they did have the power to enthrall me. He often finished off our story hour by reciting poetry. A sixth grade graduate, he'd nevertheless attended school long enough to develop a love of poems and had memorized a goodly number of his favorites. Even though I didn't grasp the nuances of many, I loved the cadence of the words, the music in their combinations. Before I entered the first grade, I knew by heart "Grey's Elegy in a Country Churchyard," "The Skater and the Wolves," and a number of other lengthy poems.

Time passed. Fluffy, like my early beloved books, eventually became worn to a rag by days of constant companionship with me. Then I discovered real dogs, our neighbors' dogs.

In the days before leash laws, I could almost always be assured of finding some dog to play with me if I stood at the end of our driveway long enough. That was as far as my parents allowed their preschooler to venture. Friendly creatures looking for companionship, they were easily seduced into our yard and, for a few minutes, I had all the joy their company could provide.

But this wasn't enough. I needed a dog that would be a regular visitor, a dog I could depend upon to come to the end of the drive each morning, a dog who'd let me hug and kiss and cuddle him to my heart's content.

I found him in Duke. An English bulldog, he belonged to a restaurant owner. His caregiver's business was situated several blocks from my grandparents' house in the small town where I lived with my mother and father.

I must admit, I added to Duke's willingness to visit by secreting bits of breakfast bacon and toast in my pockets. I loved the way he gobbled up the morsels, I loved the slurping noises he made as he fumbled into my hand, I even loved the slobber he left behind. But most of all, I loved the way his big, squishy face felt when I put my arms around his neck to plant kisses on it. Whoever said a child could die of dog germs was way off base.

Influenced by my parents' pleasure in stories, I developed tales of my own. Duke and I had wonderful fictional adventures. We'd find our way through vast forests, across grassy fields full of daisies, into dark caves, and make wonderful discoveries. Just what those wonderful discoveries were, I can't recall. Perhaps they were never all that clear even back then.

For two years Duke and I enjoyed a wonderful relationship. While there are many people and events from those years I've forgotten, Duke and his visits aren't among them. Summer, winter, spring, and fall, Duke arrived at our gate, and each time he found me waiting.

I began to worry about Duke's visits when I turned six in May of 1950 and knew I'd be entering school in the fall. His appearances at the end of the driveway became more precious to me. What would I do without them?

In July a big yellow truck arrived in our town. On each side were painted images of two giant green peanuts in the guise of nattily dressed men-about-town complete with top hats, monocles, and walking sticks. Bags of peanuts, peanut coloring books, and peanut men salt and pepper shakers were distributed to the crowd that gathered around the vehicle when it stopped at my father's gas station across the road from Duke's family's restaurant home.

I didn't get to attend. My mother had a dress rehearsal that afternoon. I always went with her. My father brought home a set of the peanut men salt and pepper shakers and set them on the windowsill above the sink. We'd recently moved into our new home next door to my grandparents. In the sparsely furnished house, even those silly condiment holders were welcomed as decorations.

The next morning I was in place at the end of the drive waiting for Duke. I waited and waited and waited. Finally, dejectedly, I went back inside the house and up to my room.

At noon I heard my father arrive for lunch. His

hushed tones from the kitchen below told me something was wrong. Something he didn't want me to hear. Curiosity pricked, I tiptoed to the top of the stairs and listened.

"I just don't know how to tell her," he was saying, his voice soft and shaky. "She loved him so much."

"But you have to." My mother's equally emotional response came back. "If she hears it from someone else…"

"I know, I know. It wouldn't have happened if it hadn't been such a hot day, if they hadn't treated him to those peanuts, if he hadn't tried to follow the truck out onto the highway…"

For the first time in my life, I believe I felt my heart truly plummet. Duke. They were talking about Duke. He'd followed the peanut truck; he'd been hurt!

I bolted down the stairs. As I yanked open the front door, my father's hand covered mine.

"Where are you going, Gail?" he asked.

"To the vet's! I know Duke's been hurt! I have to go to him!" I tried to wrench free, but my father's hand, stained with grease and oil from his service station, held me firm.

"He's not at the vet." I looked up and saw his blue eyes swimming with tears. "Gail, Duke died of heat exhaustion on the highway."

I stared up at him, dumbfounded. My six-year-old brain had never yet encountered death this close and personal. I staggered, and my father caught me up and carried me into the living room, where he put me on the couch. My mother sat down beside me and slipped an arm around my shoulders. Absolute silence filled our new home.

"No, no, no!" Recovering sufficiently to jump to my feet, I yelled at my parents as I'd never done before. "It's not true! Dukey isn't dead! He can't be dead! He's my friend, my very best friend!" Blinded by tears, I fled my parents' attempts at comfort and stumbled up to my room, the pain in my chest the most excruciating I'd ever experienced.

With every ounce of strength in me, I slammed the door shut and fell on the bed sobbing.

"Dukey, Dukey, oh, my Dukey!"

I'd never again feel his soft, slobbering muzzle in my hand as he gobbled up toast crusts and bacon bits; I'd never again throw my arms around his big, thick neck; I'd never again plant kisses on his snuffling face.

My wise parents let me have my grief. They didn't try to diminish it with promises of a puppy or even another Fluffy. And they never questioned what had happened when they found the Mr. Peanut salt and pepper shakers smashed to bits on the back door step.

Life is full of difficult lessons, and this was my first horribly painful one. Sometimes we lose loved ones and we have to learn to go on without them. In later years I'd be able to look back and recall those times with Duke as memories so warm and beautiful they were almost worth the pain of his passing. Almost.

The Ultimate Betrayal

A pain-filled summer without Duke passed. In September I entered Grade One. In the turmoil and excitement of those life-changing days, the heart-hurting pain of loss became mixed with delightful new experiences. School meant books and learning to print and read. Finally, gloriously, I would be free to enjoy books on my own. As many books as I chose. No more begging to be read to. No more making up stories only in my head. Now I could put them to paper. These revelations eased the sting of Duke's passing somewhat, but not—no, never—entirely.

One day, during the third or fourth week of school, an event occurred that would very nearly forever change my love of dogs.

I was walking home from school when a black cocker spaniel darted out of a yard near the corner of our street. I stopped and turned to him. And saw a side of dogs I'd never experienced. Growling and baring his teeth, he began to circle me.

Startled but deciding this dog simply didn't want to become my friend, I once more started for home. The moment my back was turned, he seized my ankle.

I screamed and kicked, and he released me. Shrieking, I ran toward home, the black curly ball in hot pursuit. Just before I reached our drive, he gave up and set off at a gallop back up the street.

Bursting into the house, so incoherent that for a few moments my mother couldn't understand what had caused my bloody ankle, I fell into her arms and sobbed out my terror and disillusionment.

Later, with my wounds cleaned and bandaged, I told her the story.

"He bit me, Mommy. He grabbed me, and it hurt, hurt, hurt." By then my words reflected more my sense of betrayal than pain or fear. One of the creatures I loved most in the world had attacked me, had caused me pain for no reason. "I'll never, never trust another dog as long as I live."

"Never is a long time, sweetie." My mother stroked my braids. "And that was only one dog. You can't judge them all by one that made a mistake."

I presume my mother must have called the spaniel's owners, because from that day on, the dog was tied in their backyard whenever I passed on my way to or from school. It didn't prevent a dark fear from rising in my chest every time I saw the animal someone told my mother was named Robin. What if the rope broke? What if he came after me again? I dreaded passing that house as if it were haunted by the vilest of ghosts.

I must have had nightmares about the incident, because I recall my mother gently waking me to tell me it was all right, that Robin was safely tied up at his house.

The trauma worsened. I refused to visit my grandfather on his farm because he had a St. Bernard/Collie cross named Buster, whom I'd formerly loved and couldn't wait to see each Sunday afternoon.

Finally my fear became so debilitating my mother

had to walk with me past the dreaded corner house each morning and meet me before I came to it each afternoon. My days in school were haunted by a black horror named Robin. I couldn't concentrate. My teacher contacted my mother.

"Gail, you have to get over this fear," she said the following afternoon as we were walking home from school together. "You remember my friend Emma, who lives two houses beyond Robin's?"

I nodded, dread rising in my heart. Where was this conversation going?

"She has a lovely Black Lab named Chips." I tightened my grip on her hand. "She's invited us to stop by this afternoon and meet him."

"No, no, Mommy, please no!" I stopped and stared up at her, begging with all my heart and soul. "I hate dogs. They're bad. They want to hurt me!"

"Not Chips." My mother smiled gently down at me. "I promise. Have I ever broken a promise to you?"

"No…"

"Then trust me now. You know I'd never take my darling girl anywhere she might be hurt, don't you?"

I hesitated. Finally I nodded.

"Good. Let's go. Emma said something about baking sugar cookies this afternoon."

Moments later we stood on Emma's front step. My already pounding heart leaped at the sound as my mother rang the bell. Footsteps approached, the door opened, and there stood Emma, a big black dog slowly wagging his tail by her side.

"Opal, Gail, how lovely. Come in, come in. I'm just taking the last batch of cookies from the oven. Chips, sit."

Obediently the big dog dropped to his haunches and sat watching us, tongue lolling out of his mouth in what probably was a canine grin but which I only saw as fang baring.

"Hello, Chips." My mother addressed the dog. To my surprise he raised his right front paw. As my mother laughingly accepted the greeting, my breath caught in my throat. He was going to bite her. I longed to lunge forward to save her, but I was frozen by fear. He didn't, and a moment later, when we headed down the hall, Chips followed at a respectful distance, tail still moving slowly back and forth.

Once in the kitchen and seated at the table with milk and cookies while my mother and her friend drank tea and chatted, I glanced at Chips. He'd lain down against the back door. Our gazes met. The speed of his tail beat upped, and the opening that was his mouth widened. Could it be he was smiling…like Duke used to smile? But Duke's mouth was wider, and his teeth were all crooked and funny-looking. This dog had big, straight, white fangs. But he did appear to be friendly. Hmmm, maybe he wasn't such a bad dog after all. Maybe…

I slid off the chair and stood staring at him. His tail wagged just a notch faster but not too fast. Not like he was getting excited or ready to rush at me. I took a step closer. He stayed lying by the door, watching me, and now I was close enough to look into his big, chocolate-colored eyes. There was nothing bad and frightening there. I took another step and held out my hand. Chips hesitated before carefully stretching forward to sniff. When I managed to hold fast, he licked it.

Terror ebbed away. I sat down beside him on the

floor and offered him the last of the cookie I'd held clutched in my hand. He took it with such a measure of gentleness that I've never forgotten the touch of his soft, wet muzzle on my fingers.

Only then did I realize that at the table Emma and my mother had stopped talking and were watching us.

"Chips is a good dog, Mommy." I stroked the soft fur. "A really good dog."

Thus ended my fear of dogs.

After that day, it was Chips that waited for me three houses beyond Robin's, Chips that walked me past that fearful place, Chips that saw me safely home. And one day when Robin slipped her tether and charged out of the yard as I was passing, it was Chips that faced the smaller dog down and sent it scuttling back into its yard.

I learned a lot about dogs from Chips and Robin. I learned that all dogs are not the same, that while most are kind and loving and loyal, others are not, and I had to be circumspect in my choice of canine friends. I also learned that trust, although once broken is difficult to restore, with kindness and love it can be repaired, even if it would forever bear the caveats of wisdom and experience.

Years later, I'd realize it wasn't the fault of dogs that they became aggressive but that it was due to mishandling by their owners. That would be years in the future. For the time being, Chips and Robin had taught me all I needed to know.

For several years Chips continued to escort me safely home. I didn't notice his muzzle graying, his steps slowing. One day Chips wasn't waiting for me. A twelve-year-old by then, I went up the front steps of

Emma's house and rang the bell.

"Hello, Gail." Emma answered, her eyes red and watery. "Come in, please. I have something I have to tell you."

Christmas of the China Dog

The autumn following Chips' death passed without my acquiring another serious canine friend. My grandfather's old Buster, with whom I'd reconciled, also died. The advent of the Yuletide season found me alone with my dog books and pictures and magazines and dreams. Alone, this is, except for dozens of stories written in Hilroy scribblers hidden in a box under my bed.

Christmases have a way of becoming monikered, I discovered that year. For example, I recall The Christmas Aunt Molly Visited and The Christmas Janet Got Engaged. For me, a stellar one would be the December 25th I named The Christmas of the China Dog.

Formerly when I'd asked, begged, and pleaded for a dog of my own, my parents simply replied that I was too young for the responsibility. But that year, age twelve, I'd reached the age of babysitting maturity. Surely someone who could be trusted alone with young children could be judged capable of caring for one small, chewing, piddling puppy.

I had good reason to hope that December. All the signs were there. My parents, being especially secretive, definitely were conspiring something big and exciting for me.

Oh, sure, there was only one small, mysterious box

for me under the tree (the rest with my name on them readily identifiable as books and clothing) but that, I deduced in my fanciful mind, contained a collar and leash. On Christmas morning my Collie puppy would be brought into the living room, a big red bow around his neck. I'd already named him Prince. He and I would never again be separated…except for the demands of church and school. In fact, I'd already written a story about our adventures together.

I didn't think I would survive the final seven days prior to Christmas. Plans for my dog overwhelmed my every waking minute. Dreams of my precious pooch replaced the legendary sugarplums (whatever they were) when it came to things dancing through my head.

I tingled, I hugged myself, I burst into song at odd—and often, for those around me, inappropriate—moments. Although I occasionally caught my parents casting puzzled glances at me, then between themselves, they appeared too absorbed in their own secret exuberance to be overly concerned.

Sometimes, when I felt no one was looking, I'd steal into the living room, take the small box from beneath the tree, and stroke it gently, a smile tugging up the corners of my mouth.

The big day arrived. My father, distributing the presents as usual, kept glancing over at my mother, a bemused but constant smile tipping his lips. In my memory, they'd always had the ability to communicate without words. Now I was certain I knew what they were both anticipating.

Finally all the gifts had been distributed, unwrapped, exclaimed over, and laid aside…all except the small box. The best for last, I thought, and wondered where they'd kept the puppy hidden. At our neighbors'? That had to be it. Bob and Hilda loved dogs. Reassured, I tried to will myself to stay calm and relax.

After what seemed like hours, my father picked up the little box. I held my breath.

"Gail," he said, looking over at his wife, his expression mirroring all the happiness I was feeling in my soul. "Your mother and I have something to tell you."

Yes, yes, oh, yes, please get on with it! My heart hammered. I was barely able to breathe.

"You're going to have a baby brother or sister this spring."

Astounded, I gaped at them. A bucket of ice water hitting me in the face couldn't have come as more of a shock. What was my father saying? I'd been an only child all my life. Now suddenly…

But then my father was handing me the little box.

"We know how much you love dogs…" he continued softly.

Apparently he and my mother had feared a negative response to their announcement and so had been saving the puppy presentation until afterwards. I revived sufficiently to tear off the wrappings, my prospective sibling momentarily unimportant. They could have their baby; I'd have my dog.

I pawed through the tissue paper inside the box— Where was that collar and leash?—and found at the bottom a gold-and-white china dog.

My heart plummeted. I'm sure an x-ray taken at that moment would have shown it dropping floorward at the speed of light.

I held the cold bit of glass in my hands and looked up at my parents. Utter disappointment must have laid a pall over my expression.

"I thought…" I let the dog fall back into its tissue-paper bed. Overwhelmed by grief, I jumped to my feet and fled to my room.

My father found me there a half hour later. He was carrying the china dog.

"I wanted a real dog!" I was sobbing as I had for the past thirty minutes. "Nothing else! No baby, no china dog! Just a real, live dog!"

"Gail, real dogs get old and die." My father's voice was soft, and I remembered him telling me about the husky named Jack he'd had as a boy and the terrible pain he'd suffered when the old dog died. "I don't want you to get hurt. My father recited a bit of a poem to me just before I got Jack. I wish I'd paid attention. It went something like this, 'Brothers and sisters, I tell you, beware; never give your heart to a dog to tear.' He was right."

"Oh, but Daddy, think of all the love and happiness in between!"

With a weary sigh, he stood, took out his wallet, and handed me a crisp twenty-dollar bill. A child of the Great Depression, he still believed money could heal a lot of ills.

"Buy whatever you want," he said resignedly, handing it to me.

With a pang of guilt I realized I'd let my distress color what for him and my mother must have been a glorious time. They'd wanted another child for over a decade and now, finally, they would have one. I took the money, knowing to refuse it would only wound him further.

After he'd left my room, I sat down amid stacks of dog books, magazines, and pictures and fingered the money absently. My father's words echoed back to me: "Buy whatever you want…"

Suddenly, as it had so often done and would continue to do throughout my life, inspiration struck. The next morning, Boxing Day, I donned warm clothes and headed up the street to our town's only veterinarian's house.

"Dad, will you drive me to Douglastown tomorrow?" I asked him over supper that evening. Filled with a violent mix of trepidation and anticipation, I fancied my words trembled.

"Why?" he asked looking up from his turkey pot pie. "Do you have a friend you want to visit?"

"Yes, well…no…well, sort of. But not just visit. I want to bring him back here…to live."

Both my parents stopped eating and stared me.

"Live?" my mother, not easily daunted, this time obviously was.

"Yes." I drew a deep breath and summoned all my courage. "He's a puppy…half German Shepherd and half Collie…with something wrong with his tail. I bought him yesterday."

Two forks clattered onto matching Christmas plates. I have never to this day been stared at again in such an astounded fashion.

"You what?" My father was the first to find words.

"You said I could buy anything I wanted with that twenty dollars." I felt alternately hot and cold, shaky and solid, but I'd come too far to turn back now. "So I went to see Dr. Jarvis. I told him I wanted to buy a

Collie pup, but he said a purebred would cost more than twenty dollars. He thought for a while, and then he said he knew a lady in Douglastown who had one puppy left for sale. It was a German Shepherd/Collie mix. She might let me have him for twenty dollars because he'd been born with a crooked tail. So he called her, and she said yes, and I told her I'd pick him up tomorrow."

At that point I ran out of breath and words simultaneously. The tightness in my chest and throat had overwhelmed me. I could only glance from my mother to my father and then down at my plate. I couldn't bear to let them see my expression if they vetoed my purchase.

For the longest hiatus in the history of my twelve years, silence held our kitchen in its grip. Cars swished by on the street outside, the refrigerator started, and the furnace kicked in. I felt as if I would surely die if they didn't speak soon.

"You did say she could buy whatever she wanted," my mother said finally. "And we are having the baby. She deserves something special of her own, too. And you did say…"

My heartbeat began to upgrade from a weak flutter to a steady drumbeat.

"Yes, yes, I know what I said." My father went to the stove to refill his teacup. He poured slowly while my pulse pounded in my ears. *Please, please, please.* My thoughts were a chant.

When he finally turned back toward the table, he paused, then sighed and let a cautious smile seep over his face.

"Okay," he said.

All but upsetting his tea, I leaped up and rushed to

hug him to within inches of strangulation.

"Thank you, thank you, thank you!" I cried, my joy so intense I didn't think I could bear it. "I promise I'll take care of him. You'll never have to do a thing…after you take me to Douglastown, that is."

The next morning we headed out to get my very own dog.

When I saw Prince (as I'd already named him), I became a lifelong believer in love at first sight. It didn't matter that he was the leftover of the litter because of his crooked tail. It didn't matter that he was almost one hundred percent German Shepherd except for his golden brown color. It only mattered that he was mine and I was his and we'd be friends as long as both of us lived. As a twelve-year-old hugging her first very-own puppy, I believed I was as close to nirvana as I'd ever be on this earth. In later years, reading Agatha Christie's autobiography, I fully understood her reaction on receiving her first dog. Her feelings were so intense she had to run away and hide.

That spring my brother was born. Our family was complete and happy.

But it was not to last. Six months later my mother was diagnosed with cancer. Eighteen months later she died.

I overheard people commenting on how brave I was as I went about caring for my little brother and helping my aunt move into our home to become our housekeeper. My father, overwhelmed by grief, barely seemed to notice. He'd been in his late thirties when he'd married. I think he'd been afraid to give his heart to anyone. His mother had died young, leaving his father a lifelong grieving widower. And then, of course, there'd been Jack.

But then he'd met my mother, and love must have overcome his fear of loss. The bond they'd formed had been deep and unfailing…until now. Immersed in sorrow, he left my brother in my aunt's care and me largely on my own.

During the day I appeared stoic, handling my grief, I believed, well and with dignity. But at night, alone in my room with Prince, I vented my sorrow. I'd put my arms around his neck and sob into his soft, warm coat as I clung to his broad, solid shoulders. The leftover puppy with the crooked tail never let me down. He'd snuggle close and let me release my pain for as long as I needed him by my side.

In the months and years that followed, Prince continued to be there for me. He shared the joys and pain of numerous teenage romances, long walks with a girl and later a young woman with a penchant for thoughtful solitude, and the words read aloud from the pages of multiple Hilroy scribblers kept hidden under the bed of his aspiring-writer friend.

And when my father slowly began to surface from the pain of my mother's passing, Prince unobtrusively moved in to companion him as well. Dad owned a service station downtown, and often, while I was in school, Prince would accompany him to work.

But I eventually would fail Prince. In those days, dogs went to the vet only when sick or injured. Injections for disease were just beginning to become a part of canine care. In ignorance of these life-saving preventatives, we didn't have Prince immunized against distemper. He fell victim to it, and by the time we recognized the seriousness of his illness and got him to the vet, it was too late. Two weeks before Christmas a few short years after my mother's death, he left us to join her.

That evening I found my father sitting alone in the kitchen staring down at the old dog's collar he held clutched in his hands.

"You were right, Dad," I said, my words choked with tears and bitterness. "Real dogs just die and break your heart. I should have been content with the china one."

He looked up at me, turning the worn old collar over in his hands. There were tears in his eyes.

"No, you were right," he said softly. "You understood that all the love and joy that comes before is worth it." I knew he was speaking of more than Prince.

I also knew that never, never again would I fail to get a dog immunized. Never again would I fail in my care of a best friend. Another lesson painfully learned.

Love and Marriage

My father's fear of uninhibited commitment to love would once again darken my world when, at eighteen, I met and fell in love with Ron MacMillan. A devil-may-care university student four years my senior, Ron was a free-wheeling type of young man who seemed totally unconcerned about anything but enjoying life in the moment.

My father, a child of the Great Depression, serious and with the Calvinist soul of a true Scot, was constantly looking ahead, planning for a future that would never again see him living under the conditions his early years had afforded. "God helps those who help themselves," he'd say as he worked hard at his service station. Another of his favorite sayings was "God forgive me if I whine, I have two feet, the world is mine."

The two men in my life couldn't have been further apart philosophically than if they'd been from different planets.

On the day I told my father I was going to marry Ron, now a teacher at the small rural high school in Tabusintac, about forty miles from our home, he turned away from me without a word.

"Well?" I pressed, fearing his response yet having to hear it.

"You're a little girl. He's a man who's lived more

than you can imagine." He gripped the edge of our kitchen sink in both of his big, work-hardened hands.

And that was it. His disapproval expressed in two sentences.

"I love him, Daddy!" I flung the fact at his back and stormed out of the kitchen.

The next Saturday night I loaded my most treasured possessions into my small car and drove off clandestinely to marry the man I loved. As I drove across the bridge spanning the mighty Miramichi, the words of Crystal Gayle's then hit song echoed in my mind, "Chasing my dreams down River Road."

Indeed, that was exactly what I was doing.

A Dog in Our Lives

Ron MacMillan, the man I married that cold February night and would forever love, was, like me, an avid dog fancier. We'd hoped to get a dog shortly after we were married. Finances didn't stretch to the purchase of the purebred Collie I still fancied. My pregnancy added expenses to our single-income family, so the idea of having a dog once again became a dream.

Then a crisis struck. Ron rushed me to the hospital one rainy night with severe pains in my side. After tests and evaluations, we were told an emergency appendectomy would have to be performed. The baby most likely wouldn't survive.

The days that followed were touch and go. I was rushed back to surgery several times, with a miscarriage believed imminent. Each time, baby and I survived, but those days took their toll on both Ron and me.

Finally I was allowed out of bed and managed to shuffle along the hospital corridors, feeling as limp as overcooked spaghetti but with our baby still safe and well. The ordeal had left me emotionally fragile. I wanted to go home to our little house in Tabusintac, to bury my head in the blankets, and sleep for days and days and days. Sometimes I fancied my distress was a punishment for having defied my father and marrying Ron. But I couldn't be sorry or contrite. I loved Ron too much to label what I'd done as "wrong."

During my illness and convalescence, my father never once visited. Obviously true forgiveness was still a distance away.

****

"Mrs. MacMillan, your husband wants you to come to the window." The nun who was head nurse on the floor stood beaming at me one sun-bright afternoon. "He has a surprise for you."

Surprise? What surprise? Mustering what little interest and energy I had left, I struggled from the bed, thrust my feet into my slippers, wrapped my robe around me, and shuffled to the window.

Standing two stories below in the parking lot with my husband was the most beautiful white dog I'd ever seen. She was big, she was fluffy, and her tail was wagging slowly as Ron tried to convince her to look up at me.

"He said you wanted a dog." The nun standing by my side smiled broadly. "Would you like to pet her?" she whispered, leaning close to my ear.

"Yes, oh, yes!" My lethargy lifting, I turned to the Sister. "Please! But how?"

"Wait here." She put a finger to her lips and swirled away.

Five minutes later she returned with a wheelchair.

"Get in," she hissed. "If anyone asks, we're on our way to x-ray."

Bemused, I obeyed and shortly found myself being whipped out of the room, down the corridor, and into an elevator, with all the speed of an emergency. No one stopped to question Sister Jean-Marie. Her stern countenance brooked no comment.

Within five minutes we were in a small office near

the back door of the hospital.

"Wait here." With a swish of black cloth she was gone.

Seconds later the door opened, and she escorted Ron and the white dog inside. Beaming, the nun left the room, easing the door shut behind her. I guessed she was going to act as lookout while we enjoyed our time together.

"I know she's not the Collie you wanted," Ron said, scrunching down beside the wheelchair as the dog nuzzled my hand. "But I heard about this man who was terminally ill and looking for a good home for his Samoyed husky, and I thought…"

"Yes, oh, yes!" I leaned forward to hug this gorgeous white girl. "She's absolutely perfect. Thank you, thank you, thank you." I caught Ron by the collar of his jacket and drew him close to plant a kiss on his cheek. "Now I have to get out of this place and go home where I can enjoy her and care for her and…"

"First you have to get well." Ron stood and looked down at me with that stern, do-as-teacher-says look he'd perfected. "Now Star—that's her name—and I have to go. Sister Jean-Marie is taking a big chance letting us in here." He kissed my cheek. "See you soon."

"Goodbye, Star." I gave the dog a final hug. "I'll be home soon to take care of you."

After they'd gone, Sister Jean-Marie returned.

"He must love you very much." She smiled gently.

"I believe he does," I replied as she took the handles of the wheelchair and headed back to my room.

The words of fifteenth-century educator Theodorus Gaza sprang into my mind. "The gift I am sending you is called a dog and is, in fact, the most precious and most valuable possession of mankind."

Once again I was ignoring my father's advice and giving my heart to another dog to tear, but I wasn't about to let that deter me. This beautiful white dog had had the power to revive my spirit. Dogs have that ability, I'd learned and would continue to learn from all the dogs that would enter our lives over the years.

Four months later we experienced the birth of a perfect baby girl. She had her father's wonderful blue eyes and ability to make me fall hopelessly in love at first sight.

My father, who up until that time had absented himself from my life, visited and was instantly captivated by the little girl.

We were a family again.

A Case of Fowl Play

The following spring I found a Rhode Island Red hen on our back doorstep, in perfect condition except that it was dead, its neck broken. For a few moments I was puzzled. I glanced around for a possible source of the corpse and saw Star lying on the lawn a few feet away. She wagged her tail, tongue lolling happily over snow-white fangs.

No! It couldn't possibly be. Not that beautifully gentle dog, the dog who loved our baby daughter Joan as if she were her own offspring, the dog that wouldn't kill the mouse I'd cornered in the kitchen one morning.

Later we'd learn that Star, like many huskies, had a passion for poultry. The trait, we were later informed, was inherent in the breed. On this first occasion, she'd apparently left our yard, snatched one of our neighbor's chickens, killed it, and brought it home.

I knew how such dogs were regarded in a farming community like Tabusintac. I knew their fate if they were caught in the act. Terrified that someone would discover Star's horrible predilection, I ran to the barn, picked up a shovel, gathered the hen onto it, and hurried into the field. Just beyond the barn, in the soft, rotting sediment that had once been a manure pile, I dug a hole and buried the evidence.

Sick with fear, I showed Star the grave.

"You must never, never, never do that again!" I

warned her. "And this," I pointed to the newly turned earth. "Has to be our secret."

She looked up at me, brown eyes widely innocent, tail wagging slowly. She had no idea what I was saying. My heart and hands shaking, I headed back toward the house.

****

During the next three weeks I buried a dozen hens. As I dug I prayed that no one would see the white marauder entering or leaving their chicken coops. Since Star always brought her victims home while he was at school, I'd been able to keep the truth from Ron.

Unfortunately, Star must have taken pride in her kills and was not above grave-robbing to display her prizes. Late one afternoon Ron entered the kitchen where I was trying to cook supper on the ancient, cantankerous oil stove. He asked a question that made my blood run cold.

"What is that dirty, dead hen doing on the doorstep?" he asked. "It looks as if it's been buried and dug up."

As he spoke, over Ron's shoulder, through the window I saw Star dragging another feathered remains toward the back stoop.

"It's Star." Trapped, I had to confess, my stomach roiling. "She killed a couple of hens and brought them home." I couldn't tell the complete truth. "I buried them behind the barn."

"You did what?" Ron's stricken expression made the full magnitude of what I'd done hit me in a giant epiphany. He was supposed to be one of the three most respected men in our community, the other two being the Mountie and the minister. Now here stood his wife confessing she'd covered up what in a farming community would not be considered a misdemeanor. Words like theft and conspiracy made hot flashes gush over me.

"Please, please." Nevertheless I couldn't help begging. "It won't happen again. I promise. I'll tie her to the porch. I'll make sure she never leaves the yard."

This was an extreme concession. Dogs in rural New Brunswick in the 1960s were never restrained. If they didn't stay on their own property and misbehaved on other people's land, they met a quick end. But I was desperate. I'd never lied to Ron or hidden anything from him…until those fowl murders. I told myself I was justified. I loved Star and owed it to her to protect her even though she was a proven serial killer.

"Well, okay." He loved the big, gentle dog, too. Furthermore, he still didn't know about the other ten hens in unmarked graves behind the barn. "But you can never let her loose unless you're with her and you can keep her in sight at all times."

"I promise." I kissed him, hoping he'd never have to know the full extent of my duplicity, praying that this would be the end of the killings.

The next morning I tied Star to the porch and went about my housework. I felt infinitely better. I didn't condone the brutal killings. Now they'd be at an end.

At ten a.m. I went out to check on Star. And found her gone. Somehow she'd slipped her collar. Desperately I looked up and down the road…no dog.

I couldn't leave the house with Joan sleeping in her crib. Ron had our car at school, so I had no vehicle into which to bundle her and drive in pursuit. My heart riding high in my throat, I returned to the house to wait.

An hour later Star returned. My breath gushed out in a wheeze. No dead bird dangled from her jaws. Indeed, she was panting as if she'd simply had a good run.

"Good girl," I said bringing her into the house. Indoors with me there'd be no way for her to escape, and I'd personally supervise her bathroom breaks in the yard for the rest of the day.

"Everything went okay today?" Ron looked up from his lumpy mashed potatoes that evening. He didn't have to get more specific.

"Fine." I avoided his eyes and sawed at a piece of leathery steak. "Joan had her nap right on schedule and…"

"You know what I mean." He used the dreaded schoolteacher voice that could make a saint feel guilty.

"And that…was fine, too." The meat skidded off my plate, and gentle Star looked up at me, asking permission. "Sure, girl, you can have it," I smiled at her.

The phone rang.

Ron got up to answer it.

"Yes." I half-listened until his words caught my full attention. "When? You're sure it was our dog? Yes. Well, I'll come up to see you after supper and pay for the damage. Thanks for calling."

If I expected outrage when he returned to the table I was wrong. My husband was about to surprise me, as he was to do so often over the years where our dogs were concerned.

Instead of bursting into a long string of justifiable recriminations, he began to stir his vegetables around on his plate, his gaze on the inedible mush he was making.

"That was Betty McLean," he said after one of the longest hiatuses I'd ever experienced in his company. "She says a big white dog killed four of her laying hens this morning. Was Star with you all day?"

"No." I couldn't look at him. The rose pattern on the tablecloth became etched in my mind during those horrible moments. "I tied her to the porch, but she got away. I don't know how long she was gone before I noticed she was missing."

"Okay." He drew a deep breath and got up. "I'm going up to Betty's. I'll pay for those chickens, but you have to make sure, absolutely sure, it never happens again."

"I promise, oh, I promise, even if I have to tie her to my belt!" I jumped up and kissed him…again.

For the next couple of weeks, I managed to keep Star under my control. One day while a repairman was fixing that terrible old kitchen oil stove, she slipped out when he made a trip back to his truck for parts. That day the carnage she wrought eradicated our meager savings account.

There was only one solution. Ron and I cried together as we came to the conclusion. We couldn't find another home for Star. A third home would be too much. It wouldn't be fair. If it was in the country, she'd have to be chained; if in the city, confined to a small yard or apartment. Worst, of all, would her new caregivers think harsh or even cruel punishment might cure her of what was indelibly rooted in her DNA?

We cried again and all the following night when our beautiful, gentle, murderous Star was put down. She wasn't guilty. Genetics were to blame; genetics that apparently gave these wonderful dogs an unquenchable thirst for domestic birds. Our ignorance of predilections of her breed had been responsible. It was a bitter lesson.

This time I vowed, through my tears, that I'd follow my father's advice and never ever again give my heart to another dog to tear.

I diminished as much of my grief as possible by immersing myself in my still-secret passion for writing. Secret until one day Ron discovered my surreptitious habit.

Confused and embarrassed, I tried to explain that I'd won prizes in high school for my stories, that it was really nothing, just a pastime. He made no comment.

Smokey

When Ron brought home the gregarious, six-week-old Yellow Lab pup, I was, for the first and last time in my life, dismayed by the acquisition of a dog. By that time we had two children, ages one and two, and were expecting a third. The idea of a big, full of vim-and-vigor puppy thrown into the mix, with Ron frequently away from home taking university courses, overwhelmed me. I wanted to tell my duck-hunting, dog-fancying spouse to take that toasty warm, sweet-smelling bundle of buff-colored fur right back to the breeder. I wanted to tell him I couldn't, wouldn't manage any more responsibilities. Then I saw the look on his face, and the thought melted like ice in a microwave.

While I'd always held a special place in my heart for Collies, Ron has always admired retrievers. Now here at last was the dog he'd always wanted. I remembered his getting Star for me when I thought I'd never own a dog again, when I desperately needed a dog to bring me out of my doldrums. *Okay.* I sighed inwardly. *I'll give it a try.*

"What are you going to name him?" I asked as the puppy snuggled into my arms and heart.

Glancing past me at the television screen where the children were watching cartoons, he shrugged. A forestry commercial flashed on, featuring Smokey, the big, amiable, fire-prevention bear.

"Smokey," he said. "I'm going to call him Smokey."

So Smokey joined the family that cold April afternoon. He loved the big hayfield we called the backyard of our rural home. A good dog, as big, clumsy puppies go, he housebroke easily and was amazingly gentle with the children. Although I tried to keep such unfair treatment to a minimum, small hands in his fur or on his ears or tail didn't deter him in the least. In fact, he reveled in being with the two little ones, Joan and Carol. Carol learned to walk by pulling herself upright on Smokey's hindquarters.

That first autumn, as a green pup, Smokey further distinguished himself by proving to be an excellent retriever in the marsh a couple of miles from our back door. Ron was delighted.

But Ron was frequently away from home, and I didn't have the time or stamina to train a pup, to work him into an obedient, well-socialized companion. Although generally a non-roamer, he sometimes left our property and used the neighbor's lawn as a bathroom. This, of course, brought immediate complaints.

In November our third child, a son we named Steven, was born. The pot of my ability to cope bubbled over. Three babies and a big, largely untrained puppy proved more than I could handle.

At Christmas, Smokey in a fit of good-natured exuberance knocked over the tree. When he ate an entire box of chocolates (an incident that has always made me wonder about the truth of the supposedly toxic effect of chocolates on canines) with absolutely no ill effects, I felt we, as a family, had to address the problem, but how?

To be fair, Smokey wasn't getting the attention and training he needed to become an enjoyable or even acceptable family member. He was like an undisciplined child whose annoying antics weren't his fault. Under present conditions, there appeared little hope of his improving.

As spring came, I became exhausted by the care of three babies and one large, high-spirited Yellow Lab. Something had to give.

It did. Fate stepped in and gave us a shove into the decision we were so reluctant to take.

In May, Ron's friend Dan and his wife Mary came to visit. They immediately fell in love with the gregarious Yellow Lab. A young, childless couple who lived on a farm about fifty miles away, they'd been looking for a dog, a Labrador retriever, in fact. When they saw our situation, they cautiously dropped the suggestion that they'd be willing to take Smokey to live with them.

At first neither Ron nor I would consider the idea. In spite of our problems with children and young dog, we loved the Lab with the good-natured grin and constantly wagging tail. We'd adopted him as surely as if we'd adopted a child. He was family.

The following week our decision changed when Smokey wandered out of the yard and was very nearly struck by a car. Lacking supervision and attention, he'd begun to roam.

His brush with death startled us into facing reality. Smokey needed more time and care than we could give him. If we truly loved him, we'd let him go to a place where he'd get just that.

Bright and early the next morning, Dan and Mary arrived, eager to become Smokey's new caregivers. As they drove away with the big pup in the back seat, we were brokenhearted. It seemed as if we'd given away a family member and betrayed Smokey's boundless love and devotion. We'd utterly failed him, we both agreed.

After the car had vanished around a bend in the road, we consoled ourselves with a single fact. We'd done what we had to do, what was best for Smokey. Our family situation hadn't been suited for a dog. It was another sad lesson learned.

Now, for most people who give up a dog for adoption, the story ends there. But Smokey was to prove exceptional when fate once again stepped in.

The rural school where Ron was principal was suddenly slated for permanent closure in June. We'd have to move. We didn't welcome the idea. We loved the little community we'd called home for the past six years. We knew we'd want to return to it, so just prior to leaving we managed to purchase a dilapidated little cabin.

In the meantime, Ron had looked over the available teaching jobs for which he was qualified. He decided to accept a position as chemistry teacher in the city ten miles from the farm that was Smokey's home. We didn't foresee this proximity as being a problem. We'd never let the Lab know where we were.

September saw us ensconced in our new urban home, a basement apartment in a residential subdivision. After living in the wide-open spaces with an entire house and several acres of farmland at our disposal, it took a good deal of adjusting physically as well as mentally to become accustomed to the restrictions of a small flat and a postage-stamp-sized backyard. Left each day with three preschoolers in a totally foreign environment, I suffered pangs of loneliness. I continued my secret writings but longed for a familiar face.

Early one October evening, I got my wish. I was working on yet another story, alone in our sunken living room—Ron was at a school meeting, the children safely tucked into bed—when I glanced up to see a pair of glowing eyes peering in at me.

My first instinct was to swish the drapes shut and rush to check the locks on the door. Then I recognized the lolling tongue and good-natured canine grin.

"Smokey!" I couldn't believe it.

Hearing his name, Smokey sent his tail into a wild whirl. A welcoming "woof" erupted from his throat.

By the time I got to the door, he was already there, ready to burst in, all his typical *joie de vivre* intact.

"Smokey!" I knelt to take him into my arms, tears blinding me. Here, at last, was a familiar face; a happy, lovingly and reassuringly familiar face. I buried my face in his soft, strong neck and cried.

I took him into the kitchen and, even though I knew it was the exactly wrong thing to do, gave him a slice of roast beef from the refrigerator. Then I sat down at the table and tried to decide what I should do.

Call Dan and Mary, of course. They must be frantic with worry. Reluctantly I picked up the phone. I knew in my heart that I didn't want to send Smokey back.

"Smokey!" Three-year-old Carol toddled into the kitchen, footed sleepers having silenced her approach. She'd been dragging her favorite teddy bear, but the minute she saw her old friend, she dropped it and rushed to hug him. Smokey began to lavish long, wet-tongued kisses over her little face as she laughed and pressed herself against him. "Smokey, I lub you!"

I found a tissue, blew my nose, and tried to tell myself not to let emotions overcome common sense. I remembered Dan and Mary telling us in telephone conversations that Smokey never left their farmyard even though they knew he could easily have cleared the rail fence that surrounded it if he'd made a decent effort. They'd taken his lack of interest in running away to mean he was content.

What, then, had aroused him to action that beautiful October night? Had he somehow sensed our relative nearness? Or had the full hunter's moon awakened memories of the previous autumn in field and marsh with Ron? Had those flashes provoked such overpowering longings that he'd been driven to desert a loving home for the dangers of the open road in an overpowering yearning for his former family?

More puzzling still was the question of how he managed to find us. We'd conscientiously avoided visiting him. Dan and Mary hadn't been to our apartment since we'd moved, to carry our scent back to him. I finally got Carol back into bed and sat down in the living room with the Lab that looked up at me with bright, expectant eyes.

Please, please, Smokey, don't!

While I was waiting for Smokey's new family to arrive to pick up the dog, Ron came home. I'll never forget the look of utter joy on his face when he saw his hunting buddy. It put the Christmas morning expressions of our children to shame.

"We have to talk to Dan and Mary," I said.

"I know." Ron was down on one knee, ruffling Smokey's neck.

"But how did he ever find us?" I sat down on a chair at the table again. "I can't imagine…"

"I went to see him yesterday." Ron's confession caught me totally off guard.

"You what? But I thought we agreed…"

"I know, I know." He avoided my eyes and concentrated on straightening Smokey's collar. "But I wanted to see him, just for a few minutes. I never thought he'd try to find me…us."

Dan and Mary arrived a few minutes later. We knew we couldn't take him away from them. They loved him; he was their baby. We also knew our landlord had a strict no-pets rule. Anyhow, this small apartment and yard was no place for him. We had to give Smokey back once and for all.

Smokey lived out the rest of his life—happily, we hope—with Dan and Mary as devoted caregivers. But I will never forget that October night when, with a crooked grin and flapping tail, like a canine guardian angel, he drove out the loneliness in my heart simply by being a loving, familiar face.

Sometimes a dog is sent into our lives, even if only briefly, for very specific purposes. Another lesson learned.

The Best Ten Dollars He Ever Spent

After Smokey's visit, my loneliness returned, stronger than ever. I think Ron must have seen it in my eyes.

"I've signed you up for a writing class at the high school," he announced one evening at supper the following week. "I paid the ten-dollar registration fee this afternoon."

"You did what? We can't afford it! Who'll watch the children? I wouldn't belong there. I definitely can't go." Words tumbled out. The audacity of what he'd done overwhelmed me.

"It's on Tuesday evenings, I'll watch the children, and the registration is non-refundable."

"But no one except you knows I write!" A blush flushed up my cheeks. My collection of Hilroy scribblers full of stories had been *our* secret, *my* guilty secret. It was brazen of me, with no college education, no courses in creative writing, not even a friend who was a writer, to ever presume to be an author, let alone allow the world in on my silly efforts. Now my partner had divulged my secret passion to the world...or at least to the registrar for night classes.

"Well, maybe it's time other people did," he said, turning back to his mashed potatoes. "Maybe it's time you did something with your talent."

My talent? I very much doubted I was possessed of

any of that heady stuff. But I did enjoy writing and maybe, just maybe, it would be nice to meet other people who shared a similar joy in the magic of creating stories out of thin air. I sat up straight, took a deep breath, and decided not to waste the precious ten dollars that represented a goodly chunk of our weekly budget.

The following Tuesday evening, clutching one of my dog-eared notebooks and with two brand-new Bic pens in my purse, I paused outside the classroom door labeled "Creative Writing Tonight at 7:00 p.m." Sucking in one of the deepest breaths of my life, I stepped inside.

Four students had already taken their places near the front of the classroom. A silver-haired lady with one of the softest, most welcoming smiles I've ever encountered sat behind the teacher's desk.

"Come in," she said. "You must be Gail. Your husband has told us lovely things about you and the stories you write. We're delighted you've decided to join us. I'm Jackie, and the others are Charlene, Norma, Nin, and Mary Jane." She indicated each as she introduced them. They smiled and voiced welcomes.

"Thank you." Blushing (one of my life-long handicaps), I took a seat behind the student she'd identified as Norma and tried to settle comfortably to listen, learn, and be as unobtrusive as possible. The list of student names I'd conquer later. At the moment I was suffering from severe "fish out of water" syndrome.

"Tonight we'll be discussing more markets." Jackie stood and went to the blackboard.

Markets. The woman actually expected this class, me included, to send out stories...stories that would be judged by strangers, accepted—or more probably rejected with scathing words—by these unknown individuals? No way!

Two months later, when I received my first acceptance for a short piece submitted to a regional farming publication, I changed my tune. My "career" as a writer had left the starting gate.

Best of all, I'd met five amazing people, five women who would be my friends for life, friends who shared each other's triumphs and disappointments, friends devoted to writing and to one another. We'd encourage, defend, and assist each other not only in our fledgling careers as writers but in our everyday lives. We were soul mates, individuals who understood the desire to write and the need to have our work accepted and published in a difficult and often discouraging marketplace. We held parties when we made headway, met to commiserate when the going got rough, and overall enjoyed each other's company.

The road to publication for each of us proved a unique journey, sometimes smooth, more often bumpy, but always filled with adventure and challenge. Best of all, along that amazing journey, six friends joined spiritual hands and pushed ahead.

I believe it was the best ten dollars Ron ever spent.

Ben

Shortly after I joined the writing group, we moved into our first new home. With it came a decently sized backyard sufficient to be a playground for children and a dog. But the children, ages seven, eight, and nine, were still too young for a pet, Ron and I decided. We'd wait until a dog would be fairly dealt with as a living creature and not as a stuffed toy.

One day in early September, a note came home from Steve's teacher. She believed he was having difficulty seeing the blackboard. She suggested an eye exam.

Our son protested vigorously, the mere possibility of eyeglasses making him stubborn as a Missouri mule. He wasn't about to suffer the indignities of the name-calling such despicable devices would evoke among his peers.

In order to get him to consent to a visit to the optometrist, I suggested a treat at the newly opened McDonald's Restaurant afterwards. That wasn't enough. I searched my mind for some other affordable enticement. Steve loved animals. We had no zoo, but we did have an animal shelter. If he'd consent to go for an eye exam, we'd pay it a visit, I promised.

He hesitated. His love of animals finally won out, and he buckled under this final enticement.

The following morning we set off, first to the

optometrist, then to the local SPAC. As I chatted with the lady in charge, Steve wandered among the cages and pens. He didn't attempt to play with any of the animals or even lure them within reach. I should have at least suspected what that intense expression on his seven-year-old face meant.

"These puppies were found abandoned in a ditch," the lady told me, indicating a pair of adorable brown fur balls in a nearby cage. "We believe they're part beagle. And this dog"—she moved along the row—"was turned in for adoption because her owners were moving and couldn't take her with them."

I knew I had to leave the shelter soon. The dogs and their sad stories were breaking my heart, inspiring me with such irrational thoughts as adopting the entire kit and caboodle.

"Come on, Steve," I called. "It's time for lunch."

I thanked the kind lady for her time and the tour. Taking my son by a hand, I hurried out to the car.

"Fasten your seat belt," I instructed, struggling to put the memory of all those loving, needy dogs from my mind. I glanced over to the passenger seat to make certain he complied. Only then did I notice the protrusion in the front of Steve's jacket, and the strange movements it was making. The next instant a small brown head appeared above the partly zippered garment.

"Steve, what have you done!" Appalled I could only stare at what I recognized as one of the ditch puppies.

"He needed a home." Boy and dog gazed up at me, yanking at my heartstrings, making refusal a horrible cruelty.

"Oh, Steve." I sighed, released my seat belt, picked up my purse, and got back out of the car.

"Where are you going?" The apprehension in my son's voice made me turn back to reply.

"Back inside. To pay for the puppy."

We named him Ben, and for the next two years he was an integral part of our family. In the city, we kept Ben in our fenced backyard and, growing up to be a small dog, he didn't appear to mind.

In spite of his adorable countenance and small size, Ben was not a particularly cuddly or affectionate dog. Quite possibly the attentions of three young children were overwhelming for him. He often remained aloof, ignoring the family and sometimes growling when he preferred to be left alone. Ron and I realized we'd been right in our plan not to get a dog until the children were older.

During the Ben era, we spent summers at the little shack we'd purchased before leaving Tabusintac. With no indoor plumbing, its water supply came from a spring across the field, where milk and other perishables were kept from spoiling in the cold flow. The children loved the freedom of fields and streams, and I enjoyed the freedom to sit on the front step with a clipboard full of looseleaf paper and write, in longhand, what was to become my first published novel. When we came back to the city in the fall, I transcribed the words with my manual typewriter into submitable form.

One day during his second summer with us, Ben escaped our supervision and headed out (we believe) to visit a neighbor's female in heat. In those early years of dog caregiving, we were too inexperienced to realize that all pet dogs should be spayed or neutered, and we hadn't gotten Ben properly amended.

Panic ensued when we realized Ben was missing. We searched for days, often deluding ourselves into thinking we saw him far off on the edge of a field or among trees at the side of the road. Two weeks later a lady stopped by the cottage to tell us the sad truth.

She was a worker at the children's day camp a couple of miles from the cottage. On the day Ben had gone missing, the children in her care had found a small brown and white dog dead in a ditch beside the road. Apparently he'd been hit by a car on his way to visit that alluring lady dog. The children had buried Ben. They hadn't known who owned him at the time. Several days later the lady had chanced to overhear a conversation in the local co-op store about a family who was missing their dog.

No words could describe the pain of loss or the amount of tears this knowledge evoked among the children and me. Ron alone remained stoic. Dry eyed and silent, he went back to his job shingling the cottage roof. Years later, he confided Ben's death had been such a blow he couldn't face us.

The tragedy had taught us a harsh lesson. Spaying and neutering are absolute necessities to pet safety.

A Little Ball of Baby Fur

If anything ever came into my life in leaps and bounds, it was Brandy the Beagle. His *joie de vivre* from the moment we met was immense and infectious. Unlike any other dog I had ever encountered, Bran celebrated life to the hilt and was determined to enjoy every ounce of fun he could squeeze out of it. The tale of his remarkable life began with the loss of Ben.

Our second daughter, eight-year-old Carol, was especially hurt by Ben's death.

On the night after the camp lady informed us that Ben definitely wouldn't be coming home, in a vain attempt to quell her flood of tears as well as those of her brother and sister, I promised we'd get another dog. I even agreed it would be a Beagle, in honor of that possible bit of heritage in Ben's gene pool. Carol had always fancied the breed, but I knew absolutely nothing of the little Hounds beyond Snoopy of cartoon fame.

Anticipating that finding a male Beagle puppy would take time (thus giving me time to study up on the breed) and pressed on by my daughter's interminable tears, I telephoned a lady I knew who, although she did not breed Beagles at her kennel, was familiar with a number of reputable puppy producers Canada-wide.

"Funny you should be looking for a Beagle today," she said. "A man called me just last night asking if I knew of anyone who could furnish a good home for an eight-week-old male Beagle. He had saved this one, the pick of the litter, for a man who changed his mind when the time came to take it home. I don't know this breeder personally, but I've heard only good things about his dogs. They're said to be tough, handsome, and sharp as tacks."

I'd have to put my plans for dog study in Beagle 101 on hold. This particular breeder lived within a two-hour drive of our home and probably wouldn't hold the pup too much longer.

Early the next morning we started off—two sleepy adults, three fit-to-burst children, and a Campbell's Soup box lovingly lined with a blue baby blanket and outfitted with a squeaky toy and chew bone.

As we drove north along Highway 103, I felt as if fate had taken a hand in our lives, and I was still in the whirl of the spin it had given my family and me. Moving on to acquiring another family member within forty-eight hours…it was almost as if that Beagle puppy had been waiting in the wings. I shook my head in disbelief. I was letting my writer's imagination run with the bit in its teeth again. Fate didn't preplan lives to that extent.

If life offered the foreshadowing present in some novels, warning bells would have sounded the instant we drove up to the neat, white mobile home with the tidy kennel at the rear. Evidence existed to warrant suspicion. One should have been given to speculate why an eight-foot chain link fence which appeared to be dug into the ground should be required to contain relatively small dogs.

But then *he* appeared. After scrambling out of a hole (which we later had good reason to believe he had dug) under the doghouse, he drew himself up to all his ten inches of height and struck a pose that would have captured the eye of the most discerning of dog show judges. As proud as a Prussian prince and, from his stance, master of all he surveyed, he made the other dogs in the pen pale in comparison.

I handed over the last twenty dollars of the small advance I'd received for my very first novel and bade farewell to the jovial gentleman who had been his owner. As we drove away, the small, long-legged, long-eared creature seated on the blanket in the box on my lap gave the juvenile version of the war whoop that would become his trademark, gathered wiry limbs beneath him, and, long ears flying, leaped clean out of his container.

In that single gesture (although we, innocents that we were, were not aware of it at that time), he presented us with the theme of his existence. Life is an adventure: go out and give it hell!

A Beagle in Your Bed

The first incident in what would turn out to be a lifelong series of incidents occurred on his first night in his/our home. At the corner grocery store we had picked up a large toilet paper box to serve as his bedroom until he was sufficiently toilet trained and otherwise trustworthy to have the run of the house. Surely a three-foot-high, four-foot-square box would make a safe, comfortable, escape-proof place for a small (albeit long-legged) Beagle puppy.

When a trio of exhausted but happy children finally fell into bed (a new puppy has that effect), I gently placed what I believed to be an equally exhausted puppy into his cardboard bedroom. Lined with a soft blue quilt (he was a *boy* Beagle, Carol had explained as she chose it), a small clock ticking outside one corner to imitate his mother's heart, and a warm rubber water bottle securely wrapped in towels to prevent his missing his litter mates too badly, it seemed a cozy, inviting place.

From his place in the corner of our bedroom, I could hear him shuffling about, sniffing, exploring, examining his new accommodations, and finally seeming to settle for the night. With a sigh, I eased into bed beside Ron.

Argh! My head had barely touched the pillow when there arose from the box such a clatter I sat bolt upright to see what was the matter. Small white paws clutching at the rim appeared in the darkness amid great scrambling sounds that indicated the back ones were not far behind. The newly top-heavy box swayed eerily in the shaft of moonlight flooding into the room. Finally, with a soft, dull thud, it toppled, spilling one small wiry Hound out onto the carpet.

In a single bound he was at my side of the bed. Ivory paws latched over the edge of the mattress as he demanded to be brought up to join me.

"What's going on?" Ron asked sleepily.

"Nothing," I muttered, dragging myself from the bed's pleasant warmth to gather Brandy into my arms. Gently I replaced him in his bed. "Stay," I said with only the faintest belief that he would understand and obey.

Three minutes later he was back at my bedside. The next time in two minutes, and finally it was close to only one minute before he was requesting my attention.

As the mother of three children, I knew only one solution. I pulled on my robe and, Beagle in arms, headed for the living room.

Soon we were moving gently to and fro in the old rocking chair by the window. In less than a minute, the little ball of baby fur cuddled into my neck and, with a burp, a yawn, and a sigh, settled to sleep. I looked down at the small brown-and-white face so innocent and trusting and wonderful in its vulnerability. The image lodged in my heart at the exact point where long-term love is centered.

Ten minutes later I eased us both into bed.

"What's going on?" Ron asked again, half awake.

"Nothing," I whispered. "Go back to sleep."

Trusting, he rolled over and obeyed.

Brandy grunted. Later I would understand this was a sign of contempt for anyone or anything that obeyed anyone or anything unprotestingly.

"Shhhhh," I cautioned my companion as I snuggled him in beside me. "Remember, it's only for one night."

He yawned again, lengthened out in a stretch that succeeded in pulling most of the blankets off both humans ensconced beside him, gave me a quick lick, and fell asleep.

Bran and the Bumblebee

The following morning, their puppy's newness worn down, the children went off to play with friends. Another lesson learned: never get a dog unless YOU ARE PERSONALLY prepared to care for it. Brandy was left in peace to explore his new surroundings.

This investigating took the form of sniffing each and every nook and cranny of the fenced backyard. Even at the tender age of two-and-one-half months, the Beagle puppy seemed to be aware that his nose would be his ticket to all things interesting.

I sat in my lawn chair and watched him ferreting out new scents. A sweet little creature, so easily amused, so content in his confinement, I thought innocently. Indeed, our eighty-foot-by-one-hundred-and-ten-foot suburban plantation appeared to contain more than sufficient sources of interest to keep him happy.

For example, flower beds with soft, squishy earth just waited to be excavated, and various forms of cloth hanging from a string called a clothesline made great swings for an agile Beagle puppy with strong jaws and teeth. A thing called a garden hose could keep the rest of his family at bay if a small dog could seize it near its spouting head and run around the yard with it clamped between his teeth. .

Also during these early days, one of Brandy's most

exasperating and also one of his frequently nerve-fraying characteristics revealed itself. The little Hound, we discovered one fine spring day, possessed a revengeful spirit.

This revelation became apparent one morning after Brandy was caught swinging, not from a star but from a pair of Ron's favorite fishing pants hanging on the clothesline. After observing this infamy from the kitchen window, Ron grasped the nearest weapon, a flyswatter, and rushed out of the house.

The next day we found that flyswatter chewed to death and half buried in a flower bed. Poor, inanimate thing! The light tap it had given a Beagle bottom swinging in the breeze hardly seemed grounds for such a horrible demise.

Several days later Ron made a second mistake. He chuckled a trifle diabolically when, in the course of uprooting a geranium in full bloom, Bran annoyed a bumblebee.

"That will teach him not to dig in the flower bed," he said, satisfaction coloring his tone as I hurried across the yard to comfort the yiking Beagle.

It didn't. Although Bran would retain a lifelong abhorrence of anything that buzzed, his fascination with flower beds and their easily excavated soil resurfaced every time he could find nothing better to do. Some dogs have long memories, we discovered, and should never be underestimated.

Lost in the Woods

Brandy did display one most desirable domestic trait. He appeared to have house trained himself. In spite of the fact that he had been born and raised in an outdoor kennel for the first ten weeks of his life, he never once soiled our floors. What a clever pup, we thought.

But then came the day he used this desirable feat to his own advantage. We were moving to our summer cottage—three children, two adults, a mountain of food, clothing, etc., and one wiry Beagle pup all crushed into our '74 Volkswagen Beetle. Suddenly Brandy, seated on my lap where he had been staring out the window, seemingly mesmerized by the scenery, let out a yelp and began to whine.

"He needs to make a pit stop," I said, proud of this naturally clean little dog.

"No problem." Ron, equally impressed by the little dog's conscientiousness, pulled into a campsite we were conveniently (we thought) passing.

Once inside its entrance and a safe distance from the highway, I opened my door to let Bran out. I expected him to make a modest, careful exit. I had much to learn about Beagles.

The moment the door swung open, he crouched, dug his nails deep into my lap, and launched himself, with a war whoop, out of the car.

Bran seemed to remain airborne for the next couple of seconds…until he landed right into the center of a totally innocent, totally unprepared group of picnickers! In retrospect, I'm sure he didn't. He couldn't possibly have jumped that far. The awfulness of it has simply expanded the distance in my memory.

Before the bucolic diners comprehended what had hit them, Brandy had sprinted through their food and off at full speed, the rabbit we hadn't seen near the entrance of the campsite racing ahead of him. Deaf to the shrieks and expletives that followed, he bolted in hot pursuit of the first bouncing bunny of his career.

How does one apologize for upset cold cuts, scattered dinner rolls, and, perhaps most terrible, a paw print sunk deep into a bowl of potato salad?

Returning to the car after trying to set matters (people and food) to rights, I found an exasperated husband and three wailing youngsters. Brandy was gone forever, they sobbed. We'd never find him. Ron looked as if he hoped that would be the case.

"He'll be back." I tried to reassure them much more confidently than I felt.

Without comment, Ron pulled the car out of the driveway and parked to wait.

"Remember, Beagles are equipped with homing instincts surpassed only by carrier pigeons," I told the children, hoping I'd correctly recalled this bit of information acquired nearly a decade previous from a dog-eared *Reader's Digest* in a doctor's waiting room.

Ron looked over at me warily, skeptically. He knew my habit of digging up half-accurate facts, gleaned over my many years as a bookworm, to support needy situations.

Minutes turned to a quarter hour; the wailing I'd managed to suppress to the level of sniffling rose again. I, too, I can now admit, began to despair of ever seeing our Beagle again.

As the half hour dawned, out of the alders at the edge of the campsite came a mud-drenched little critter, a long slice of pink (which later proved to be his tongue) hanging far down its front. Trotting toward our car in as sprightly a manner as his state of exhaustion would allow, he raised a chorus of cheers from the rear seat and even a muted sigh of relief from Ron.

"Brandy, come," I called opening my door.

"Hurry up, get in," Ron urged the dirty, panting creature. I assumed he, like myself, was anxious to get away from the disdainful looks of the picnickers before they decided to make us pay for the carnage.

Bran hesitated a moment. "Come," I said gently to soften Ron's command. He looked up at me, gathered his legs beneath him, and leaped up into my lap.

Tan shorts metamorphosed to mud brown, white T-shirt to a tie-dye of earth tones.

He paused and looked up at me, his expression one I will never forget. The sense of satisfaction I saw reflected in his golden brown eyes astonished me. An epiphany burst over me. I was in the presence of one of those rare beings who had no doubts about his purpose in life and was willing to give it his best shot no matter what.

Understanding and admiration sprouted on top of the love I already had for the little dog. Here was a soul mate, one as dedicated to the chase as I was to my writing. I hugged him, he twicked the end of my nose with a quick, wet kiss, and our partnership was sealed.

A Contest with Two Horses and a Great Dane

The perilous picnic prank heralded a summer of unique, often boisterous, frequently shocking, usually dangerous, occasionally exasperating (for Ron, at least) incidents. The one thing Brandy could not be accused of was being dull. And I (generally alone) delighted in his high-flying escapades. If he'd been human, he'd probably have been Napoleon Bonaparte or some similar type of unique personage—small in stature but large in vision and overflowing with confidence in his own invincibility.

Fearless, reckless, incorrigible, and daring, he soon illustrated that he gloried in living on that edge of life I'd always conscientiously avoided. Our summer in the country gave him ample opportunities to ferret out adventures suitable to those character traits. Rabbits, foxes, and even mice unwillingly helped him hone his skills of the chase. Although he never caught a single critter, his joy, like mine in writing, was as much in the pursuit of the dream as in its actual attainment.

The hot, sultry dog days of August arrived. Intense heat kept the children indoors on several 90-degree-plus days. After a few hours of lying across one of their bunk beds watching them read and color and nap, Brandy grew restless. A whine at the screen door gave him his freedom. Shortly I noticed him loping off across the crisp stubble of the newly mown hayfield bordering our property.

His leaving home territory gave me pause, but he was soon too far away to hear me call him back. He probably wouldn't have responded if he did. By that time I, basically at least, knew my Beagle. All I could do was hope he'd be all right.

Suddenly I realized where he was headed. Our neighbor's meadow two fields away held a pair of beautiful palominos. With nothing else to chase...

"Come on!" I yelled to the children. "Bran's headed for the Harpers' horses!"

"Mr. Harper has a hu-mongous Great Dane!" Steve cried, following me as fast as seven-year-old legs could carry him barefooted across brittle stubble. "He'll eat Bran!"

Too engrossed in trying to run and keep three children close at the same time, I didn't reply.

Long before we reached the wire fence that contained Trigger and Bullet, I saw two golden flashes streaking around the paddock, snowy manes and tails extended in flight. Mere feet behind them, narrowly avoiding flying hooves, Bran gave chase to the biggest critters he had ever chanced upon. The Red Baron in fearless pursuit, spirit souring, he'd thrown caution to the winds and was having a whale of a good time.

"Bran!" I yelled as the children and I stumbled up the fence. "Brandy, come!"

He didn't spare me a single glance. Super Beagle was not about to be called off a chase of this magnitude.

The Harpers' humongous Great Dane appeared. Streaking out of the farmhouse and across the pasture, Brutus looked as dangerous as a grizzly, only leaner and meaner. We later learned he had an almost maternal attachment to the horses and was inordinately protective of them. Even without this knowledge, we knew Bran had gotten into deep, deep trouble.

"Bran!" I shrieked, in a cry that rivaled any of Jamie Lee Curtis' best in *Halloween.*

For a split second he paused and glanced in my direction, exactly the wrong thing to do at that moment. Unobserved by the Beagle, Brutus had overtaken him. When Bran turned, the Great Dane opened his mouth.

Bran's head disappeared inside.

"Brandy!" All three children screamed in unison.

The situation was out of my control. There was only one thing I could do. Desperately I tried to shield my children from the horrible sight of their beloved pet being devoured alive.

"Brutus, stop! No!" Jim Harper's gruff roar sounded as sweet as a chorus of angels as he came running across the field. Brutus, apparently an obedient canine, immediately ceased his attack. Bran flew from his mouth like a cuspidor-aimed tobacco wad.

"Bran, get here!" I ducked under the wire, waved the children not to follow, and hurried across the field to catch the regurgitated creature by his collar.

"I'm sorry, Mr. Harper," I said, trying not to show my fear of the two horses still bucking and prancing about the field—or of Brutus slavering profusely as he glared at Bran. Hatred glowed from his yellow eyes, reminding me of the Hound of the Baskervilles in the throes of a major snit. "He ran away."

"No problem." Jim Harper was a good-natured, animals-will-be-animals type of man. "But maybe you should keep the little fellow home. Trigger and Bullet might get him with a random kick. The other problem is

Brutus. As you've seen, he's very protective of the horses, and if I'm not around to call him off…"

"Yes, of course," I agreed and started toward the fence, stooped into Quasimodo position as I clung to Bran's collar. "Thanks for calling off your dog."

That night, as I paused outside the children's bedroom door, I heard Steve whispering to Brandy curled up in his bunk with him.

"I bet it was really neat," he said to the little dog by his side. "I wish you could talk so you could tell me all about it."

"What was really neat?" I asked, stepping into the room and snapping on the light to see the Beagle cuddled up against the seven-year-old in Superman pajamas.

"What Bran saw when Brutus tried to swallow him," Steve said, sleepily hugging the family pet closer. "I bet the inside of a Great Dane has some really neat stuff in it."

His eyes closed, and his regular breathing told me he slept. Bran let out a squeaky yawn and settled comfortably beside "his" boy, the trauma of that eventful day apparently successfully placed behind him.

This was one lesson we'd never learn from a dog.

Ticks Without Tocks

On the afternoon of his run-in with Brutus, we took Bran to the vet to be treated for four fang holes around the perimeter of his neck. The vet patched the marks, gave him a shot of antibiotics, and advised us not to replace the flea-and-tick collar we had deemed appropriate canine country wear.

"The repellents on that collar might have a detrimental effect on his wounds," he said. "Wait until he's fully healed to replace it."

We agreed, thinking that a Beagle suffering from such a traumatic incident would be content to stay, if not indoors, at least close to home and therefore hardly vulnerable to fleas and ticks.

We should have known better. The next morning when he stepped a trifle shakily outdoors to relieve himself, I watched for a few minutes and then, deciding he wasn't going to leave the yard in his weakened condition, went back inside to start breakfast.

When I returned no more than two minutes later, he'd vanished. With the knowledge I had acquired over the past few weeks, I decided I knew exactly where he had gone…to revenge himself on Brutus and the horses. Leaving Ron and the children to fend for breakfast on their own and giving no explanation for my sudden departure, I set off at a run across the adjoining field, my heart pounding harder and faster than my feet.

The little dog's total unpredictability was again demonstrated, when, feeling ready to collapse from exhaustion, I burst into view of the meadow. Both horses grazed peacefully in the morning sun, a perfect picture of pastoral tranquility. Bran was nowhere in sight. Then where…?

Perplexed, I returned to the cottage and the hodgepodge of cereals the children called breakfast. At the head of the table sat Bran, a dish towel tied about his neck, a bowl of Rice Krispies, complete with milk, in front of him.

Now, I've always fostered love and respect for all living things in my children, but this was going a bit far.

"What is he doing at the table?" I asked, pointing an accusatory finger at the contented-looking little Hound. Still sweaty from my wild Beagle chase, I was not in one of my most lenient moods.

"He's an invalid," Steve said, adjusting the bowl more conveniently into Bran's reach.

"What's going on?" Ron came sleepily out of the bedroom to join the breakfasting group.

He took one look at Brandy seated in his chair, carefully bibbed with the red-and-white-checkered cloth, and began to chuckle.

"Well, you've finally gotten where you apparently think you belong," he said to the lapping Beagle. "You're head of the household…at least for a little while."

The mystery of where Bran had been that morning persisted until late that afternoon when Jessie MacIntosh, one of our neighbors, called.

"Your Beagle was over here this morning," she

said, and before she could continue, I began to apologize. "Oh, I'm sorry, Jess. What did he do?"

"Oh, nothing, nothing at all," the good-natured lady quickly assured me. "He played with our new puppy for a couple of minutes, then left."

Then why are you calling? The question darted across my mind.

"The reason I'm calling," she answered my silent query, "is because we've just discovered our dog has ticks, and we noticed Bran wasn't wearing his tick-and-flea collar. Maybe you should check him out. You wouldn't want those things to get in your house."

Now, nothing is more inspirational than the mention of the presence of fleas, lice, or ticks. Dust flecks move; irrepressible scratching begins immediately.

"I will. Thanks, Jess." I hung up the phone, my palm rubbing my thigh.

"What is it?" Ron asked.

"Jessie thinks Bran may have caught ticks from her dog," I said lamely. "He was over there this morning."

"Really?" Ron's fingers flew to his scalp and wriggled into his hair. "And he's napping on Steve's bed?"

Out of the corner of my eye I'd seen Steve stealing away as we talked. By the time we got to the bedroom, a tearful little boy was clutching his beloved Beagle in his arms, his ear pressed to its sleek, furry side.

"He hasn't got ticks, he hasn't!" he sobbed. "I've been listening and listening and I haven't heard a single sound. He's not going to 'splode, I know it!"

The following day Bran made another visit to the vet and was absolved of being host to creepy crawlers.

As we left the office, Steve held Bran's leash proudly and ignored his sisters' snickers as they made copious jokes about ticks and ticking and the obvious difference between the two.

Bran looked disdainfully at us all. Through the whole of this unsettling incident, he had been the only member of our entire family who had never once scratched. He had known all along he didn't have ticks and that certainly he wasn't about to explode.

Don't Fence Me In

On returning to town that fall, Bran made a momentous (but at first unknown to us) decision. He, like Jack London's Buck in *Call of the Wild*, had tasted freedom and was not about to relinquish it to basket-weave fences or chicken wire. He'd known the exhilaration of racing across vast meadows, plunging into deep thickets, and swimming wide rivers (wide, at least, in Beagle proportions). Digging up flower beds, swinging from clotheslines, and playing hose tag now seemed deadly dull pursuits.

We already had fences: basket-weaves along the sides and chicken wire at both ends of our property. It had been sufficient to keep Ben contained. But then, Ben had had only a (possible) smattering of Beagle genes. We'd never dealt with a purebred member of the breed.

By the time we returned to town in the fall, Bran had grown tall and strong enough to clear that chicken wire in a single bound. Thus began his career as a canine criminal and mine as his personal prevaricator.

Of course, being a hedonist promoted this trait in the little tri-colored imp. Bran delighted in all creature comforts, especially food. But not just any food—fine food, take-out food, party food. Therein lay the problem when we returned to town. Suburbia in summer and early fall abounds with patio parties and kitchen doors left carelessly, invitingly ajar during same. This provided fertile territory for a bored and bottomless Beagle. By the time the leaves had turned, I had lied my way through the case of the cooling cookies and the pizza party prank. I'd also become an unwilling accomplice in the brazen barbecue raid. But worst of all had been the crafty crustacean caper staged soon after we had returned to town.

Late afternoon sunlight was dappling its way through the ripening birches in our backyard when Bran returned from an unauthorized expedition. At first I couldn't believe what I was seeing. A large, freshly cooked lobster dangled from his jaws.

Before Ron and the children could witness Bran's latest larceny, I seized the red-shelled critter, snapped a lead on the tri-colored one, and headed for the neighbor who, earlier in the day, had told me she had invited her boss over for a lobster dinner.

When I returned the crustacean to its owner, my face as red as the stolen delicacy, and offered the unlikely explanation that the Beagle had stolen it, I thought I detected a smirk on Bran's face when I glanced down at him standing by my side.

Beyond her I saw a dining table elegantly set for four and wondered if the purloined lobster would still be considered fitting fare to set before the boss. I couldn't see why not. Bran hadn't even dented the shell. True, it was slightly travel worn from having been dropped a couple of times, but… I pulled myself out of my reflections as my neighbor questioned me.

"Dogs don't usually steal lobsters, do they?" she asked, haughty annoyance coloring her tone.

"No, I don't believe they do," I said lamely as Bran

sat down and cocked his head at her. He looked cute, appealing, and totally innocent, while I appeared a clumsy, inept liar. "But Bran is…" I searched for a socially acceptable word, "unique."

"Really?" She took the lobster gingerly between her fingers and looked down at the little dog. "He looks like just another Beagle to me."

Bran's eyes narrowed. Fear fluttered to life in my heart. He'd understood! One day soon Margaret Aims would suffer the full-blown ire of a Beagle's revenge.

"She didn't mean it, Bran," I said softly, nervously, as we headed for home. "She knows you're not just any Beagle; she knows you're special."

I stopped short. Had I completely lost my mind? Here I was desperately trying to placate a small dog with inane apologies. What had this devious little creature done to me?

The Great Fencing Competition

Though I conscientiously tried to cover-up Bran's escapades beyond the boundary of our yard, tales of his misdeeds must have filtered back to Ron through some of our quisling (and/or vandalized) neighbors. How he got wind of it is immaterial. What happened after he did is the important thing. My husband immediately decided stronger security precautions were in order, and thus began what I later entitled The Great Fencing Competition.

On the day after Bran had *reportedly* chased a neighbor's cat (Margaret Aims' cat, the lady from whom Bran had previously *borrowed* a lobster and who had dared to call him *just another Beagle*) up a tree, a delivery truck rolled into our yard and deposited several large rolls of eight-foot-high, green-plated chain link fencing. Bran, now ignominiously tied to the clothesline, watched with interest.

He also watched with interest that weekend when Ron installed steel posts around the perimeter of our property and painstakingly stretched strong emerald-colored wire between them. On Sunday evening, when, in the glow of a sinking autumn sun, Bran was once more given freedom of the newly secured yard, the little dog ambled around its edge inspecting Ron's handiwork.

"There." A satisfied smirk on his face, Ron

watched him. "That should keep the little bugger out of trouble."

Confident of the truth in his words, we all trouped inside for supper. When we called Bran to join us a half hour later, he didn't respond...which in itself wasn't unusual. When we went out into the backyard to find him, he was nowhere to be seen. A deep, gaping, freshly dug hole in the far corner of our lot, beneath that beautiful new fence, told the tale.

The next day a neighbor was overheard telling how an entire foil-wrapped, shrimp-stuffed salmon had disappeared from his barbecue when he had gone into his house for a moment the previous evening. It had been purely circumstantial evidence that Bran's snout and breath smelled fishy when he returned home at dusk, I told Ron. No one had actually *seen* him take that fish, now, had they?

Nevertheless, the great fencing competition between Bran and Ron was on. The next day Ron bought tent pegs and skewered the fence to the ground. Bran jacked them out with his snout and again (at least, allegedly) chased the Aims' cat. This time it was through Margaret's tomato bed which, in September, was laden with lush, ready-to-harvest fruit. The resultant carnage made her patch look like the scene of some terrible battle, with the ground stained a horrible blood red. The purloined lobster incident paled by comparison.

Ron bought longer tent pegs. Bran miraculously (because we never discovered how) removed them. Ron dug the fence deep into the good earth. Bran dug deeper.

One day, a big delivery truck backed into our yard.

It roared and beeped, and Bran, once again tied to the clothesline, for all his bravado had the good sense to retreat up onto the back step.

Two burly men alighted and began to pile cement blocks beside the house. Looking out the dining room window, I saw Bran's eyes narrowing into slits. Perhaps he realized that this time Ron had called in the heavy artillery.

That evening Ron, puffing and sweating, piled the blocks around the edge of the yard, on the edge of the chain link, on top of the tent pegs. They proved to be Bran's nemesis. This time he was to be successfully contained.

Released from the indignity of the clothesline, he inspected every inch of this new barrier. Finding it impregnable, he affected a blasé attitude, wandered over to the back door, and asked to be let inside.

"Got him!" With those two triumphant words, Ron sank into a lawn chair as I opened the door for the Beagle. "I guess that will teach him not to mess with me!"

Fifteen minutes later we decided to go for a walk and went into the house to put on our sneakers. In the living room, Bran lay stretched out full length on his back on the couch, seemingly at peace with the world and everyone in it.

"Got ya, got ya!" Ron couldn't resist a victory tease and tickled the tan-and-white belly.

With cold disdain, Bran rolled over onto his stomach and watched from under half-closed eyelids as a jubilant Ron stuck his feet into his new sneakers. And yelled.

As the human slowly, disgustedly, withdrew his

foot, Bran heaved a bored sigh and settled into a serious nap. Using that nice, white, Ron-scented shoe as a toilet hadn't taken nearly as much time and effort as piling up those heavy blocks.

Touché! I saw the word mirrored in his golden brown eyes as they closed in sleep.

Thus ended the great fencing competition. I think it might have been declared a draw. Sometimes you just can't win with a dog.

Brandy and the Muse

Summer turned to autumn. Children returned to school. Ron went back to teaching, and Bran and I were left alone to write my/our second novel.

Each morning after the children and Ron left the house, Bran and I went for a walk in the woods and meadow beyond our subdivision. Although I didn't mention it to Ron, I felt sorry for Bran, his free-wheeling spirit confined to house and yard. He, like my imagination, had to have a chance to run free. When we returned, we would settle in a corner of our bedroom, where I'd simulated an office with a card table and a manual typewriter.

On the first day of this routine, Bran followed me into the bedroom after his romp. There he climbed up onto the bed, where he promptly fell asleep, Snoopy fashion, on his back among the pillows.

After an hour or so, he awoke, yawned, stretched, and arose. Out of the corner of my eye, I saw him looking at me, tail wagging slowly. I knew that look. Only awake a few seconds and already attention-seeking, action-ready.

Ignoring him, I typed vigorously. He had to learn this was MY time. I returned my attention to the words appearing on the page before me.

I felt a paw on each shoulder and a tickling, furry snout against my ear. Gingerly turning only my head, I saw Bran stretched out Slinky-like to a length I would have believed impossible as he craned across from where his hind paws rested on the bed to where his forefeet hung around my neck in a Beagle hug. He licked my ear.

"No," I said removing his paws and getting up to replace him on the bed. He cocked his head and looked up at me, cute as a button. "No, I don't have time to go to the meadow again right now. *We're* writing a book."

For the first time I verbally (and I can now admit, intentionally) included him in my creative endeavors.

His tail slowed, then stopped. With a final glance I could not quite fathom, he leaped from the bed and trotted in a sprightly way to the kitchen. *What was he up to?* Trepidations began to rise. He didn't easily acquiesce to anyone's wishes.

I returned to my typing, but the muse had vanished into distraction. I listened, straining for any sound that would give me a clue as to Bran's intentions.

This is irrational. He's only a little dog, my common sense muttered.

Wrong! an inner voice admonished. *He's a Beagle.*

A slight scraping sound followed. I heard him trotting back toward the bedroom. When he appeared in the doorway, he carried his largest chew bone.

Grinning behind his burden, he looked up at me. He leaped back onto the bed and prepared to enjoy a good, long gnash.

In that moment I knew he had decided to be my partner in all things literary. After all, I had supported him in all things nefarious, hadn't I? There was power in partnership, I learned.

Bran's Photos in a National Magazine

My writing career has taken many different roads over the past quarter century. I started with writing Young Adult novels, veered into short stories and poetry, swung toward historical books and articles, then lurched along a bumpy two-lane stretch of profiles and travel pieces. Under Brandy's influence, it took a fortuitous detour. This trail would lead me into an entirely different realm, one I would not previously have considered exploring.

A friend first awakened the possibilities in this new area one day after I'd told her of another of Bran's escapades.

"You could write a book about that little devil," she said with a laugh.

I laughed too. Dog stories were written by breeders, trainers, sportsmen, veterinarians, and other such experts. Against these knowledgeable individuals I hadn't a chance.

The following afternoon, as Bran and I were returning from our walk in the meadow, the Beagle paused on the lip of a hill, struck his best proud-as-a-peacock pose, and stood silhouetted for a moment between dancing emerald grass and pristine sapphire sky. The image brought a catch to my throat. He was handsome, he was devil-may-care, he'd made me his partner both criminally and creatively. He deserved to be famous…as famous as that other Beagle…Snoopy. Then and there I decided I would be his publicist.

The next morning, with Bran ensconced on the bed behind me, I began tapping out what would prove to be the first of thousands of dog-inspired words. With hopes as high as my Beagle's white-tipped tail, I sent my first canine story soaring off to Canada's largest outdoor magazine. It was promptly rejected.

Nevertheless, the editor replied that she liked the story; liked it so much, in fact, she was willing to give me a shot at being their "gun dog" columnist. Theirs had recently retired.

Barely able to keep my head out of the clouds, I rushed to compose the two sample columns she had suggested. Ron bought a Nikon to take the accompanying photos.

Since I was familiar with only two breeds of gun dogs at that time (and then on a mainly personal basis) I wrote about Beagles and Labs. Bran sat on the bed and watched. Perhaps he visualized me and my writing as his ticket to fame. At any rate, he allowed me to work undisturbed.

Much to my chagrin, those wonderful little essays filled with anecdotes, humor, and personal experiences came winging back. They lacked that certain depth of gun dog knowledge required for the person who would do the column, the editor wrote. She suggested I try more pet-oriented publications.

Insulted, I threw the manuscripts onto my improvised desk and vowed never to write about dogs again.

The pictures Ron had taken with that costly new camera tumbled out of the envelope. One of Bran leaping out of the children's wading pool, droplets of water spraying out like crystal shards around him, was especially fine. They deserved to be published. I began to repackage and re-address.

Three months later that beautiful action photo headed up my first published dog story in a national magazine. My career in canine creations was out and running. And like Bran, once off the mark, I never paused to look back.

Over the next few years my dog stories and Ron's photos appeared in an array of national and international outdoor, dog, pet, hunting, and even general interest magazines. Bran and his escapades had set Ron and me up in a cottage industry and a professional partnership that would add a long-lasting, thoroughly enjoyable dimension to our lives.

Just as with his constant pursuit of rabbits that he never did catch, Bran taught me that you should never stop trying. One man's trash is another man's treasure…or some such. The journey can be as rewarding as an elusive trophy.

Brandy and the Beasts

Those dog stories helped crack markets for my writing and Ron's photos in other magazine genres. I began to write stories for outdoor and travel publications as well as do profiles on individuals I met as a result of researching these articles. Ron faithfully snapped the accompanying illustrations.

Ron and I frequently travelled into forests and up mountains to get stories and, of course, Brandy accompanied us. During this period, we had a camp in a wilderness area known as Moose Brook. We often spent weekends there and allowed the Beagle to run free.

By this time the little dog had more or less proven he was capable of finding his way back with homing pigeon regularity. Somewhere over the months and years, we must have forgotten his little-big-man complex, his Napoleonic belief in his invincibility. Our forays to Moose Brook that fall and winter would revive the reality.

The first incident happened in the autumn of that year. At daybreak Brandy was at the door, whining to go out. I opened it, and he raced outside and down the steps.

"Don't go near the beaver pond," I called uselessly after him. I knew the beavers were busily preparing for winter and probably wouldn't welcome a howling, annoying nuisance.

Heedless as usual, he dashed into the trees. I sighed and returned to bed.

An hour later as we were eating breakfast, scratching at the door announced his return. I opened it and he marched proudly inside. As he passed me on his way to his food bowl, I noticed a large piece of fur missing from his tail.

"Lucky he's got any tail left," Ron commented when I pointed to the bare spot. "Maybe that will teach him not to bother the beavers."

Need I say it didn't?

That winter when Ron, Brandy, and I were snowshoeing in the woods, the Beagle (typically) disappeared into the trees. He was gone quite some time, but we weren't concerned. This was his general modus operandi on such occasions.

We'd returned to the truck and were loading snowshoes into the back when he came at a spritely trot out of the bush and stood waiting by the door to be let inside.

"Look." I pointed at the little dog. A long, head-to-heels bloody scratch ran down his left side.

"Looks like Indiana Jones got into another brouhaha." Ron glanced briefly at the beagle before continuing to load the truck.

For Ron, at least, Bran's near-death adventures had become normal events. I couldn't become that complacent.

We never did find out what manner of beast had produced that long ugly wound or what Brandy had done to provoke it. The incident in no way dampened his adventurous spirit. An application of disinfectant, a couple hours' snooze, and he was once more rarin' to go. Beavers, beasts, or dragons, he was ready for them.

A Moment of Victory

Brandy exuded pride. I believe he might have chosen death over defeat if life hadn't been providing him with such a good time.

An illustration of this pride occurred one cold, wet autumn day as Bran and I made our way out of the subdivision toward the meadow where the little dog had his daily romp. Only my devotion to his Beagle needs, the knowledge that I needed the exercise, and the belief that this type of weather, for some nebulous reason, fostered peaches-and-cream complexions (e.g. the flawless skin of so many British women) had the power to drag me from the warmth and comfort of my home on such a day.

Bran loved this kind of weather. He trotted enthusiastically along at my side, long ears glistening with mist, alert to the moment when I would snap the lead from his collar at the edge of the big field and give my own special release command, "Go play!"

A fog had drifted in off the bay. I like fog. It's cool and soothing and silent. It hushes the world and holds it suspended in a place of mystery and intrigue. Like a Victorian lady buried in layers of petticoats, it leaves much to the imagination…and I happen to be blessed (or cursed) with an extremely active one.

"You can pretend you're the Hound of the Baskervilles," I suggested to Bran, glad he'd lured me out to enjoy this morning of mysterious mist.

He glanced up at me, instant interest in his expression. Perhaps the idea of scaring the daylights out of Sir Charles Baskerville held a certain appeal for him.

On such a day, one could easily envision that great luminous Hound charging out of the mist, Sherlock Holmes in his deerstalker hard on its heels. Dr. John Watson, wielding his trusty service revolver, would not be far behind.

Not surprisingly, none of these fictional characters appeared. The man who did materialize out of the mist was much more contemporary. Tall and still athletic-looking at well past middle age, he was wearing a full-length trench coat of the London Fog variety and holding a sturdy umbrella. A tweed driving cap was pulled low over his eyes. Prince Phillip, perhaps?

"Good morning," he grunted. The thought sped across my mind: *Glad we're only passing acquaintances.*

The next instant all such contemplative meanderings jerked from my mind as I was brought to an abrupt halt by the leash. I turned to see what had happened. And gasped.

Bran had his jaws clamped vice-like onto the previously flapping coat tails of the grumpy passerby.

Scalding blasts of dismay and embarrassment shot through me. *How much does an expensive coat like that cost? Will I be sued for harboring a schizophrenic Beagle?*

"I'm sorry," I babbled, my cheeks burning so furiously in the cold air I envisioned steam hissing from them. Disgraced, I bent and attempted to pry small, determined fangs from fine, tan-colored cloth. "He's never done anything like this before."

"No need to apologize, m'dear," the victim astonished me by replying in a convivial tone. "Nothing quite like a good, keen-as-mustard Hound. Coat slapped the lad across the snout as I passed, I dare say. A proud young fellow like this stalwart little rascal cannot be expected to let such an insult go unchallenged."

His expression warm and companionable, he bent over the determined little dog still attached to his coat. "Sorry, old chap. Will try to keep this infernal garment under control in future. Now off with you! Go play!"

Whether it was the recognition of an honest apology or that of my homemade release command, I'll never know. I could only be overwhelmingly relieved when Bran let the coat fall free.

"Is there any damage?" I asked as we humans straightened up and faced each other in the mist.

"Certainly not!" he replied heartily, his former bellicose expression transformed into one of beaming pleasure. "The lad's a gentleman...would never go beyond exacting reasonable reparations. You've got a fine one there, my girl. Take good care of him."

He touched the peak of his cap...to both of us...and strode away.

When I turned back to the Beagle, the scolding I had been planning died in my throat. Bran faced me, eyes gleaming yellow-brown in the dull day. He had managed to turn a slap in the face into a moment of victory. His pride remained undaunted by the incident; in fact, it's just possible the Brit's apology had actually bolstered it.

Jet Joins the Family

"Teddi was right on point, rigid as a stake, bird just out in front of him, the best performance that pup ever turned in. Suddenly, out of nowhere, came this Beagle. Crashed full tilt into my dog and started a real donnybrook. Ruined the entire hunt."

I leaned farther back on my bench into the lengthening late afternoon shadows behind our camp and fervently hoped my husband's friend Dan wouldn't decide to come around the building to where I sat. Stretched out on the carpet of red, orange, and gold leaves at my feet lay one tired Beagle, a bloody scratch running down the length of his snout.

We were (at least, Ron was) duck hunting that October weekend near our camp. The children had gone picking apples at a neighbor's. Bran and I had taken a walk alone.

"Dan had some bad luck this afternoon," Ron commented when he came to join me a few minutes later after his friend had left. "A Beagle interfered with Teddi's point and threw the pup's concentration off for the rest of the day."

"Really?" I feigned innocence as I bent to scratch my companion's floppy ears and block Ron's view of the little dog's bloody nose.

"Yes, really." Ron stared at me with all the penetrating force of a laser. "By the way, where were you and Brandy at 2:30? Nowhere near MacKenzie's Meadow, I hope?"

"No, of course not!" I said with the best pretense of indignation I could muster. "We were at the shore. I could see him the whole time. He ran up and down the beach."

"I sincerely hope so," Ron, like all school teachers a master of the disapproving look, remarked and walked away, his brother's borrowed-for-duck-hunting, goody-goody Lab at his heels.

Bran looked up at me, tongue lolling rakishly out of his mouth. Something in those gleaming, yellow eyes told me he knew what was going on and that he wasn't the least bit sorry that he had once again drawn me into another of his nefarious escapades. It added to my series of lies that had been escalating over the past few months. But I must admit, I did feel tinges of guilt in lying to my husband.

Ron had been (mostly) tolerant of Brandy and his bohemian ways. He deserved to be rewarded. In deference to his patience, I decided after the Teddi incident to get him a dog of his very own.

His favorite breed had always been the Labrador retriever, especially its black members. For a number of years, after we'd given Smokey up for adoption, he'd borrowed his brother's Lab each hunting season and would come home to regale us with tales of Buddy the Black's amazing retrieves.

The choosing of a good hunting dog takes time and care. I shopped long and secretly for just the right pup. Finally, four weeks before Christmas, Jet of Acamac the Third joined our family.

He was adorable. Tumbling about the living room

on short, stubby legs, he looked like a black bear cub and was much cuddlier. Ron was delighted. Here at last was the dog of his dreams.

Indeed, Jet from day one was a dream come true. Good natured and obedient, he was a big, handsome creature, as laid back and easygoing as Brandy was razor sharp and impulsive. From the first moment Jet tumbled into our home and hearts on oversized puppy paws, he and Bran were destined to be an odd couple, as opposite as fire and ice.

During those early days of Jet's membership in our family, Bran largely ignored the big, gregarious pup. He did, however, develop a bizarre resentment toward Ron. It was as if he somehow blamed him for absolving his position as sole, and therefore unique, family pet. It shouldn't have been all that surprising. We were fast learning dichotomies were common in the little dog's character.

Jet had only been with us a few weeks when Bran demonstrated his resentment toward the head of the household in an original fashion.

During examination time at school, Ron brought home stacks of test papers from his chemistry class each evening, marked them at the dining room table after supper, and placed them on a footstool near the front door, ready to take to school in the morning.

One day about two weeks after Jet had joined our family, Ron woke late, dressed hastily, grabbed the tests from the footstool, and hurried off to work. It wasn't until he was returning the papers to his students that he realized something was amiss.

"What's the problem?" he asked, facing the room full of teenagers, all of whom were gingerly fingering the sheets of paper.

"Do you own a dog, sir?" one of the boys in the back asked.

A mass snicker erupted.

"Yes, as a matter of fact I do," Ron replied, puzzled but not without pride. "My wife just gave me a CKC registered Black Lab. Why do you ask?"

"Well, it looks as if he thought these papers were still part of a tree," came the reply. Full-fledged laughter erupted as a half-yellowed sheet of exam paper was held aloft.

Since Jet was still at the squatting puppy stage, there could be no doubt as to the identity of the leg-lifting culprit.

The words Ron had for Bran that evening were definitely not for publication.

Jealous revenge can manifest itself in unique and unpleasant forms.

Buried Alive!

The first serious snow after Jet's arrival in our home was really semi sleet. It ricocheted off buildings, fields, and windows like popcorn in an overheated machine. It stung cheeks and nipped noses and made people and puppies glad to be warmly ensconced at home.

Brandy and Jet sat in the dining room window and watched. What a picture they made, I thought, a warm fuzzy feeling coming over me as I gazed at the incredibly cute, velvet-eared tri-colored Beagle sitting close to the ebony-coated bundle that was Jet. The caption "Friends forever" raced across my mind as I hurried in search of our vintage Kodak (only Ron used the Nikon). How wonderful that Brandy had accepted Jet so fully, so uncomplainingly…except for the test peeing incident, that is. What could have been a nightmare of flying fur and yowls had turned into a picture of perfect serenity.

I should have known better than to take anything in which Bran was involved at face value. I should have recalled Bran allowed no indignity or perceived indignity to pass unpunished. The peed-upon term papers had been his revenge on Ron; Jet, the source of Bran's discontent, had yet to be fittingly punished.

When we woke the next morning, the world about our house lay blanketed in purest white. Trees bowed gently under their ermine robes. As the sun broke through the clouds, the foliage sparkled with sun diamonds. Brandy stretched, yawned, and raised front paws against the back door.

"This will be fun," I said to Ron as I opened the door to let both pups bound into the fenced yard, and I hurried to the dining room window to watch the pair as they burst out into the downy whiteness.

For the first few minutes, watching the dogs explore the ivory cold softness, burrowing deep into drifts with their noses, then surfacing trimmed with winter's icing from snout to ears, it was just that. Jet was especially appealing in his dappled coat of ebony and ivory.

Finally Brandy ended his careless cavorting and embarked on what appeared to be a scientific examination of this newly arrived material. He thrust his nose deep into it, blew it out in a stream like a surfacing whale, shoved it about with his snout, finally flying into a frenzied digging that sent feathery clouds billowing up into the frosty air.

"Crazy Beagle." Ron chuckled as he returned his attention to his wonderfully sane Lab puppy shying away from Bran's apparent madness.

After breakfast both pups eagerly returned to the yard. As I cleared dishes from the dining room table, I noticed Bran had changed his location of investigation to a drift stacked against the shed. While the children threw a bright red puppy bumper for Jet to retrieve and frolicked with the playful Lab, the Beagle remained hard at work. Snow flew and a hole grew until only the tip of his tail was visible.

An hour later the children, rosy cheeked and ready

for a warm place on the couch in front of the TV, came back inside. Jet, toasty warm in his furry coat and far from exhausted, bounced back from the kitchen door when they invited him to join them.

"Leave him out," I called from where I was seated in a chair by the dining room window with a second cup of coffee. "He and Bran aren't ready to come in yet."

Jet watched the children leave, his wagging tail slowing at the loss of his playmates. Seemingly disappointed by their departure, he let the bumper fall from his jaws.

In the time it takes to slit a second, Bran whizzed across the yard from his work site and seized it. Nonplussed, Jet stared for a moment at the Beagle standing a few feet in front of him, red toy protruding from his jaws. Then instinct prevailed. The Lab lunged and the chase was on.

For a few minutes it was hilarious, with puppy Jet floundering through the feathery drifts in pursuit of wiry, long-legged Beagle.

"Ron, you have to see this!" I summoned my husband from a TV sports broadcast.

A few seconds later I wished I hadn't. As Ron joined me, Bran reached the edge of his excavation and flung the toy into its depths.

Jet, a retriever from long generations of retrievers, leaped into the hole and disappeared from sight. In a heartbeat Bran had swung about and begun to fill in the cavity with kicks as deep and mighty as his twenty-five-pound body could produce. Jet, sunk in the downy depths, struggled to escape.

"He's burying Jet!" Ron raced out the back door,

yelling a stop order at the Beagle. Caught red-handed (or, in his case, white-pawed), Brandy paused, glanced toward the source of the commotion, then returned to burial detail.

Seconds later he was ignominiously deposited at my feet, sharp words of rebuke echoing around us both.

Bran appeared to listen in bored silence and watched as Jet was dried, soothed, and petted. Finally, with an exasperated sigh, he sauntered into the living room to leap up onto the couch and stretch out on his back for a snooze.

A friend who loves dogs but is not a Beagle fan, once referred to the little rabbit dogs as small demons put on earth solely to annoy mankind. While I don't agree, after that December morning I could understand why some unsympathetic souls might come to that conclusion.

This prank proved to be the only one Bran would ever play on Jet. Maybe it had simply been some sort of weird initiation into the family or maybe, discovering Jet possessed infinite good humor and tolerance, he saw no worthwhile future in such escapades. After all, what fun could there possibly be in teasing a creature who emerged from having been buried alive with its tail still wagging?

A sense of humor can be a useful weapon of defense.

The Purloined Turkey

By the time Christmas rolled around, Brandy stories had hit home with other Beagle owners. Letters and phone calls started arriving at our house with nice comments about the articles and an amazing variety of anecdotes about other little Hounds of the Beagle ilk.

One of my favorites came from an elderly widow who had been a minister's wife in a small Nova Scotia town. An avowed lifelong Beagle fancier, she told her story with such a kindly sense of humor I knew it had to reach a wider audience.

Her tale began one snowy Christmas morning as she was placing the family turkey—steaming, golden brown, and bursting with stuffing—before her family seated around the dining room table. Vegetables, breads, and gravy already in place paled before that magnificent bird.

A scratching sound issued from outside the back door.

The minister's wife opened it to find Bartholomew, their beloved Beagle, on the step. A large cooked turkey complete with stuffing melted a puddle in the snow beside him.

When the entire family had gathered to witness the little dog's thievery, being good Christians they decided there was only one thing they could do. They brought Bart and his battered bird (it had a gnawed drumstick) into the house and packed up their own Christmas turkey. The Reverend, bird in a basket, set off along the street in search of a family missing the meaty portion of their holiday repast. His wife would later describe him as being rather like the prince in Cinderella, only his glass slipper was a turkey.

"He never did find out who lost it." She chuckled. "But a family near the end of the street who wouldn't answer the door and moved away the following week without ever speaking to us again seemed the likely victims. Perhaps they thought George was bringing back the purloined turkey and they had no desire for it after it had been dragged through slush and snow."

Later the minister and his family ate a much cooler turkey and fixings while Bart, in lieu of punishment, (and who, after all, had simply been being a Beagle) enjoyed selected slices of his loot. His people were true Beaglers, that unique group of humanity capable of understanding and forgiving the antics of their chosen canine chums.

Of course, the fact that they were first-class Christians didn't hurt. Definitely Bart had given them ample opportunity to provide a lesson in forgiveness and the spirit of Christmas.

To All the Dogs I've Loved Before

Brandy Saves the Day

Bran never ceased to be full of surprises. After the Christmas of the Bart story, I was stricken with the most painful illness of my life, inflammation of the sciatic nerve. Three childbirths, an extracted tooth that had left a dry socket, and an appendectomy during the fifth month of pregnancy...all these ailments paled before this excruciating malady. For six weeks I lay stricken on my bed. Amazingly, for the entire six weeks of my disability, Bran, the willful, the free spirited, the inscrutable, never left my side except for the basic necessities of life.

Filled with astonished gratitude, I recognized the extent of the sacrifice the little Hound was making. He who passionately loved his freedom, the chase, and the great out-of-doors had given it all up to be with me. When noises from the living room signaled Ron or the children were getting ready to take Jet (and him as well, if he deemed to go) for a walk, he would raise his head, listen for a moment, then with sigh, snuggle back down at my feet.

Sometimes at night, when the misery became too great, when I lay despairing of ever walking pain-free again, of ever sharing forest and fields with my family, dogs, and friends, Bran would crawl up the bed, lick away my tears, and then settle gently against me.

I will never forget his loyalty.

And then the miracle happened! I received a contract to write a book…a book I had been longing to write for months! Lying on the bed, I held the offer in my hand and wondered how in the world I could manage it.

I looked at Bran, sitting at attention beside me, his eyes bright with interest. As surely as Sherlock Holmes, he knew when something was afoot. *Let's get on with it,* I saw mirrored in his outlook. *Don't lie there and let life pass you by.*

Using a broom and a hockey stick as improvised crutches, I hoisted myself off the bed. It hurt—oh, how it hurt—but I had to do, I knew I could do it! Teeth clenched, I struggled to my typewriter in the corner of the bedroom and sat down at the keyboard.

Bran watched me, his stance as proud as the day we'd first met. *Go for it, buddy,* was in his golden brown eyes. And I did.

Moonrise Mystique

Like all things temporal, winter and my pain passed. Spring and health came to me almost simultaneously and, with them, a renewed anticipation of my friend's next exploits. I didn't have long to wait.

In early May I discovered he was, if not actually a dreamer, a most persistent pursuer of one particularly impossible one. This revelation came to me on a spring morning as my friend Christiana and I were entering the meadow with our dogs.

All three animals halted for a moment to survey the wide open spaces; then Christiana's Boxer, Ross, and Jet continued with their usual raucous play. Brandy alone remained rooted to the spot, his eyes gazing upward and taking on an expression of sheer wonderment you would only expect to see in the face of someone mesmerized by a miracle.

Suddenly, with his traditional Beagle war whoop now as familiar to us as Tarzan's yodel to his jungle critters, he was off, a veritable tri-colored streak crossing the field full of golden dandelions, nodding daisies, and emerald grass.

"What is he chasing?" I asked. There were no rabbits, cats, groundhogs, horses, or even squirrels in sight.

"It's the moon," Christiana said, pointing to the late-setting, bleached-yellow ball hanging low above the trees at the far end of the meadow.

Much to my chagrin, I realized she was right. Brandy, howling his cries of the chase, headed for the trees beneath the point where the moon lay pale and dying in the brightening sky.

The entire family eventually came to enjoy this eccentricity. We would even take him out to the meadow on nights of a full moon and let him chase the golden globe to his heart's content.

Each time he disappeared into the shadowy darkness of the trees beyond the field, we would wish him luck. After all, don't we all secretly admire and envy the persistent dreamer, that amazing being who fights on in spite of the impossibility of his quest, careless of how a prosaic world may label him?

Although Bran knew nothing of Cervantes' Don Quixote or his dreams, I sometimes fancied I saw windmill blades around the moon and myself as a faithful Sancho Panza, never once considering the possibility of asking my own special dreamer to abandon his quest. How could I, when he'd taught me to chase one of my own?

The Case of the Careless Camper

On my return to health and vigor, I discovered I was looking forward to whatever new adventures Bran could stir up. (I assume that bout of sciatic had affected the little gray cells in my brains as well as the nerves in my back.) True, the moon-chasing thing which came first was innocuous. What followed wasn't.

For a Bohemian Beagle who cared nothing for conventions, Brandy had an amazingly straight-laced view of how humans should conduct themselves. He brooked no actions that he, in his canine mind, deemed unsuitable. For your consideration, I submit The Nude Sunbather Incident and The Case of the Careless Camper.

June first that year was one of those dates that, like the first time your child shrills out a four-letter word in church, will forever live in your memory. Bran and I were on our usual morning meander across the meadow. On the rim of a dip in the field, he paused and froze into pointing pose.

Groundhog, I thought, unconcerned. The area was full of them. Most never ventured so far from their burrows that they could not scurry back to safety in seconds when a troublesome Beagle approached.

Bran threw back his head and gave his unique version of the Tarzan roar. That indicated something out of the ordinary was afoot. Bran never warned a groundhog of his approach.

"Bran, wait!" I broke into a run, leash at the ready to capture him in my hand. My attempt failed. Like a one-dog contingent of the Light Brigade, he charged down the slope and out of sight.

I will never forget the sight that greeted me when I arrived at the top of that knoll. Streaking up out of the hollow, clutching an armful of clothing, a nude sunbather alternately ran and stumbled, indignant Beagle in hot pursuit at his naked heels.

Here, finally, I will reveal the truth about what I did on that humiliating day. I turned and hurried away in the opposite direction, hoping that poor harassed (actually his-assed) soul would not glance back, see me, and expire from embarrassment.

That was not to be Bran's only attempt at reforming errant outdoors people. A couple of weeks later, when Ron and I took both dogs for a walk in the woods in one of our provincial parks, Bran's judgmental nature once more surfaced.

In a little depression between rolling hills, we came upon a group of campers. They had set up several tents in a small clearing beneath lofty pines beside the proverbial babbling brook. When we paused for a moment to talk to them, I saw Bran gazing about the neat campsite and thought, for once, I knew what was going on between those long, velvet ears. No unprotected food, he was probably thinking. And there wasn't a rabbit in sight. I almost sighed aloud with relief. Bran the Brash was checkmated.

We wished the campers fine weather and few bugs and started on down the trail.

We had gone only a few hundred yards, when

Bran, trotting ahead of us, paused and sniffed intently. With the thrust of an atomic missile, he dove into the alders a few feet from the trail. His accompanying howl all but drowned out the expletive of the gentleman who had been using nature's answer to the Gents in that thicket.

Frantically pulling clothing back into place, the camper stumbled out into the trail to greet us, red-faced and fumbling. Bran howled at his heels.

"G-good morning," he stammered above the noise, trying to muster a smile and look as if nothing were amiss. "Beautiful day, isn't it?" He stuffed bits of shirttail into his jeans and furtively tried to check his fly.

"It was," Ron said between clenched teeth as he caught the howling little Hound by the collar and snapped a lead onto it with a resounding snap. "And it will be again," he said, glaring down at Bran. "Won't it." (No question mark required after a rhetorical question.)

We started off once more, two thoroughly chagrined humans, a confused-by-all-the-upset Lab, and one undaunted Beagle, tail and head held high. Once again he was the hero who had fought for the right. He would brook no fouling of the natural environment by human kind and would bear his resultant imprisonment like the Count of Monte Cristo, with unbowed dignity. No member of Green Peace could have exhibited a greater sense of accomplishment on saving an entire whale species from extinction.

Lesson learned: Never back off when you're convinced you're in the right.

Joan, Jet, and Joy

It happened in the early autumn of Jet's first year. Our daughter Joan had just been diagnosed with a rare and potentially life-threatening blood disease. In the hospital, bruised and weak from transfusions, she begged for a day's reprieve to go to the country with her parents and her pup. After much deliberation, the doctor agreed.

In spite of it being a gray September Sunday, with clouds hung low in a charcoal sky, girl and dog thoroughly enjoyed their time together. They visited old haunts, then sat together side by side as the afternoon waned. When Joan came to help us pack up to return home, Jet wandered off in search of Brandy, who had, of course, gone away in search of rabbits.

It happened as we were loading the last of our supplies into the car. A squeal of tires, the yelps of dogs. Before anyone could stop her, Joan raced off toward the road in the direction of the sounds.

When I reached the road, I found a deathly pale teenager kneeling in the ditch, an immobile black pup clutched in her arms. The Beagle stumbled about by the roadside, dazed but mobile. Jet had buffered the blow, being between Brandy and the vehicle. A distressed motorist stood over them, muttering, "I'm sorry. They ran right in front of me. The Beagle was chasing a squirrel. Are they going to be okay?"

Jet was breathing, but just barely. We wrapped him in quilts and loaded him into the back of our station wagon. Joan climbed in beside him, holding his head, whispering words of love and encouragement. Not once did she give in to the panic she must have been feeling. Her concern centered on her dog, nothing else.

I tried to pick Brandy up in my arms. Confused and hurting, he snapped at me for the first and only time in his life. Demonstrating his typical independence, he staggered into the car on his own.

Ron kept glancing into the rearview mirror as we drove toward the city; when our eyes met, I knew we were both wondering what would happen to our fragile daughter if she lost her friend. The doctor had warned us against exposing her to emotional stress.

Sunday is the worst day of the week to find a vet. Ours proved no exception. He was out of town, his answering service informed us. In case of emergency, please contact his retired predecessor.

That veterinarian, a kindly but outdated old gentleman, took one look at the Beagle, declared him fit except for a few days' soreness, then turned to the Lab. After a cursory examination, he declared nothing could be done for him.

"Have Tom put him down when he gets back tomorrow morning," he said, referring to our regular vet. "It'll be best. He's paralyzed."

Joan expressed no emotion at his words, but her blue eyes turned sapphire-hard. My husband and I both knew that look. She wasn't about to give up without a fight.

We drove home in silence.

"Put him on my bed," Joan said when we arrived.

Her tone allowed for no argument or refusal.

When the pup lay as comfortable as possible in the center of her bed, I turned to her.

"Honey, it's only for tonight. Tomorrow…"

"I don't want to hear it!" She threw up her hands to cover her ears. Her arm hit her bedside lamp and sent it crashing to the floor.

Startled out of his shocked state, Jet staggered to his feet, falling over the edge of the bed onto the floor. Leaning against the wall, his eyes glazed with shock, pain, and confusion, tongue lolling out of his mouth, he stared up at us.

"He's not paralyzed!" Joan on her knees beside him, covered his snout with kisses, tears coursing down her cheeks. "He's going to be all right, I know!"

An hour later, she remained cradling Jet in her arms when I gently broached the subject of her return to the hospital.

"Let me talk to Dr. Henry," she said. "He'll understand. He'll know I have to stay with Jet tonight."

Ten minutes later, she handed the phone to me. "He wants to talk to you," she said before hurrying back to her dog.

"I've decided to let her stay home tonight," the doctor informed me. "She'd never rest away from him. Bring her in tomorrow for a blood test. I'm concerned about how all this stress is affecting her condition. We'll have to keep our fingers crossed for the dog. She can't afford to lose him at this point."

That night, girl and dog slept in a tangle of quilts and pillows on the living room floor. Early in the morning, we eased Jet out of her arms and carried him to the car. If he had to be put down, better to have it done before she awakened, before she had to say goodbye.

Our vet gave us wonderful news. After examining Jet, he told us he believed that with hospitalization and a lot of TLC, Jet could recover. How fully, Dr. Larsen couldn't be sure, but he believed the Lab deserved the chance to explore the possibilities.

Over the following months and years, the girl and her dog required much specialized care, including lengthy periods of hospitalization. Jet lost part of one paw to infection and Joan needed multiple blood transfusions. Both had to take life much more slowly and cautiously than the average girl and dog. But each time they beat their illnesses, life became just a little more precious to them. Struggling back to health, they were drawn inextricably closer in their quiet celebration of *joie de vivre*.

They even discovered there could be plusses to their disabilities. At this reduced pace, they had time to savor the hamburgers, to study the birds and flowers and bullfrogs along the way. Together they enjoyed summer showers, autumn sunsets, Christmas snowfalls, and the first pussy willows of spring. What if one was a little too pale and the other walked with a limp? Their days overflowed with the joy of lives full of precious moments, moments they might never have been granted.

When Joan's disease finally went into remission, she attended university and became an elementary school teacher. The friendship between young woman and aging dog never once flickered. When Joan came home for weekends and vacations, she and Jet immediately fell back into their old role of being inseparable.

As the years passed, the big, black dog, graying about the muzzle, hobbled happily at her side, worshipping her with soft brown eyes and never once giving in to bad humor or self-pity. He became an inspiration of uncomplaining acceptance of life lived to the best of one's ability.

Brandy, of course, remained Brandy, not an iota of his *joie de vivre* tarnished by his near-death experience. Although he couldn't possibly have been aware of the old adage about getting right back on the horse after you fall off, he did go right back to chasing anything that would move in front of him. No setback, no matter how great or small, should dull one's dedication toward one's purpose in life.

Just Doing His Job

If anyone ever tells you oil and water are impossible to mix, you can top them with the mixture of bears and Beagles. These little Hounds probably are near the top of the list of breeds that conscientiously disregard the inherent danger in this concoction. My father-in-law Wilson was very nearly a victim of this Beagle disdain for these omnivores on two occasions during Bran's second summer and autumn.

The first incident happened on a hot June afternoon the year following the car accident. Bran had accompanied Ron and his father to a wilderness area on a fishing expedition. We had not yet moved to the cottage, and Bran had had a long winter of suburban living. I'd decided to send him along with husband and father-in-law to give him a chance to stretch winter-cramped legs. By this time I was sufficiently confident of the Beagle's homing abilities to feel he would come back no matter how far he strayed into the hinterland.

So off my soul mate went, seated proudly between Ron and his father on the truck's bench seat, to what would prove an outing indelible in our memories.

As Wilson later told the story, he was contentedly fishing along the edge of the lake, intermittently slapping at those chemically insensitive bugs undeterred by his layers of repellent. My father-in-law later described the scene as being one of those still, hot, muggy days so quiet in the forest you could hear a bird burp.

Shattering as the pistol shot that killed Archduke Ferdinand and started the Great War, the peace blew apart. The silent, sweltering bush came alive with roars, crashes, and yikes.

Before Wilson could comprehend the situation, Bran burst out of a thicket, yowling, a huge black bear hot on his heels. With his remarkable homing instincts as keen as mustard, Bran headed straight for Ron's dad.

For you to fully appreciate the moment, it is necessary that I describe my father-in-law in his traditional fishing attire. His garb was classic Norman Rockwell, complete with Tilly hat adorned with his most prized lures, the strap of his wicker catch basket slung across the chest of his plaid shirt, L.L.Bean hip waders fastened to the belt of his khaki bush pants. His fly rod, a special edition, had cost more than the advance on my first novel.

As he turned to see what was happening, Bran hit him full speed amidships. Rod and hat were launched skyward as man and dog plummeted backward into the lake.

Wilson's roars and flailing arms as he toppled, a Beagle stuck to his chest, apparently discouraged the bear. With a disgruntled roar (as clearly as Wilson can recall), it turned and galloped back into the forest.

As Wilson struggled to right himself in waders half full of water, Bran released his stranglehold and swam back to shore. There he shook himself, stretched out on his belly to catch his breath, and listened to his savior using language that would make a drunken sailor blush as he searched for that fancy rod in the mud and grass at the lake's murky bottom. His beloved hat with its lifetime collection of special lures had landed too far out on the water to be rescued by a man in water-logged waders. Bran, being neither a water dog nor a retriever, didn't attempt its rescue. Anyway, he was too involved in rolling about in the grass and weeds on the shore in a carefree effort to dry himself.

You would think that after such an experience, Wilson would not welcome Bran on any further hinterland excursions. But my father-in-law (rest his soul) was a remarkable man. He had spent five horrendous years in the European theatre during World War II and managed to return home with little animosity toward the enemy.

"Just doing their job," he'd say of the Axis soldiers with a philosophical ease I found difficult to understand knowing only a little of the horrors he had endured. I submit this bit of background so that the reader might understand why, that autumn, Brandy again got invited to share another woodsy outing with Wilson.

Ron and his dad had planned a partridge hunt. Wilson suggested Bran might be able to flush a few birds. Jet, recovering from paw surgery, was not able to go. Reluctantly Ron agreed. Even a brash Beagle would be better than no dog at all.

Once in the bush, Ron and Wilson separated to walk two different overgrown logging roads. Wilson, the magnanimous optimist, took Bran with him.

About ten o'clock, Wilson sat down on a mossy stump to rest. Warm autumn sunlight filtering through golden birches in the quiet forest shed a pleasant lassitude over Ron's dad, and he believes he may have dozed.

Suddenly, *deja vu*! Roars, yikes, and crashing bushes shattered the stillness with the impact of a rifle blast. Wilson leaped to his feet just as Bran hit him full force against the knees, a huge black bear once again mere feet behind him.

As the enraged bruin reared on its hind legs to tower above man and dog, Wilson stumbled backward over his stump seat, discharging both barrels of his shotgun into the air.

The racket proved too much for the marauding omnivore. With an echoing roar, he swung and lumbered back into the bush.

This time Bran had the good grace to remain where he'd landed on Wilson's chest and, before his rescuer could try to get up off his back, give him a gigantic kiss.

This adventure turned out to be Bran's last safari with Wilson. My wonderful, forgiving father-in-law, a man who had been able to see the entire German army as just doing its job, had had all he could take from one small Beagle doing what the little dog saw as his job.

Sometimes you just have to admit some things won't work.

The Lady in the Pink Snowsuit

Winter rolled around, and Bran was once again presented with a fresh, new season in which to amuse himself. One of his escapades that second winter became indelibly etched in my mind. Until now, it has remained a secret shared between only a profoundly trusted friend and myself. The reason is simple: criminal charges may, for a time, have been pending.

It began one gorgeous day in early March, that time of year in northern New Brunswick when the snow crust is as hard as pavement and sun-glazed to the slipperiness of an eel's back. Skiing conditions, both downhill and cross-country, varied between the treacherous and the suicidal.

Christiana and I never ceased to walk our dogs in spite of this challenging footing. Ross, her Boxer, and Jet and Bran were best friends. They should not be denied their daily socializing.

One glorious Monday morning, we set out through the woods and across a meadow alive with snow diamonds, framed by spruce trees iced in ivory, and topped with sapphire skies. A benevolent sun smiled down, warming our faces, awakening thoughts of spring, and glazing the snow's hard surface with a treacherous liquid sheen. Several times Christiana and I caught at each other's sleeves to prevent falling. Even the dogs found it difficult to run without an occasional spill.

At the far end of the meadow the land dipped downward into a long, sweeping slope of virginal white that terminated in a cluster of alders and dogwood. When we reached a vantage point, all five of us paused to savor the panorama.

Then I saw Bran's ears prick into that frightening stance that indicated "the game," as Holmes would say, "was afoot." Following his line of vision, I saw a rotund lady in a pink ski suit perched atop the hill some distance away. On her feet was a pair of cross-country skis.

"What can she be thinking?" Christiana, a veteran skier of the Austrian Alps, breathed as she, too, caught sight of the object of Bran's interest. "Cross-country skis…on this crust…on a hill?"

As we watched, the lady plunged her poles into the crust and squatted to adjust her boots, pink bottom hanging between her widespread skis.

An unearthly howl went up from the smallest in our company. Before I realized what was happening, Bran was off, charging toward that pastel bundle as if he'd discovered the Energizer bunny well within his reach.

There was a scream, a wild scratching. The lady, still in squat position, and her skis were off down the slope, pink rear end bouncing over each natural mogul with an accompanying shriek.

I watched, horrified. This was the first time it appeared one of Bran's pranks would result in serious bodily harm. As fast as we could scramble, Christiana, Jet, Ross, and I half slid, half staggered down the slope toward the crumpled mound that had come to an abrupt halt in the thicket at the bottom.

By the time we reached her, the lady was fumbling to her feet with the aid of limbs and branches. Her face bore a much deeper hue than her suit.

"Are you all right?" Christiana, a nurse, was instantly at her side to assist.

"Yes, yes…I think so." Slipping and sliding on skis still miraculously tacked to her boots, the woman clung suspended between my friend and a dogwood like a pink personification of that rotund cartoon creation used in Michelin tire commercials. "But who owns that miserable little dog?"

She pointed to Bran standing proud and alert at the top of the hill.

Christiana and I exchanged glances, and then my friend, a quicker thinker than I am, replied, "We have no idea. He's been following our dogs through the woods all morning. He really should be contained."

We helped the woman unclamp her skis and assisted her to her car, parked on a road below the meadow. As she drove out of sight, Christiana turned to me.

"Bran couldn't have foreseen the outcome," she said looking into my stormy countenance. "I'm sure he didn't want anyone to get hurt."

"Right," I snapped. "Defend his deviousness. You've already lied for him."

"Good Lord, I did…I have!" She gasped. "You don't think he's turning me into one of his co-conspirators like you, do you?"

The idea of Bran's being able to cast some sort of sinister spell over the mind of my pragmatic Austrian friend broke the boil of annoyance pressing down on my sense of humor. I burst out laughing.

That was not the last we were to hear of the sinister ski accident. The next morning when Christiana returned to work at the hospital emergency room, a colleague told her of an unusual case she had treated the previous day.

"This lady had bruises and lacerations all over her bottom," she said. "She tried to tell me it was the result of some kind of weird skiing accident involving a dog. Now, I ask you, do I look gullible enough to swallow a crazy story like that?"

Sometimes practical jokes can go wildly awry. Best not get involved.

The Battle of the Birds

Over the years, I frequently compared Bran to Napoleon Bonaparte, small in stature but large in vision and overflowing with confidence and sense of invincibility. I will continue this analogy by describing Bran's actions under a state of bombardment.

It was the summer after the great skiing incident. With the family once again living at the cottage, Ron had purchased a secondhand (polite description… preowned) outboard motor boat to add to our summer's enjoyment. Instead, it became the bane of our existence. Sometimes it worked like a charm; mostly we ended our voyages wading home through the shallows for miles, the not-too-good ship *Undependable* in tow. Needless to say, with such unreliable transport we seldom ventured out into big or deep water.

One beautiful July morning we decided to take a trip out to one of the nearby islands at the river's mouth to dig clams. Soon the entire family—which, of course, included Bran and Jet—were aboard, with pails, shovels, and lunches stowed away aft. Or is that amidships?

Undependable ran beautifully on the outgoing voyage. Jet lay relaxed and happy, sunning himself near the rear (I think I probably should say stern) with the children, while Ron captained at the steering wheel and controls in the front, me beside him. Bran, true to form, had to be more of an adventurer than the rest of us. He stood with front paws braced against the dashboard (or whatever its nautical equivalent is called), head over the windscreen, ears streaming back in the breeze.

His delight in our mini-adventure was contagious. We foresaw a great day ahead. Even old *Undependable* seemed to be humming along better than usual.

Once on the strip of sand and grass we called an island, even the tide, we discovered, had cooperated and gone out to allow us access to the clam beds. We set to work at once to dig for our supper.

With Bran penned in by water on all sides, we didn't bother to keep track of him. Soon he disappeared into the tall marsh grass that grew thick and rich along the island's elevated spine.

We had only been digging a few minutes when we heard screams arising from that vegetation. Looking in the direction of the commotion, we saw a cloud of herring gulls rising out of the grass, their cries shrieks of shock and outrage.

"What could have happened?" Ron asked. "There're no foxes out here to disturb them…"

At that moment a flash of black, white, and tan burst out of the three-foot-tall grass, the cloud following in incensed pursuit.

"But there is a Beagle!" I muttered.

"The little beggar must have gotten into their nesting site!" Ron breathed.

Homing instincts working perfectly, Bran headed for his family at top speed, hoards of enraged gulls screaming and diving after him. Scenes from Alfred Hitchcock's classic *The Birds* flooded into my mind, and I was suffused with an urge to throw myself bodily over my children in an heroic effort to save them. Ron, as always, took a more practical approach.

"Run!" he yelled, and we were off *en masse* to hit the deck of old *Undependable* in a rush that all but capsized the sixteen-foot plywood craft.

Bran leaped aboard, too, bringing his squawking, dive-bombing entourage with him.

As Ron struggled to push and paddle us to water deep enough to employ the motor, the birds had time to reconnoiter, hover, and begin to do what herring gulls do best. We reached sufficient depth to lower the motor as the first volley of guano hit us amidships.

True to form, *Undependable* chose not to start. With Ron frantically trying to crank her twenty-five-horsepower Johnson into life, she floated calmly out toward the bay, uninspired either by the barrage of bird bombs or the cries of shrieking children.

Bran alone seemed to be weathering the battle well. He had dived under the front seat.

When Ron had finally managed to force *Undependable*'s propulsion system into life—with a combination of brute strength and his own special selection of expletives—and we were able to leave the ballistic birds behind, Bran emerged from his bunker and disdainfully examined our spattered deck. He yawned, stretched, and glanced disparagingly at the rest of the crew as we tried to wipe long streaks of smelly white goo from hair and clothing.

With a sigh he returned to his shelter to sleep out the remainder of the voyage. He had reviewed his troops and found them wanting, it appeared.

As our beleaguered boat struggled away from the Battle of the Birds, I realized I was much wiser in nautical terminology. Now I definitely knew why a part of a ship was called the poop deck. The only thing I couldn't quite understand was how sailors got the gulls to confine that activity to one special area.

Brandy's Dose of Rabbit

The following winter, Brandy became ill. In spite of our vet's best efforts the Beagle grew progressively weaker. What had begun as gastritis had escalated to such a disabling level Bran could barely manage to go outdoors for necessities. By April, the normally vivacious little dog had deteriorated into a weak, despondent creature with glazed eyes and only enough strength to sniff his food before staggering back to his bed to rest.

Our vet could find no explanation or cure. Reduced to giving the little Hound pain-killing injections, Dr. Larsen admitted there was nothing more he could do.

"He's simply not responding to treatment," he said.

That year, a dark, cold winter had reluctantly evolved into an equally dismal spring. Rain, unseasonably low temperatures, and mounds of late-dissolving snow had helped intensify my feelings of hopelessness for my little friend. A hard lump formed in my throat as I recalled other springtimes when warm, sunny days had seen him racing about the house and yard, eager to be taken out to the woods and meadows to hone his hunting skills on the first rabbit crop of the season.

Rabbits! How their scent had set his nose twitching, his tail flagging like a deer on the alert. It had been months since he had been out in the forests and fields he loved; weeks since he had done more than languish in his wicker basket in the living room. I recalled a friend's Pointer that, after simple surgery and apparently on the road to recovery, had suddenly lapsed into a deep melancholy. Eventually he had died in his bed. I shivered. I couldn't let that happen to Brandy.

One morning, when we were halfway home from another vet visit, the first sunshine in more than two weeks broke through the heavy cloud cover. It sent a golden beam through the windshield to bathe in its warmth the small furry body curled up beside me. At its touch Brandy stirred but did not bother to look up.

We were nearing a side road that led to the meadow, the same meadow where Bran had enjoyed some of his best adventures and pursuits. I remembered another spring and a book contract and that immense, incredible desire to struggle back into life no matter how much it hurt. When we reached the lane, I turned into it, a glimmer of hope rising in my heart.

As I drove slowly and carefully over the lumpy dirt trail, I rolled down my window and let the forest scents of pine, spruce, and leaf mold waft into the cab.

I felt a slight movement on the seat beside me. Glancing down at Bran, I saw his head come out of the cocoon-like ball into which he'd rolled himself. His nose twitched.

I stopped the truck, turned off the engine, and lifted the shaky little body into my arms. Carefully I carried him out into the field's reborn grass, placed him on the ground, and waited.

For several long moments he lay still. Finally his head came up, his nose wiggled, and he gazed about, eyes brightening.

"Rabbits, Bran," I whispered.

The nose wiggled again, the old familiar golden glow ignited in his brown eyes. With a grunt he pulled himself to his feet and staggered over to sniff droppings under a small spruce. Legs trembling, he tottered to the next bush, which he inspected thoroughly before he had to sit down and pant. He had taken only five steps, but it was a beginning. I remembered shaky fingers slowly tapping out a first sentence, one springtime past, while Bran watched. I smiled.

"That's enough for today, Buddy." I gathered him up in my arms. "We'll come again tomorrow."

He and I returned to the meadow each afternoon for the next three weeks; each afternoon Brandy managed to move about more and more, with more and more confidence. By the time maples and birches were in full leaf, he was trotting briskly across the fields, flesh on his bones, a gleam in his eyes. Life simultaneously returned to the woods, the meadows, and the little dog. It brought memories of how good I'd felt at the end of that first chapter.

One afternoon in the first week of June, as Brandy and I crossed a meadow rich with daisies and robins, we spotted a brown lump in the trail ahead of us. I didn't have to say "rabbit"; my buddy was off in a modest cloud of dust. A completed manuscript boxed and ready to be shipped came to mind.

The Beagle I took home that evening was indeed a happy camper. It didn't matter that the rabbit had made it safely to its burrow or that Brandy was panting like an 1850s steam engine. He had once again experienced the reason for which he lived…the joy of the chase.

When he arrived home, he glanced disdainfully at

his pillow-filled wicker basket and leaped up onto the couch to assume Snoopy position on his back for a snooze.

Perhaps Brandy's recovery was a miracle. Or perhaps whatever mysterious virus he had contracted had simply run its course. I will never know. But I do know he received no medication during the weeks of his revival.

Bunnies and book contracts? Perhaps both hold some mystical cure for those possessed of certain eccentricities. I believe Bran and I had both learned a sense of purpose could be a major ingredient in returning to health.

Chalk Another One Up to the Beagle

"There's absolutely nothing wrong with him a little more exercise and a lot less food won't cure," Dr. Larsen informed us.

Bran, once recovered, seemed to have decided to make up for each and every meal he had missed during his illness. Now, halfway through the following autumn, his girth told the tale.

"No more treats," Dr. Larsen said sternly as he lifted the thickening, tri-colored Beagle off the examining table.

Once more on *terra firma*, Brandy looked up at the vet, ears cocked to catch every syllable. As he listened, his round teddy bear eyes slowly narrowed and turned a glowering gold. The humans were using the word he most abhorred and which he had conscientiously managed to ignore all his life. That word was "no."

Denying himself anything he really enjoyed had never been Bran's idea of living. Iron-willed, sensuous, free-thinking, and totally arrogant, he was not about to buckle under to whatever the human society decided he must not have or do.

As we drove home, Brandy sat quietly between Ron and me, staring straight ahead. Normally he would have been prancing across the seat, watching for stray cats and pigeons. Ron and I glanced apprehensively at each other. He was plotting; we just knew it.

At supper that night, Brandy got his first hint of his food future. No table scraps to flavor the Doggy Diet Delight in his bowl, no television-advertised treats to enhance the meal. He sniffed the dry, bare kibble, glanced up at me—at first reproachfully, and then when I made no move to change his meal, with contempt. Slowly he turned narrowed, covetous eyes toward Jet's matching bowl topped with roast beef gravy.

"Don't even think about," I warned. Jet, although forty pounds heavier than Brandy, had been raised by the Beagle to respect the Beagle. He would have allowed Brandy to drive him away from his supper, and I knew it.

His thoughts read, his plan thwarted, Bran gave his bowl a disgusted shove that sent it flying into his water dish. As its contents splashed over the kitchen floor and Jet shied away from the clatter, a thoroughly disgruntled Hound turned and headed into the living room. A few minutes later I found him stretched out on his back on the couch, staring at the ceiling.

"Playing starving Beagle won't work," I said. "Dr. Larsen said this diet stuff is perfectly edible and incredibly good for you. At any rate, it's all you're getting. It's for your own good, you know." I finished lamely with the words that are every mother's last resort in urging her children into something disagreeable while at the same time soothing her own sense of guilt.

The simulated corpse on the couch remained unmoved. I turned and walked back into the kitchen, where Jet was licking the remains of his supper from his bowl. He looked up at me and wagged his tail good-naturedly.

"Why didn't the Powers That Be see fit to give us two agreeable creatures?" I asked. "Instead of one sweetheart like yourself and the other that nemesis playing dead on the couch."

Nemesis was the correct name for a dieting beagle we found out that night. Formerly bedtime had meant four or five dog biscuits washed down with a bowl of water. Hoping to spare the fasting Beagle (he still hadn't touched the Doggie Diet Delight) complete food withdrawal pangs, I gave him a single bone-shaped crunchy.

He munched it eagerly. Ah, at last, real food, his satisfied eating noises declared. Licking his lips, he looked up at me for the rest of his bedtime snack.

"Sorry, chum, that's it. Dr. Larsen says there's sugar in those little munchies. You have to cut down."

Expectant round eyes narrowed into those familiar glowing yellow slits. Nervously I turned my back on his glare and went to bed.

I was drifting off to sleep when I felt his paw on my shoulder, tap, tap, tapping.

"No." I rolled away from the appealing little eyes inches from my nose. "No food. Go to sleep."

Front paws dropped to the floor and slowly, with calculated deliberateness, padded across the shadowy bedroom to our antique dresser. In the moonlight streaming into the room I saw a white paw come off the floor to hold threatening claws extended before the one-hundred-and-fifty-year-old furniture front.

"No!" Ron bounded out of bed. "Don't you dare!"

A muted thump announced a hand connecting with furry bottom. "Now forget your chubby little belly and go to bed! You've stored up enough fat to hibernate until spring!"

Indignant little paws clicked a staccato rhythm back into the living room and leaped up onto the couch.

"That's that," Ron said with satisfaction as he climbed back into bed. "All he needs is to be shown who's the boss."

"I hope so, but…"

"You know so. The proof is right in front of you. Now good night and sweet…uninterrupted dreams."

3:01 A.M. I know the exact time because when my eyes flew open at the crash I faced the luminous dial of our bedside clock radio.

"Someone's broken in." I heard Ron's tense whisper. "He tripped in the dark and fell down the basement stairs."

My husband grasping a flashlight, we made our way stealthily into the living room. On the couch Jet had awakened but had not been sufficiently concerned to get up.

"Great watch dog," Ron muttered as we continued cautiously into the kitchen.

As the beam of light fell on the top of the basement stairs, golden canine eyes glared back at us. A non-repentant-looking Beagle stared up at us for a moment before returning his gaze to something at the bottom of the steps.

When Ron turned the flashlight downward, we saw a yellow dog dish lying upside down at the bottom. Doggie Diet Delight lay scattered over every step.

"He pushed it over here and shoved it down the steps," Ron breathed in astonished outrage. "Get back to bed right now, you furball, and don't let me hear another sound until morning!" he ordered the Beagle.

Tail held high, back straight, obviously undaunted, Brandy gave us a final disdainful glance, then ambled back to the couch.

"Maybe he really is hungry," I said. "Maybe…"

"No way. We're not giving in to his evil little tricks. He can't torture us with sleep deprivation. We're the masters here. He's only a little dog."

But as the flashlight beam swept over the two dogs lying on the couch, the smoldering animosity in the eyes of the smaller one told me this battle of wills had not yet reached its climax.

4:17 A.M. Again the luminous radio face assured me accuracy of time. Shuffling noises in the kitchen. A big mouse? A rat, perhaps? We'd never had any rodents, but there is always a first time. Sweat broke out over me. I feared both more than any burglar. I wondered if I dared awake the cranky creature snoring beside me.

Deciding it was safer to face anything by myself rather than another false alarm with an incensed spouse, I slid from the bed. Flashlight in hand, heart pounding like a sledgehammer, I crept to the kitchen and splashed the light over the room.

It came to rest on a pair of glowing eyes. Bran stood proudly amid the mess of an overturned garbage can.

Looking up at me, he kicked a butter wrapper from a hind paw. The only positive thought I had at that moment was that I had had the good sense not to awaken Ron.

The next five nights proved no better. Finally, worn to a nub from broken rest, I opted for a modified diet. Taper him off his regular food instead of forcing him to go cold turkey. After all, Doggy Diet Delight must be quite a shock for a Beagle that knew every take-out in town and had not infrequently feasted on a vast variety of purloined goodies.

Gradually I put a little less of the good life in his bowl and each night a little more Doggie Diet Delight. By the end of five more days, I was able to leave Jet and Brandy alone in the kitchen, each at his own bowl. Best of all, the night noises had stopped. *I've won,* I thought gleefully, having difficulty not to break out into a Snoopy happy dance.

At the end of the month I took both dogs to the vet for a check-up.

"Have you been giving Bran the diet food?" Dr. Larsen frowned as he weighed the Beagle.

"Oh, yes. I had to taper him off scraps and junk food gradually, but now he's totally on the diet formula," I said proudly.

"Strange." Dr. Larsen set the little dog on the floor. "He's gained three pounds. Jet, on the other hand, has lost four."

I looked down into those round, innocent teddy bear eyes. It wasn't possible. He couldn't have bowl-switched. But yet, who really knows what diabolical plots can be spawned in the mind of a hungry Beagle?

"You are lucky I love you," I said later as I loaded both dogs into the cab of our pickup. "You're also fortunate Jet is an affable soul with a great deal of misplaced respect. Otherwise, nothing would have saved you from some kind of food-based punishment and a good canine thrashing."

He looked me squarely in the face as I settled behind the wheel, gave his tail a couple of perfunctory wags, twinked me with a quick kiss on the nose, then pranced to his position in the center of the seat to watch for stray cats and wayward pigeons.

With a sigh so deep it seemed to come from the tips of my toes, I turned the key in the ignition. Not only had my dieting plans for Bran proven futile, I was now three pounds on the plus side of square one. Chalk another victory up to the Beagle. Moral to this story: Sometimes you don't succeed no matter how hard you try.

Calm in the Face of Crisis

One huge advantage of having three children barely over a year apart in age (as time goes on, after diapers, three a.m. feedings, and non-simultaneous naps) is that they can share the same activities as they grow.

When ours reached the ages of ten, eleven, and twelve, they simultaneously (for once) became obsessed with the desire to tent out of doors. Our children, from toddlers, had been enthralled with the structures. They'd draped sheets and blankets over every inch of available furniture on rainy or stormy days in their efforts to simulate their outdoor counterparts. Now they wanted the real thing.

In June, Ron and I decided to buy them an actual (if profoundly economical) tent. They had done well in school. They deserved a reward.

Such delight when Ron carried the awkward oblong box into our backyard that beautiful spring evening! Such scrambling to put it up! Such heartfelt pleas to be allowed to sleep out in it that night!

Finally we acquiesced. After all, they would be in our fenced backyard, and what point had there been to buying them the tent if we weren't prepared to allow them to enjoy it?

The evening that followed was filled with a constant procession of goods and materials (not to mention food and drink) from house to tent, until I thought our home would be emptied.

At ten o'clock, as soft summer darkness descended over the canvas edifice in the center of the yard, Ron and I were prodded out of our lawn chairs and herded inside. It was time for us to leave them alone.

I whistled to the dogs to come along. Three indignant faces appeared in the tent's mesh doorway.

"Bran and Jet are sleeping with us!" came the chorus.

A shadow of foreboding wafted over my mind, but it was so nebulous, so apparently groundless, I forced myself to brush it off like a cobweb. But, like a cobweb, bits of unrest persisted in clinging.

"Come on." Ron put an arm about my shoulders and guided me into the house. "They'll be fine. We'll leave the back door open, the screen one unlatched. If anything goes wrong, they can be inside in a split second. But," he continued, catching my concerned glance, "nothing will. There's not a cloud in the sky, it's a beautiful twenty-five degrees C, and the gate is securely latched."

"You're right." I tried to sound confident, but every negative nerve ending of my woman's intuition tingled. "What can happen." (Again, no question mark was required at the time, since it was meant to be rhetorical.)

Try as I might, I could not quell those uneasy feelings. Straining to hear any hint of trouble from the yard through our open bedroom window, I lay awake for hours. All I heard were muted voices and giggles, the subdued (on strong parental suggestion) tones of rock music from a ghetto blaster, the rustle of celluloid snack bags, and the occasional admonition, "Bran, get your nose out of the chips/cheezies/etc."

About 1:30 a.m. silence descended. I sighed, rolled over, and prepared to sleep.

Suddenly out on the lawn there arose such a clatter I sprang from my bed to see what was the matter. The moon on the crest of the birch tree beyond gave a luster of midday to objects on the lawn.

In its illumination I saw the tent pitching and rocking like a thing possessed. Bran was howling. The screams and cries of my children made my blood run cold. Some horrible creature, human or otherwise, was attacking my darlings, all five of them. Like a tigress in a faded cotton nightgown, I raced out of the house, ready to fight to the death.

I got into the yard just as, accompanied by terrible ripping sounds, Bran burst through a corner of the tent and bolted, baying at the top of his lungs, across the yard. Margaret Aims' tabby, the cause of the catastrophe, paused a moment on the top of our basketweave fence just long enough to hiss disparagingly down at the frustrated little dog howling and leaping up at her. She vanished, unscathed, into the night.

"[Expletives deleted] Beagle!" Steve at ten had recently been testing the shock value of four-letter words. The incident had presented him with a golden opportunity.

His voice coming from the capsizing tent was no experiment this time. It sounded totally sincere.

Dismayed, I could only stand on the doorstep and watch as children and Lab extricated themselves from the crumpling structure. Besides the gaping hole Bran had made, the tent's pegs had been ripped from the ground with resultant tears in the cheap canvas. Now the entire thing slowly collapsed like a punctured hot air balloon until only a rumpled pile of weather-resistant cloth lay on the lawn.

Ron joined me as Carol burst into tears. Bran, still baying, had his front paws braced against the point in the fence above which the cat had vanished, Joan fumbled about in the debris trying to find her ghetto blaster, which had been knocked into life at full volume, and Steven was still spewing forth a volley of words he must have been saving for such a momentous occasion.

The only one who remained calm was Jet. He'd managed to crawl clear and now stood surveying the chaos, his tail slowly wagging in a confused but, as always, amiable fashion.

What a wonderful dog, I thought two hours later as he and I sat alone in the dining room. His calm in the face of crisis had a reassuring effect I desperately needed at the moment.

It was three a.m. The police had left a half hour before. Bran, the instigator of our "wild party," lay fast asleep, curled up and forgiven by Steve in the latter's bed. He hadn't been worried when the cruiser, lights flashing, had driven into our yard. After all, no one could arrest a Beagle for doing his job.

Later I'd write and sell the story to a national magazine. I discovered that an adventure is an event that scares the beejeebers out of you and yet you live to tell the tale.

A Beagle in Blue

Bran, for all his general impatience with the foibles of human kind, tolerated most of my fads and fancies quite well. I believe this acceptance was generated by the symbiotic nature of our relationship. To put it simply, he knew which side his bread was buttered on. He wasn't about to let it land greasy side down.

Confident in this probability, I had few qualms about including him in my latest idea when it arose bright and bushy-tailed in my mind the following November. I had recently attended a dog show and seen some totally adorable canines with not only matching collars and leashes but also color-coordinated sweaters. Bran, now famous to many readers of canine magazines both in the United States and Canada, deserved no less than such princely attire.

Royal blue, I decided. Bran's fashion statement had to be made in royal blue to capture the essence of his vibrant masculine personality and to reflect his aristocratic heritage as the companion of captains and kings. Happily I headed for our two local pet stores to realize my version of Beagle Beautiful.

There I hit a major snag. Neither store could provide the ensemble I wanted. Undeterred and as persistent as the Beagle himself, I kept looking.

Two weeks later, we took a Christmas shopping trip to Moncton, a city one hundred and fifty miles away. After visiting several pet stores, I found exactly what I was looking for…dazzling blue leash, collar, and matching sweater with white turtleneck and cuffs.

I could barely wait to parade my own special boy in blue.

The Great Groundhog Battle

Christmas came again with all the characteristic ringing rafters at our house. Due to the heavy demands on maternal time during its height, I did not have an opportunity to dress Bran in his new finery until Boxing Day.

But when I did, the effect was well worth the wait. Bran in his regal Beagle outfit easily put Gainsborough's *Blue Boy* to shame. Standing at full alert, he was handsome, distinguished...and just plain cute. I caught his snout between my palms and planted a resounding kiss on it.

"I love you, you handsome devil," I said, and stood, pulled on my mittens, and headed for the door, blue leash clasped. We were off to the meadow.

It was a beautiful winter day, bright, sunny, and unseasonably warm for northern New Brunswick. Here and there in the meadow drowsy flies—and even a few bees tricked into believing spring had come early—crawled drunkenly over the glistening snow. I let Bran off his leash and removed my mitts and hat. What a gorgeous day, I marveled, as my buddy started off at a smooth lope across a just-strong-enough-for-a-Beagle crust toward a little thicket at the edge of the meadow.

Suddenly he stopped, stiffened into his pretend-I'm-a-Pointer pose, one front paw raised. My heart lurched in a now familiar but nevertheless unpleasant manner. I knew that stance only too well. Bran had spotted a quarry.

"Bran," I yelled, typically pointlessly. Fearing a human might be his target and in full remembrance of the traumatized lady in pink and of the nude sunbather, I began to stumble after him, crashing through crust not strong enough to support a one-hundred-and-thirty-pound Caucasian.

I saw what he was stalking. A groundhog, fooled like the flies and bees by the unseasonable warmth, had climbed out of his burrow on the edge of the thicket and was nonchalantly sunning himself on his doorstep.

"Bran, no!" I cried, knees already bruised and aching from breaking through snow shell that felt as hard as window glass.

Bran only eased stealthily forward a couple more strides before once more freezing into a perfect (no doubt learned on that fateful day from Teddi) point.

Then he broke. Like a ground-to-ground missile, he was off. He got to the drowsy groundhog a split second before it could dive into the safety of its hole.

Now, groundhogs are rodents, possessors of sharp, strong, terrible teeth. They've been known to seriously injure and even kill dogs much larger than Beagles.

"Bran!" I screamed, crawling toward the skirmish in an ineffective attempt to distribute my weight over the crackling crust.

Shrieks, yowls, and screams made my blood run cold. All I could see was a whirling mass of fur not unlike those Tasmanian Devil eddies common in Bugs Bunny cartoons.

As suddenly as it had begun, it was over. The groundhog, apparently having had enough but seemingly unscathed, vanished down into his burrow. Bran threw back his head in a resounding howl of victory.

By this time I'd reached the scene of the battle and gone weak-kneed with relief when I saw no blood marring the virgin whiteness of the snow. The battle must have been as Shakespeare had once written, "A tale full of sound and fury signifying nothing."

Then I saw the coat. That once beautiful, lovingly purchased royal blue sweater hung in rags and strings about Bran's heaving middle and dangled in strips around one front leg. Bits of curly wool squiggled from every inch.

When we returned home, the look I gave my children muted them. Only Ron sitting peacefully with Jet in front of the TV dared venture a comment.

"Looks like the Red Baron got the beejeebers beaten out of him this time," he said mildly. "Rogue rabbit?"

Isn't it written somewhere in the Bible that "pride goes before destruction and an haughty spirit before a fall"? This proverb applied to me, not Bran. His spirit remained as haughty as ever.

Thornton W. Burgess Never Met This Beagle!

Did I mention I sometimes half accurately remember things I've read? This weakness very nearly caused me to have a heart attack one fine spring day when Bran was about four years old. To fully understand the situation, it's necessary to first take a ramble down memory lane.

During my childhood, from earliest recollection, in fact, I have been an ardent admirer of writer Thornton W. Burgess. His children's stories of nature and loquacious wildlife were an integral part of my intellectual development during my most impressionable years.

From time of earliest memories, I lumbered along sylvan trails with Buster Bear, delighted in the exploits of Jimmy Skunk, thrilled to the hairbreadth escapes of Chatterer the Red Squirrel, and sobbed over the loss of Poor Mrs. Quack's drake.

My favorite tales involved the exploits of Reddy Fox and Bowser the Hound. Stories of Bowser's relentless pursuits of Reddy imbued in the sure and certain knowledge that the clever fox would always escape the Hound had always been paramount on my list.

Reddy's most brilliant checkmate of the swift and diligent dog had been the episode in which he eluded the dog by running nimbly across a railway bridge. As I remembered the tale, canines are afraid of railway bridges and will refuse to cross them. Certainly any dogs I had seen encounter such structures would not.

That beautiful spring morning Bran enlightened me.

Bran, Jet, Ross, Christiana, and I, in honor of the burgeoning season, had taken an exceptionally long walk across the meadows and into new, unexplored territory in the woods beyond. Brooks, giggling in delight at being freed from winter's ice, interspersed the small, overgrown fields.

Eventually we emerged into an open area to discover railway tracks that extended to and across a trellis bridge before once again disappearing into the trees. The bridge stretched over a small valley above one of those happily liberated streams. We'd paused to rest when we heard an approaching train. Turning in the direction of the sound, we saw it bearing down upon us.

"Catch the dogs!" Christiana cried. She slipped collar and leash on obedient Ross. Jet, a sweetheart as always, came to sit at my side while I performed a similar service.

"Where's Bran?" my friend asked, straightening from attending to her dog. Then, "Oh, no!"

I looked in the direction she indicated and saw Bran a few feet out on that terrible railway bridge. The train, a fast-moving passenger type, bore down on him with dreadful speed.

"Bran!" I screamed. In that instant I came as close to clinical death as possible and still live to tell the tale.

Bran glanced back at the mass of steel and locomotion charging toward him. There was no possible avenue of retreat for the little dog. The valley beneath, which appeared the Beagle's only possibility of escape, appeared horrendously deep.

"Jump!" I screamed.

As usual, Bran did the totally unexpected. Taking to his heels, he galloped nimbly across that awful bridge, mere yards in front of that murderous train!

On the far side, he leaped from the tracks and watched the train roar past, tongue lolling rakishly out of his mouth.

That evening, older and grayer and just about nodding in my sleep from nervous exhaustion, I took down that half remembered, dearly beloved, dog-eared book and re-read the section on foxes, hounds, trains, and trellises. And discovered that once again I had been half correct.

Indeed, Reddy Fox had eluded a very young, inexperienced Hound through the dog's fear of railway bridges. The second time with Bowser, now a veteran for the chase on his trail, he hadn't been quite as successful. The story, *in précis*, follows.

One day the wily fox, pursued by the much wiser Hound, came upon what had in the past proven a perfect escape situation. Reddy burst into an open area to discover a railway bridge crossing a ravine as a train lumbered toward it.

Leaping onto the bridge, he raced to perceived safety on the other side.

Once across, Reddy jumped from the tracks and sat down laughing (remember these were loquacious animals), eyes closed to avoid the smoke and cinders as the steam engine roared by him. Only when the entire train had passed did he open his eyes to look directly into the baying mouth of Bowser the Hound. Bowser, like Bran a veteran of the chase, knew a trick or two himself. He had waited for the train to pass, then loped across behind it. Of course, in spite of this calamity, Reddy once again managed to escape and lived to rob Farmer Brown's henhouse yet another day. That was one of my major reasons for loving the words of Thornton W. Burgess. No animals were seriously harmed in the making of his stories…except perhaps the odd chicken.

What was I saying about half remembered facts? Bran taught me it's always best to get one's information straight.

A Skunk by Any Other Name…

The family matured. Carol and Joan headed off to university; Steve entered his last year of high school; Ron became vice principal at the city high school; I returned to work as a secretary to help support the college couple but managed to write magazine articles at night and on weekends; Jet mellowed into loving, obedient canine maturity; and Bran…remained Bran.

During Carol's first year at university Bran inadvertently did her one of the biggest favors he could…although it was months,—nay, years—before she was able to honestly thank him.

At university Carol began to date a young man whom the entire family less one regarded within moments of meeting as a pompous ass. Convinced of his and his family's superiority, he proved a royal pain from the moment Carol brought him home for Thanksgiving weekend. She apparently saw something in him, so we all settled down to try to do likewise for her sake.

I admit I did spend most of breakfast time on the first morning of his visit shooting silencing looks across the table at Ron, Joan, and Steve as Pompous Peter (an alias) expostulated on the virtues of apple over orange juice and strawberry jam over blueberry.

Shortly afterwards, Ron and I took Bran and Jet for a run in the meadow. The golden-ripe season offered ample examples of why we should give thanks for this wonderful earth we're privileged to share with all God's creatures.

"Have you noticed how good Bran has been lately?" I remarked as we walked along the perimeter of the meadow enjoying the sunshine. Would I ever learn not to make such outrageous statements? I wondered later. "There hasn't been an incident in ages. Do you remember last week when Bob told us the terrible mess his dog got into with that skunk? Bran has never once bothered a skunk."

Four sentences back I should have stopped talking.

Ron merely looked at me, the skepticism produced by ten years in Bran's company in his expression.

Bran, as usual, ignored us. Involved in ferreting out rabbit scent, he kept dashing in and out of the dogwoods, alders, and raspberry bushes along the path. I smiled, remembering Wilson, who had passed away the previous winter, and his description of the Beagle as doing his job.

Suddenly the peace of the day shattered. Bran had darted into dense cover. The entire clump of bushes reverberated with roars, screams, yikes…and then that terrible, unmistakable stench rose in a thick, choking cloud to envelop us.

Bran burst out of the bushes, his snout dripping with that awful liquid. In a frenzy he flung himself into the grass at our feet and rolled and contorted.

"No, no, no!" Ron backed away, shaking his head. "No, this time I'm not taking him home!"

For the first time in twenty-five years of marriage my spouse deserted me as he set off in long strides back down the trail.

I cannot say I wasn't tempted to join him. But then I looked at Bran. My beloved little dog was in abject misery and for no more nefarious reason than doing his job. I remembered how he had stuck with me during my bout of sciatic, how he'd stood by me through countless edits. I couldn't leave him in distress.

I moved off a few paces, struggling to ignore the orange juice, blueberry jam, and scrambled eggs beginning to churn in my stomach, and waited while Bran rolled and kicked and grunted.

Finally, apparently convinced he'd done all he could with such rudimentary ablutions, he stumbled to his feet and looked at me, the acidy skunk solution making his golden brown eyes painful-looking bloodshot pools.

"Poor sweetie." My heart went out to him, although physically he definitely wasn't. A sweetie, that is. Holding my breath, I approached and snapped the leash on his collar. Turning away, I exhaled in a burst. The reflexive gulping intake made me gag. The stench had become a taste.

Trying to breathe just enough to sustain life, I started toward home with Bran pausing periodically to roll and kick at the end of the leash. As usual, he was unbowed by the experience. In fact, I feared he might be plotting some way to make that skunk pay.

At the edge of the subdivision I found Ron waiting. I didn't say anything when he silently fell into step with us, albeit several feet away.

It does give one a disconcerting feeling when people who have been one's friends and neighbors for years suddenly begin crossing the street to avoid you, some of them actually holding their noses.

When we reached the house, I took Bran into the backyard. My plan was to fill a tub with tomato juice and set to work on the Beagle's problem before he got into the house.

Once inside the enclosure, I released him. He raced into a flower bed and flung himself in the moist, dark soil for a good roll. Ron, possibly relenting in view of the little dog's distress, said nothing.

Carol opened the back door.

"Hi," she smiled in her usual cheerful manner. "Did you have a nice…?"

"Close the door!" I yelled.

"What?" she asked as Bran jumped to his feet and sped past her into the house. "God, what's that awful smell?"

Inside, draped over a corner of the couch was an expensive leather university jacket. It belonged to Pompous Peter. Bran chose it as the appropriate item on which to clean flower bed mud and skunk odor from his coat.

Although Carol missed Peter for a while, even cried a bit over their ensuing breakup, she recovered and went on to love again. After all, she finally reasoned, if Peter had really loved her, a bit of dirt and a permanent skunky odor on a brand-new three-hundred-dollar jacket wouldn't have mattered, would it?

Bran taught us that true love has to be nose blind.

Last Post

The inevitable was happening. Bran was growing old. And with age came illness, an alarming tumor on his right shoulder.

At first it was dime-sized. When it became the proportions of a quarter, our vet decided to remove it for a biopsy. Now fifteen, Bran came out of the surgery amazingly well. When test results indicated no cancerous cells, our family rejoiced.

A few months later, that ugly growth returned, this time larger and more insidious. Bran again underwent surgery for its removal. Although once again a biopsy revealed no cancer, our vet told us the problem was escalating.

"It's like tree branches spreading out through his body," he said. "I can't get it all."

I understood what he was saying, but with all my heart I didn't want to.

Bran spent Christmas swathed in bandages but nevertheless at the center of festivities. He loved life as much as ever. He would celebrate every last day.

He opened his presents, enjoyed a small bowl of turkey, carrots, and gravy, and fell asleep on the couch in Steve's arms as he had done for so many Christmases for so many years. I looked at the twenty-two-year-old young man and the old gray Beagle and felt the lump in my throat turn to tears in my eyes. This would be the last time I would enjoy that scene.

Spring came and Bran seemed to rally. The growth hadn't reappeared, and I tried to believe it wouldn't. I read and re-read every story I could find about dogs that had lived to be nineteen and one even to twenty-three. Bran could do it if any dog could, I thought, knowing his fierce determination.

That summer we didn't move to the cottage. We had obligations that held us in town. Perhaps it was just as well. Travelling might have proven too much for Bran. Then, too, being in rabbit country and unable to give chase would have been like myself with a great story idea brewing in my brain and no way to record it. I couldn't frustrate him in that way.

Instead, Bran and I, along with Jet, also a senior by now, were content to loll about in the backyard with the squirrels and robins. Bran even dug up one of Ron's favorite petunias, for old time's sake.

In August the tumor returned. This time it grew huge with horrifying swiftness. Dr. Larsen looked grim as he examined Bran. He had known the Beagle since we'd first brought him home and had developed the same kind of amused pride I had in his exploits.

"I can try one more operation to relieve the pressure," he said. "But he has no more than two months left."

Although the surgery took a heavy toll on Bran's diminishing strength, the old Beagle survived. Joan and I went to pick him up afterward and found tired yellow eyes above a body swathed in bandages.

It was a beautiful late summer day when we took him home from that last surgery. Ron was waiting for us and carried Bran to a little bed of quilts and pillows he had made for him in the shade of a birch tree in the backyard. Then he sat down in an old lawn chair beside him, the old Black Lab at his feet.

At four o'clock I looked out to see the trio still there. Ron's hand hanging over the arm of the chair could just reach Bran's head on its pillow. A lifetime of annoyances and challenges forgotten and forgiven, he stroked the gray head.

Amazingly, Bran rallied for a short time after that final operation. Nevertheless, knowing that his days were growing few, Ron and I decided to take him for one last trip to the cottage, to the forest and fields he loved.

We made him a bed between us on the truck seat and set off. Once there, we placed him carefully on the ground and watched as he walked slowly, painfully, about the property, sniffing every nook and cranny, savoring every odor, every sensation. He knows, I thought. He knows this is the last time.

Confident that in his weakened condition Bran wouldn't leave the yard, Ron and I went into the cottage. Looking back now, it seems incredible. Hadn't we learned anything from Bran's sixteen years?

Suddenly we heard it—the familiar Tarzan-Beagle yell. Looking out a window, we saw the old dog taking off at a lope, nose to the ground, baying all the way. He'd found a rabbit track!

We didn't try to stop him. He deserved this one last time of joy. As I watched him disappear into the forest, I hoped someone would be kind enough to grant me pen and paper in my last hours. And somewhere deep in my heart I hoped he wouldn't return from this last chase, that he would die happy, doing what he had loved best.

Two hours later he staggered back, barely able to walk, tongue hanging almost to the ground. He didn't stop at the camp but puttered slowly to the truck door.

"You can take me home now," his golden brown eyes told me.

A week later, on a beautiful, bright October morning, I carried Bran out to the truck for our last trip to the vet. For once I was glad the children were no longer living at home. Their farewells to their childhood friend would have been too much to bear.

"'Bye, buddy," Ron said simply, patting the old dog's head. We didn't look at each other. We couldn't and remain brave for Bran.

Before we went to the vet, I knew there was one last thing Bran and I had to share. I turned off the highway and drove down an old road that led to the meadow where we had shared so many adventures. On the edge I stopped the truck and helped Bran to a sitting position against my shoulder so that he could see it one last time.

Nude sunbathers, plump pink ladies, groundhogs, a pale moon riding high in a morning sky, three dogs and two good friends…sixteen years of memories. I knew then why he had come back from that last chase. He and I were to have this time together.

The sun coming up over the birches turned the ripening trees and frost-killed grasses to purest gold. Bran stared at it for a few moments, then looked up at me and sighed sadly. A moment later he slid down onto the seat beside me.

We didn't have to continue on to the vet.

Lucy Maude Montgomery, that wonderful First Lady of Canadian Literature, once wondered if animals, like her beloved, long-lived companion cat Daffy, could somehow develop souls through years of loving association with human kind. I hope her musings are fact. That way, I can forever picture Bran in heaven or whatever the good hereafter is called, cavorting through meadows rich with daisies, dandelions, and bouncing bunnies. While he waits for me...

****

Years after Bran had passed away, our daughter Carol wrote the following thoughts about her beloved Beagle. It seems fitting that Carol, who was responsible for bringing the subject of this story into our lives, should finish it.

"In our lives there are always a few characters who manage to steal a special place in our hearts no matter what. One such creature was our Beagle, Brandy.

"Brandy came into my life when I was a little girl and left it when I was a woman. His exuberant, high-flying lifestyle brightened my childhood and influenced me as an adult.

"His motto was 'Enjoy life for all it's worth.' Being, like my mother, a confirmed conservative, I had much to learn along those lines. Mind you, this attitude often got him into trouble, but through it all he remained undaunted, ready to take on the next adventure the moment the opportunity arose.

"Given the above, people have asked me why I enjoyed this willful, free-wheeling little creature so much. I explain that Brandy and I had a special relationship. I would test his devil-may-care nature by telling him something he wasn't allowed to do, then watch as he plotted and manipulated to break that rule.

"For example, he knew he was not allowed in my

bedroom. And, indeed, while I was in residence, I never once saw him venture past the door. However, reports from other family members informed me that the minute I left the house, he'd make a beeline for my room and have a grand, old time frolicking on my nice, neat bed!

"I learned a lot about living from Brandy. He taught me to seize the possibilities in each moment; opportunities seldom come around twice. He was right.

"Brandy also taught me to think for myself, trust my own judgment, and then be willing to live with the consequences.

"Brandy lived a full, eventful sixteen years. His picture hangs in my stairwell. Sometimes when I'm tiredly making my way upwards after a bad day, I pause and look at him standing gray-haired and proud in old age among the yellow autumn marsh grass behind our cottage, and my heart lifts. I smile.

"'You're right, Bran,' I say. 'It's not worth worrying about. Tomorrow is another day.'

"I loved that crazy Beagle. I cried as a little girl on the day before he came into my life, and I wept as a woman on the day he left it. I will always remember him simply as 'the best.'"

****

Brandy's passing cast a dark pall over our home and family. He'd been the devil-may-care little rake that brought adventure and laughter into the house. And while we all missed him acutely, perhaps the one who fell deepest into mourning was Jet.

The Lab's devotion to the little scamp is a tribute to a dog's ability to forgive and continue to love even after a companion has gotten him into more than a few scrapes. Certainly Jet demonstrated he held no grudges against his companion of nearly fifteen years. In fact, he fell into a depression so deep he stopped eating. Six weeks after Brandy's passing, I decided something had to be done, and so off Jet and I went to visit Dr. Larsen.

"He's suffering deep mourning," he said. "I'll prescribe medication that should bring him around, at least enough to start him eating again."

It did, but it failed to revive his *joie de vivre*. By this time arthritis was another of his problems, along with his lameness. Physically and mentally, our wonderful dog that had always been the soul of optimism had become a sad, depressed spirit.

As the winter drew on, I thought perhaps a companion might help, a youthful companion that could revive memories of the good times he'd shared with Brandy.

For some time I'd been interested in a relatively rare breed from Nova Scotia called Nova Scotia Duck Tolling Retrievers. I'd learned the most famous of the breeders were Erna and Avery Nickerson, from Yarmouth, Nova Scotia. These medium-sized red dogs were reputed to be fine companions as well as excellent hunting dogs and, best of all, after sixteen years of trying to find and catch Brandy, non-roamers. So I called the Nickersons…a call that would change my life.

****

It had been love at first sight when I saw the photo of Nova Scotia Duck Tolling Retrievers in a regional outdoor magazine six years previous. The picture of Avery Nickerson of Harborlights Kennels with his corps of flashy little fox-like dogs had mesmerized me.

The word "tolling" equally intrigued me. I knew that toll, in a hunting context, meant to lure game, but how could a small, red dog do this?

The dog's fox-like appearance was responsible, the article writer informed me. Once upon a time, the story explained, men had observed the hunting techniques of a pair of wily foxes. When the foxes sighted a flock of ducks rafting far out on the water, one would begin to prance and caper about on the shore while the other secreted itself in the long grass nearby. Dancing and leaping, the visible fox proved to have a magnetic effect on the birds. As if hypnotized by the fox's behavior, they'd turn and swim toward it and their hidden fate. The foxes' success rate was so great, the advantage of using fox-lookalike dogs as a similar lure went on like a light bulb over the heads of observing humans.

Fascinated as I was by this tale, the time hadn't been right for a deeper involvement with one of these canines.

For a while after Brandy's death, in dealing with Jet's mourning, I shelved the idea of becoming caregiver to one of these amazing little red dogs. I needed time to mourn. Several months later, I finally did dig out that dog-eared article and considered the possibility. Perhaps a young dog would do Jet some good, help to draw him out of his sadness with a puppy's seemingly endless enthusiasm.

At the dawn of the new year following Brandy's passing, I called Erna Nickerson. The voice that answered the phone at Harborlights was warm and motherly. Erna Nickerson sounded exactly like the kind of person who should be responsible for my next companion's earliest days.

We asked each other questions for the next hour, my curiosity boundless, Erna determined not to let one of her puppies go to anything less than an excellent home.

"I'll send you our video," she said finally. "If you're still interested in a spring puppy, you can send a deposit."

I'd passed her stringent test. I hung up and whooped with joy.

The video arrived within six days. The deposit was on its way to Harborlights within seven.

The winter passed slowly. Jet recovered to the point where he ate regularly and even managed to go on short walks in spite of his worsening arthritis, but he didn't recover the optimistic, calmly happy outlook of the past. The puppy would change all that, I told myself as Jet moved into his fifteenth year.

On a rainy morning late in May, I drove to our local airport to pick up a puppy we'd already named Harborlights Highland Chance. Her first name was for her birth kennel, the second reflected her New Scotland heritage (and, by coincidence, her new address at our home on Highland Avenue), and the last recognized the many possibilities dogs of her breed offered.

Finally the flight carrying this wonderful puppy was announced. Within minutes, a flight attendant handed me a small, beige cage that had a pair of the most intense blue eyes I'd ever seen staring out at me. When I opened the door, an adorable ball of tan-colored fluff tumbled into my hands and heart.

Chance proved to be no chance at all. She was a definite winner. At forty-nine days of age, true to Avery Nickerson's forecast, she retrieved in the house like a little trooper. By the time she was three months old, the commands of Sit, Down, and Come had become pieces of cake for her. Her willingness to please amazed us. The only rules that had to be consistently followed (as the Nickersons had stressed) were to incorporate training into the dog's naturally playful nature and to be lavish with praise.

"Very little pressure is needed to make the dog respond," Avery had said. "They love to work."

Socially, Chance proved a great hit. She went to school during the month of June with Joan, a third-grade teacher at the time, and became unofficial mascot of a local amateur baseball team. Her gregarious personality soon made her social puppy of the year wherever she went and demonstrated she would be an excellent family pet and companion. She loved people and life, and she showed it in leaps and bounds.

This social effervescence could, at times, become a trifle unruly. One evening when Ron had invited the local softball team into the backyard for a barbecue, Chance, busily playing with Jet in the house, wasn't immediately aware of visitors, creatures both human and canine, in which she delighted.

When she did realize we had company, she tore out of the backdoor and leaped for the hot dog one of the players was raising to his mouth. Unfortunately, this sportsman and a friend were seated on our garden swing. When Chance landed full speed and twenty-plus pounds on his chest, the entire thing upset backwards, taking Nova Scotia Duck Tolling Retriever, third baseman, and pitcher for one wild ride. Fortunately no one was injured, and Chance scrambled from the wreckage, dancing and prancing in true happy Toller fashion.

Later that summer we took her to our camp and introduced her to water and marsh. From Jet she learned about retrieves in and under the water. She also developed a jealous need to outdo the old guy.

This might have been all fun and games, but Jet, old and wearied by his aches and pains, appeared frustrated in his attempts to keep up with his exuberant new companion. When Chance's antics stretched to galloping around him, barking sharp little fox-like barks, jumping on him, and nipping at his paws and ears, I began to wonder at the wisdom of getting him such a youthful friend. Proving to be more nuisance than inspiration, the pup frequently had to be separated from the senior in order for him to get rest and much-needed peace and quiet.

If Jet had been a few years younger, if his body had been in better condition, perhaps the idea of a rambunctious pup might have been a good one. Under the present conditions, it was proving a vast mistake, another lesson learned from my dogs.

By the following winter Chance had calmed down sufficiently to leave Jet in peace when he indicated he didn't want her attention, but his health was deteriorating. Shortly before Christmas he celebrated his sixteenth birthday with a small steak. It was a venerable age for a Lab. He settled into sleeping away most of his days on the living room couch.

One morning in March, he got to his feet and began staggering around the house in circles, panting, exhausting himself with the effort but seemingly unable to stop. We rushed him to the vet. By that time his inane actions had stopped, but once at the vet's another fit overcame him. Watching him, Dr. Larsen didn't take long to diagnose major seizures.

"I'll keep him with me today for observation," he said, his expression grave. "Then I'll be able to decide if there's any medication that will help."

At five o'clock he called. Jet had had sixteen more seizures during the day. There was only one answer to the gallant old Lab's dilemma.

Later that evening when Joan arrived with gourmet dog food for her faithful companion, I had to tell her the sad fact.

I'd expected a violent outburst of tears, of recriminations for not having tried a few more medications. Instead, her blue eyes looked at me with sad understanding.

"He couldn't go on like that," she said, voice breaking over the words. "We had to give him comfort and peace."

Jet will always remain an inspiration. His courage in the face of disability, his constant good humor, his will to carry on, his love for all creatures, two- and four-legged, can never be forgotten. He taught us that each day is a gift and we must glory in it as best we can.

Harborlights Scotia Ceilidh

I wanted her to love me. But, more importantly, I wanted her to know how very much I loved her. It would be years before I realized it couldn't happen. Her heart belonged to someone else, and for all of the nine years I was privileged to share with her, she remained fiercely loyal to her first love. Although I called her *my* Ceilidh, she was never really mine. This is the story of her unfaltering quest for the man who would always be the most important person in her world.

****

Ceilidh came into my life as a gift, the result of Jet's passing. Chance had suddenly become an "only" dog in our household. We recognized her loneliness and decided she needed a new friend asap. I called Erna Nickerson at Chance's birth kennel and asked her about another dog. (We'd already decided it had to be another Nova Scotia Duck Tolling Retriever.)

Erna was a remarkable woman, fiercely loyal to the conscientious breeding and care of her beloved Nova Scotia Duck Tolling Retrievers. She and her husband Avery had been pioneers in having the breed re-established with the CKC in the 1960s after registrations following the Club's 1945 initial recognition of the dogs had lapsed.

Since my husband Ron and I had gotten Chance from the Nickersons, we'd continued our relationship with the couple. Frequently in need of advice and guidance in dealing with this unique breed of dog, we'd often called the knowledgeable pair for help. Avery was inclined to be gruff and outspoken, whereas Erna was quiet and reserved. Both had been generous with information and assistance.

Then Avery died.

Left alone with a large kennel that included seventeen adult Tollers, Erna didn't hesitate. She immediately took over its full management.

I admired her courage as much as I admired her extensive and intimate knowledge of Duck Tolling Retrievers. Then in her late sixties, Erna worked long hours to keep Harborlights Kennel afloat and viable. She downsized only when she realized it was impossible to continue to operate the facility at its current capacity. I remember, with acute sadness, the night she called to inform me she'd had to sell off part of her breeding stock.

"They've gone to a good home," she said, the shakiness in her voice betraying her sense of loss. "It was the best I could do for them."

So it was to Erna that we turned when we wanted a companion dog for our beloved Chance. This time we were interested in a mature dog but didn't expect to be able to get one with the prestigious Harborlights bloodlines.

"I have a three-year-old female that might interest you," Erna surprised and delighted me by replying to my query. "Her name is Harborlights Scotia Ceilidh. She's been returned to our kennel because her family can no longer keep her. She's housebroken and even obedience trained. Her father is Gator, her mother Meg-a-Duck. If you think she's what you're looking for, I can send her up to you at the end of the week."

"She sounds perfect." I was thrilled. Her breeding couldn't have been better. Not only was Meg-a-Duck also the mother of our wonderful Chance, her dad, Ali Gator was probably the most famous living Toller stud in Canada. "Can you put her on a flight to Bathurst this Saturday?"

"Yes," she replied. "Now, I must tell you. Ceilidh is Chance's half-sister. Sometimes dogs in this situation have what I call a Queen Complex. There may be some squabbling for supremacy."

"I can deal with that," I said confidently. After all, I had twenty-five years of dog handling to my credit. How much havoc could two little forty-pound bitches cause? "How much will I send you to pay for her?"

"Just pick up the cost of the plane fare at your end," she surprised me by replying. "I only want to be sure Ceilidh goes to a good home. I could have placed her several times—she's been with me for about three months—but I was waiting for just the right people. And now they've come along. Consider her my gift to you."

Welcome Home

March 11, 1992, was a snowy, overcast day. Afraid the inclement weather might delay flights, my daughter Joan and I kept calling the airports in Halifax and Bathurst to chart Ceilidh's progress. When we knew she'd successfully made the final transfer and was on the last leg of her journey to Bathurst, we cheered. Harborlights Scotia Ceilidh was coming home!

Joan and I were at the Bathurst airport when Flight 421 from Halifax touched down. Breathless with excitement, we waited by the baggage shunt for her crate to slide out. Getting a new canine member for our family is always a momentous event.

Even at that, our first glimpse of Ceilidh was a never-to-be-forgotten experience. Peering out from her travel kennel was the sweetest, most angelic little dog face we'd ever seen. Harborlights Scotia Ceilidh was beautiful! Joan knelt, snapped open the door, and let her out.

"What a gorgeous Golden Retriever puppy!" one of the people in the small crowd that had gathered to see the new arrival commented.

"She's not a Golden," Joan replied a bit indignantly as she attached a leash to the little red collar on Ceilidh's neck. "She's a Nova Scotia Duck Tolling Retriever."

I could barely tear myself away from the gorgeous

little creature long enough to pay for her flight. I wanted to hug her, to kiss her, to welcome her with all the joy and love in my heart. As I stood waiting for my receipt at the reception desk, I watched, smiling with pure delight, as Joan led our new family member proudly around the waiting room. How fortunate we'd been that Erna had seen fit to entrust us with this lovely creature.

Ceilidh didn't seem to have any interest in becoming acquainted with the young woman at the end of her lead. Instead, she strained at the leash, sniffing, searching each person, nook, and cranny for something she appeared in desperate need to find.

With the paperwork complete, we loaded Ceilidh into the car for the short drive home. Inside the vehicle, she once more began her frantic investigations. She leaped from seat to floor and even tried to scramble up into the rear window area, her nose and gaze roaming over every inch of the car.

"She'll settle down," I assured Joan, who was driving. "Everything is just so new to her."

When we arrived home and opened the door to be greeted by Chance, I was slightly apprehensive. Erna's words about queen complexes echoed in my mind as I kept a firm hand on Ceilidh's leash.

I needn't have been concerned. Ceilidh, when I freed her from her lead, simply rushed into the house and resumed her search. Chance dashed about behind her in an effort to get a decent sniff at the newcomer, apparently no more understanding Ceilidh's behavior than I did.

When Ron arrived home a couple of hours later and I tried to introduce him to Ceilidh, my efforts failed. Deeply involved in her investigations, she had no inclination to make new acquaintances.

On a positive note, Chance had lain down on the couch, content to watch her half-sister's antics from a distance. So far so good, I thought…no fur flying, no snarling, not a single bit of evidence of the queen complex about which Erna had warned me.

Ceilidh's first night in our home proved a chore. I don't think she slept a single minute. Instead, she raced up and down stairs and through all the rooms like Don Quixote in her puzzling quest, with Chance in the role of Sancho Panza at her heels.

"How long is this going to go on?" Ron muttered as the luminous numbers on the bedside clock indicated it was 2:31 a.m. "Is that dog never going to sleep?"

My spouse was reaching the exasperation point. Over the years, he'd shown amazing tolerance for me and my dogs—not all that difficult, when I believe he loves all of us—but this new dog seemed a veritable ball of never-ending nervous energy.

"Not much longer," I assured him without the faintest idea if I told the truth.

But it did…until the dawn's early light. Exhaustion from the flight and all that frantic searching must have overcome her. In the earliest rays of her first full day as our girl, Harborlights Scotia Ceilidh fell asleep by the front door.

As I looked at her little face finally peaceful in sleep, I wondered what I'd gotten into. Already I loved her, already I knew she was home to stay, but how could I convince her of those facts? And how in the world would I be able to find out what it was she was so desperately seeking?

Getting to Know You

As Ceilidh slept, the morning brightened into all the diamond-sparkled beauty of a perfect March morning in northern New Brunswick. A light overnight snowfall had covered everything with a brand-new blanket of purest white. As I drank my tea and polished off my toast, I looked forward to taking our dogs for a run in the woods.

"I wonder if we should let Ceilidh free," I asked Ron as we bundled up to leave the house. "After all, she's new and might get confused and…"

"We've got to trust her." He handed me my snowshoes. "Otherwise she won't trust us. If we keep her on a leash while Chance runs free, it could start a resentment that will lead to that queen complex thing Erna mentioned."

Ron has always been much more willing to take chances with the dogs than I am. Yet, almost without exception, he's been right. Once we were sufficiently deep in the woods to be a safe distance from roads and traffic, I snapped the lead from Ceilidh's collar and thought a silent prayer.

Off she streaked across the meadow and into the trees at the far side. My heart plummeted. We'd lost that beautiful little dog. What would I tell Erna? More importantly, how would I ever forgive myself?

"She'll be back," Ron said confidently, setting off

with Chance trotting at his side.

I followed them, fear-induced nausea roiling. Catching up with Ceilidh, on snowshoes, wasn't an option.

Miraculously (possibly in answer to my repeated mental prayers), a few minutes later, as we started along a trail that led into the woods, Ceilidh appeared out of the trees to our left.

"See?" Ron pointed. "She was just stretching her legs after the flight."

For the rest of our walk, Ceilidh (generally) stayed a part of our group. She made numerous short sidetrips to sniff and again search and search but each time returned. The situation appeared to be settling into place.

Nevertheless, our adventures with our new family member weren't yet over for the day. Galloping along beside Chance, Ceilidh suddenly flipped, then staggered to her feet, right hind leg stuck out behind her.

"Look!" I cried to Ron, the dog panic to which I'm prone skyrocketing.

"Just a cramp…something left over from a rough flight," he said calmly, but I saw concern mirrored in his face.

Strangely, it didn't appear to inconvenience her. She kept pace with her half-sister on the three remaining operational legs, even though her condition looked excruciatingly painful. This was the first indication of a facet of Ceilidh's character that we would become familiar with over the years. She was a stoic.

As we reached the end of the trail, Ceilidh's disability vanished as suddenly as it had appeared. Her leg returned to normal position. Once more on her lead, she trotted back to the house on all fours as if nothing untoward had happened. Maybe it had been, just as Ron had suggested, a cramp left over from her flight.

Although she seemed undeterred by the incident, I couldn't get the painful-looking image out of my mind. Once inside, I placed her on the couch and settled her among pillows before heading for the kitchen to get her a dog cookie.

I'd gotten half way when I heard a thump. By the time I'd turned to look at her, she'd stretched out on the hardwood floor beneath the bay window.

"No, no, no, Ceilidh!" I replaced her in the cozy corner of the couch. "You have to rest. Be comfortable. I'll be right back with your snack."

I started back toward the kitchen. Once again the distinctive thump. I turned to see her once more stretching out on the floor.

A light bulb of understanding flashed on in my mind. In her former home Ceilidh probably hadn't been allowed on furniture. She didn't feel comfortable in a formerly forbidden place.

Well, I thought, as I took cookies from the dogs' special can on the cupboard. If I couldn't convince her that in the MacMillan household dogs had permission to sleep on beds, chairs, and couches, I'd make sure she slept in another place almost as comfortable. That afternoon I went to the local fabric store and bought mattress foam and material with pictures of retrievers decorating it.

The next day Harborlights Scotia Ceilidh had two new foam-filled floor mattresses…one for the living room and one for our bedroom where she would spend her nights beside our bed. In the summer, I'd make two more for the cottage. I would see to it that Harborlights Scotia Ceilidh was as physically comfortable as possible.

As for her leg problem, I decided to try a remedy that had proven effective for Joan when she'd injured her leg in a skiing accident. I began to treat Ceilidh with a combination of vitamins and herbs. I'll never know for certain if my potions worked, but within six weeks Ceilidh no longer went lame. For the rest of her years with us, her leg appeared to be perfectly normal.

Another of Ceilidh's problems bothered me much more. She'd only lived with us a couple of days when I became aware of it.

Her tail never wagged.

Oh, she was obedient, came when she was called (except outdoors when her constant searching during the early part of our walks would draw her away from us for a bit), sat instantly on command, and heeled like a trooper. On the other hand, she expressed no joy in the profuse praise and heartfelt hugs she received for her flawless performances. It was as if she lived inside some sort of hard, psychological shell, impervious to our love and approval.

Determined to break through this barrier, I'd sit beside her on the floor, my arm about her sturdy little shoulders, and hold her against me, hugging her and rubbing her back and telling her how very much she was loved and wanted in her new home. It was all to no avail. Ceilidh had closed the door to her heart and wasn't about to let us in…not yet, at least, I thought optimistically.

Shortly we learned Ceilidh had yet another

problem so acute we were at a loss of how to cope with it. Harborlights Scotia Ceilidh suffered from severe separation anxiety.

Each time we tried to leave the house without her, she'd get between us and the door and bark sharply, aggressively at times. The only way we could peacefully exit our home was to bribe her with a dog biscuit.

Those panic-stricken responses to our leaving gave me the first real clue into my beautiful little dog's troubled thoughts. Someone she loved very much must have left her once upon a time and never returned. She wasn't about to let it happen again.

Getting to know Harborlights Scotia Ceilidh wouldn't be easy, we realized, but we were determined to do it. After all, she was our girl now, and we loved her, and anything worth achieving takes time.

The Gulping Gourmet

One of the first things we learned for certain about our new girl became blatantly obvious on her first day in our home. She loved to eat. In spite of any homesickness or queasiness from her flight, on her first night in our home Ceilidh devoured her supper with gusto and continued to do so unfailingly every day afterwards. In fact, food seemed the only thing in which she took any real pleasure.

And when, on her second day in our home, she discovered Ron baking homemade dog biscuits, we saw the first sparkle in her beautiful brown eyes. She seated herself beside him in the kitchen and proceeded to watch intently as he mixed whole wheat flour, eggs, oxo, margarine, and milk into the tasty concoction all our dogs have loved. She refused to leave the kitchen while they were baking.

Once they were cool, and she received her first sample, the best vacuum cleaner in North America couldn't have sucked it up faster or more efficiently.

The temptation to overindulge her with food became difficult to avoid when it seemed it was the only thing that could bring a gleam to those gorgeous teddy bear eyes. I often had to turn away to avoid giving her "just one more treat."

I must admit I enjoyed feeding Ceilidh. Always beside me at the cupboard at the first signs of doggie supper preparation, she made each meal a much-anticipated experience. When I turned to put her bowl on the floor, she'd whirl in joyful circles of anticipation that would have made a carousel operator dizzy.

Once the dish was on the floor in her corner of the kitchen, she'd shove her snout into it and snuffle and burrow like a starving piglet. As I watched her, Jed Clampett's words of bucolic wisdom echoed through my mind: "Don't get twixt that critter and the trough!"

****

Ceilidh's penchant for food was to get her into several scrapes over the course of our years together. The first involved a half-empty bag of flour.

On the morning after she'd first watched Ron making those delectable dog biscuits, she disappeared into the basement. I didn't pay much attention to her being missing. I knew she was somewhere inside the house and assumed she was off on her continuing quest for whatever it was she was seeking.

About twenty minutes later she entered the small office where I was busy writing. I glanced up from my computer, ready to greet her with a hug and kiss. I gasped. Her face had turned pure white! I knelt and gathered her into my arms. What terrible thing had happened to make my dog go gray within minutes?

The "gray" came off on my hands and arms. What was the stuff? Then it dawned on me. Flour! Ron had placed a bag beside the dryer in the laundry room instead of up on the shelf yesterday when he'd finished baking the dog biscuits. How much had she eaten? What would be the effect?

I grabbed the phone and called our vet.

"I've never encountered a dog that's eaten a large

quantity of just plain flour," Dr. Larsen said after I'd explained the situation. "Seems to me that, combined with the moisture inside her mouth and body, it could make paste. I think we'd better give her a laxative to make sure she can pass the mixture."

So, after a quick trip to the vet, home Ceilidh came to spend the next few hours mostly at the back door, asking to go out. By the next day, she appeared to be in excellent health. Her appetite and other bodily functions had returned to normal with surprising speed.

After that incident we kept the flour on the shelf at all times. Ceilidh had taught us to be diligent in returning items to their proper place.

Bubble, Bubble, Toil and Trouble

That was not to be Ceilidh's only visit to the vet that first spring. A few weeks later, after we'd taken her for a walk in the woods and she'd gone off on one of her now customary exploratory jaunts, she returned home with an appalling bout of diarrhea. After spending most of the following night letting her out, sometimes in time, sometimes not, I once again headed for Dr. Larsen. I traveled alone. Ron hadn't volunteered to accompany us.

Living in horror of hearing that abrupt bubbling sound that meant Ceilidh had had another attack, I kept my fingers crossed during the drive. Fortunately we made it and proceeded into the vet's crowded reception area. I told the receptionist our problem, and she instructed me to take a seat and wait.

I led Ceilidh to a far corner and sat down. She looked up at me, beautiful brown eyes sad and appealing.

"Don't worry, Ceil," I whispered. "Dr. Larsen will help you. And"—I bent down to whisper in her ear—"Remember I love you."

I can't believe it was another declaration of my love that did it. It doesn't really matter. The fact is, at that moment, a distinct bubbling sound erupted, and my beautiful dog suddenly sat in a large, brown pool.

The resultant stench would make the strongest

stomach swirl. Within seconds, the other clients in Dr. Larsen's waiting room had fled out into the fresh air, and the receptionist was rushing toward us with a bucket of water laced with disinfectant. As I got Ceilidh to her feet, the poor woman began to mop up that vile-smelling puddle.

Dr. Larsen emerged from his consulting room and looked around. His expression mirrored surprise at finding his waiting room empty except for Ceilidh, me, and the receptionist.

He sniffed, then strode over to our corner. With a quick, efficient move he picked Ceilidh up under her front legs and started into his surgery with her dangling and dripping.

"Nothing like a good old-fashioned bout of projectile diarrhea to clear a room," he said matter-of-factly.

I had to agree.

Dr. Larsen concluded Ceilidh had eaten something foul during one of her unauthorized forays in the woods. It was early spring, the time when dead and disgusting things previously buried in the snow finally surface. Ceilidh, with her indiscriminate tastes, must have indulged herself.

It only took a bit of medication and a day's rest and she was once more ready to face the world with an unquenchable appetite and seek whatever was the object of her continuous quest. Moral to this story: Don't eat anything obviously well past its expiry date.

The Present of a Squirrel

We hadn't had Ceilidh long before we realized she had a passionate hatred for squirrels. Their taunting chatter drove her crazy. Since our fenced backyard had several large trees frequented by the furry creatures, Ceil was at their mercy. Darting up and down the trunks and out across the lawn, they defied the little red newcomer.

One morning in late April, after most of the snow had melted from our backyard, I glanced out the dining room window to see Ceilidh sitting on the patio. She watched several saucy squirrels leap from hedge to apple tree, from apple tree to sugar maple, chattering boldly. Normally she'd be racing about after them, barking her annoyance in no uncertain terms. I ventured a theory of what was going on.

Some people will tell you animals don't plot, can't reason, even that they're incapable of thought. Such concepts never cease to exasperate me. Anyone who has ever lived in close contact with an animal has seen multiple examples to the contrary. All our dogs, from the Einstein-type thinkers to the simply how-do-I-steal-the-toilet-paper ones have had the power to figure out solutions to at least some of their problems.

I watched, curious to see what Ceilidh would come up with. But as she continued to simply sit immobile, then finally stretch out full length on the deck in the warm spring sunshine, I decided I'd been wrong on this occasion and turned back to my housecleaning.

A half-hour later, I returned to the window. Ceilidh still lay just as I'd left her, while Chance nosed about in a far corner of the yard. One squirrel, emboldened by Ceilidh's continuing immobility, had jumped onto the edge of the deck, inches from the little dog's nose. Sitting up on its haunches, it stared at the supposedly sleeping dog, then burst into a saucy monologue.

It was a brief boldness. In a flash the rude rodent had been seized in the jaws of that definitely not drowsy dog.

"Ceil!" I cried as I dashed out of the house in an attempted rescue.

I was too late. The squirrel, already dead, dangled from Ceilidh's jaws. Like a conquering hero, she strode over to me and proudly placed her booty at my feet.

"Ceil!" I breathed. "No!"

As she looked up at me I saw it in her eyes—the hurt expression of a child whose lovingly handcrafted gift had been rejected. Before I could find any words to soften my *faux pas*, Ceilidh turned and shambled away.

Stung by my insensitivity, I knew I'd missed an opportunity of getting close to Ceilidh or breaking down a little of the barrier between her heart and mine.

After that incident, we had to watch Ceilidh more closely in the backyard. Whenever we saw her going into her "possum" act we'd bring her inside. She did catch a couple more of the rodents before most of the squirrels got wise to her strategy and decided not to tease her any more. They weren't dumb either.

I came out of the experience sadder but wiser, realizing you should always accept a gift, no matter how unusual, with gratitude and respect for the generosity of spirit with which it was given.

The Queen Complex

Ceilidh had lived with us for a little over two months when the problem about which Erna had warned us reared its head. By that time, Ceilidh had sort of accepted our house as her home…at least for now. She even began rushing to the door in true gregarious Toller fashion to greet us and all visitors on arrival. One day she and Chance hit the ceramic tiles at the front door simultaneously to greet a newcomer.

Wild Kingdom erupted in our living room. The two half-sisters flew into a violent battle, teeth bared, snarling, tearing at each other.

Fortunately both were wearing buckle collars. I managed to get a good, firm grip on each, pry them apart, and hold them at arms' length until the snarling subsided. When I deemed it safe to release them, they reverted to their former benign relationship as if nothing had happened. A freak incident, I told myself as I tried to reassure my startled guest that he wasn't about to be eaten by two little red wolves.

That wasn't the case. These Queen Bee altercations would continue to flare any time one of them perceived the other had garnered too much attention. Although I have never been sure who started these pitched battles (they broke out so suddenly and with such violence I could never be certain), a week after that first fight I did learn more about Ceilidh's combative strategies. It happened at our vet's office.

I'd taken Ceilidh for a routine visit. Once she'd been checked over, Joan, who'd accompanied us, took her out into the waiting room while I remained chatting with Dr. Larsen. Once I glanced out and saw a big, black, mixed breed glaring at Ceilidh across the room, but its owner appeared a competent lady with a seemingly good grip on her pet's leash.

Ceilidh, I also noticed, had gotten to her feet and was staring straight at the larger animal, paws planted, head lowered and neck extended like a gander whose flock had just been threatened. Still I didn't see any cause for alarm. Joan had a tight hold on her lead. I turned my attention back to our conversation.

Then it happened. The lady with the other dog (Joan later explained) had loosened her grip on her pet for a split second. That was all it took. It charged Ceilidh.

Canine snarls and roars made me whirl back toward the waiting room. A ball of red and black fur whirled about with the acoustic accompaniments of a major battle at the zoo.

Later, after hostilities had been squelched and Dr. Larsen had decreed neither of the combatants was in need of his services, I led Ceilidh back out into the waiting room where the black dog and her mistress sat awaiting their scheduled appointment. As we passed the pair, I was halted as Ceilidh came to a full stop at the end of her lead.

Glancing back, I saw she'd resumed her gander stance as she faced her former opponent head on. The black dog, nearly twice her size, whined and backed against her mistress. I learned, as time went by, this threatening pose would keep most future challengers at bay, Chance excepted.

Maybe even if you do occasionally choose an unwise battle, you might still come out ahead.

The Littlest Shortstop

Ceilidh, in her constant, nebulous quest, was ever watchful for any opportunity to escape our custody and have an opportunity to search on her own. Therefore we were careful to keep the gate to our fenced backyard securely latched.

But no one or nothing is perfect, and one day Ceilidh did manage to get free. It happened one spring evening when Ron was painting the fence. We would be moving to our cottage the following week, and we wanted all necessary summer repairs at the house finished before we left. When making a quick trip to the shed to get a new paintbrush, he left the gate open.

Not one to miss an opportunity, Ceilidh must have dashed to freedom.

All that spring, through the fence, she'd been watching ball games in the park that bordered our property. The words of the old Clearwater Revival song came to mind each time I watched her waiting, crouched and ready for any foul ball that might fly into our yard, something about the singer urging the coach to put him in to play center field.

The sight of spheres flying through the air while chain link prevented her from retrieving them must have irritated her no end. The moment she gained her freedom, she apparently headed for the park.

At first we didn't miss her. The back door was

open, and Ceilidh often sauntered inside to snooze or search for food. Unaware of our missing girl, Ron returned to his painting.

Only when yelling erupted from the park, yelling that definitely wasn't cheering for a home run, and a bunch of baseball players burst out of the enclosure in pursuit of a small red dog did we realize she'd gone AWOL. Softball clamped in her teeth, Harborlights Scotia Ceilidh headed for home with her coveted prize. Like a speeding amber bullet she burst past Ron, flew across the yard, and disappeared into the house.

"That dog stole our ball!" an irate player yelled at Ron as they arrived at the fence.

"Yeah, and it would have been a home run if he (Ceilidh) hadn't jumped a good three feet into the air to catch it!" another yelled.

"Sorry." Ron, an avid baseball fan, said with sincerity. "I'll get your ball. It won't happen again."

Already Ron was too late. Ceilidh, perhaps in an attempt to avenge herself on that formerly elusive, much-coveted ball, had torn it to shreds.

Ron returned to the baseball players at the gate, wallet in hand.

Ceilidh never did get to play shortstop. She did seem content after the incident, however. Sometimes all anyone needs to find satisfaction is one brief moment at center field.

Tollers Ahoy!

In July of that first year after Ceilidh had joined our family, we took both dogs to Mount Carleton Provincial Park, a pristine wilderness area about seventy-five miles distant from our home. It would be our first time canoeing with both Tollers. We were eager to see how they behaved on the water.

We off-loaded the canoe into the first of the big, beautiful lakes that form a major part of this lovely area, packed it with our supplies, and shoved it out into the shallows.

Thinking Chance would be the most relaxed in the situation, I picked her up and placed her in the boat. To my surprise, she pranced excitedly, nearly tipping our small craft. A firm command to "sit" from Ron ended her little dance, and she settled herself a bit uneasily amidships. Then I returned to shore for Ceilidh.

"Come on, girl," I said picking her up and starting out into the water. "It's all right. I'll be with you."

She felt as rigid as cement. As I placed her into the canoe near the stern, I expected an explosion of panic. In anticipation, I gripped her collar. To my surprise, she sat down in the exact center of the canoe with a contented sigh.

"Look at that," I called to Ron. "All she needs is a little sailor's hat to make her perfect."

"Let's go." Unimpressed by my fanciful

impressions, Ron waved me aboard. All four of us glided peacefully out across the water.

Chance occasionally moved, but a stern command from Ron in the rear of the boat brought her back to a sit. Ceilidh, on the other hand, remained centered in our craft, scanning the shores, searching, always searching…

As we rounded a small island, a flock of Mergansers appeared out of the tall grass on its shore. I held my breath. What would these two duck dogs do?

Both began to sniff, Ceilidh from her stationary position amidships, Chance getting up and moving to the left gunwale nearest those tempting ducks.

"Sit!" Ron touched her with his paddle to urge her back into the proper position. "Sit!"

A disgruntled gurgle echoing in her throat, she obeyed. Both dogs continued to sniff as hard as they could until the mother duck and her flock had been left far behind us. I'm convinced my vacuum cleaner has less sucking power then those two Toller noses trying to breathe in "duck."

As the incident paled into memory, Chance relaxed to once more enjoy the ride. Ceilidh continued to scan the shores.

Off the Deep End

Although Ceilidh had continued her forays away from us for about twenty minutes each time we released her near our house, she always came back at the end of that period. I hoped the old adage was true…if you love something, set it free, and if it's meant to be, it will come back to you.

In Mount Carleton Provincial Park, Ceilidh apparently decided to behave differently. Instead of rushing off on her constant quest, she remained close to us. Perhaps she realized that if she wandered off into the wilderness there would be a lot less chance of her finding us again.

Or perhaps she smelled the bears and coyotes that inhabited the area and was clever enough to know not to risk a scuffle with any of them. Throughout her years with us, Ceilidh would exhibit a survival savvy that Chance lacked.

As we returned to our truck parked beside one of the lakes, Ceilidh, who had a much heavier coat than Chance, paused and stared at a small dock jutting out into the water. Hot and tired, she saw a solution to her discomfort. Like a gunshot blast, she burst away, an amber streak flashing across the meadow and out along that little wharf. Chance raced close behind her.

At the end of the pier, exhibiting perfect canine diving form, Ceilidh made a flying leap out into the cool lake water.

Now Chance was a wonderful dog…clever, obedient, loving, all we could possibly wish for. She had only one flaw. She wouldn't swim. Since puppyhood she'd raced into the rivers and lakes only to stop dead in her tracks when the water reached her belly. On this occasion, she apparently hadn't noticed Ceilidh's ultimate destination.

As Ceilidh dove, Chance came to the end of the dock at such speed she had no choice but to follow. Her diving form was decidedly not that of her half-sister's. It resembled the worst of belly flops, and it had to hurt. After she hit the water and managed to turn toward land, her eyes reflected shock and desperation.

Recognizing her panic, I ran to the end of the short pier and knelt, ready to grab her collar and help her back to dry boards. I didn't have to urge her. Chance headed toward me as frantically as a Titanic survivor. When she came within reach, I grabbed her collar and pulled her out of the water.

Eyes round from fear, she didn't bother to shake. She simply stood staring at me as if to ask, "What the heck happened?!"

I gave her a reassuring hug and looked out across the lake for Ceilidh. Swimming in a leisurely manner some distance from the dock, our newest companion seemed to be in her element, relaxed and enjoying herself.

Chance shook, long and hard, gave me a quick lick of thanks, and dashed up the bank to join Ron beside the truck. I turned my attention back to Ceilidh. Such pure delight in such a simple pleasure. I sat down on the end of the wharf, feet dangling over its end, to watch and share in her enjoyment.

Like a lot of the things Ceilidh felt passionate about, her love of the water ended up giving her more discomfort that pleasure later that same summer. It happened when we took a trip to Fundy National Park in southern New Brunswick.

Hiking along a boardwalk over a marsh, we came to a beaver pond. A windless day in mid-July, temperatures in the upper 80s had left both dogs panting. When water-loving Ceilidh saw that still, black, stagnant pool, she didn't hesitate. With a resounding splash, she leaped and stretched out full length in water just deep enough to cover her belly. She heaved a deep, contented sigh as she looked up at us.

That evening Ceilidh's enjoyment of her exploit paled. She began to scratch at her belly. For the remainder of our holiday she never ceased to take every opportunity to claw and bite at that section of her anatomy.

Fearing she'd caught something serious or contagious, we took her to Dr. Larsen as soon as we got home. His diagnosis was quick and simple. Ceilidh had attracted some sort of lice common to beaver ponds. A bit of medication and she'd be fine.

We breathed a sigh of relief for two reasons. First, that the problem had proved so easily cured, and second (if uncharitably) that the parasites had seen fit to stay confined to a single host in our family.

The incident in no way diminished Ceilidh's enjoyment of the water. Quite possibly she didn't associate her nasty itching with the beaver pond, but even if she had, I'm sure it wouldn't have lessened her love of swimming.

If you're passionate about something, don't abandon it simply because of a single unpleasant experience.

A Clothes Fetish

Ceilidh had a number of strange little quirks that surfaced as time went by. Among them was a penchant for toilet paper and dirty clothing. If anyone left unwashed underwear or socks lying about, Chambermaid Ceilidh took possession.

At first it had its amusing moments. I recall the day the Avon lady came to my door. While I was informing her as kindly as possible that I didn't use the products because of allergies, I noticed her looking beyond me into the house, apparently more interested in something beyond me than my explanation. Turning, I saw Ceilidh a few feet away, a strapless bra clamped in her teeth, a stiffly wired cup protruding from either side of her mouth.

When we had guests, Ceilidh never failed to turn up in the living room to present them with a roll of toilet paper confiscated from the bathroom. If they didn't accept the offer, she'd find a quiet corner and rip it to smithereens.

For a while we tolerated her eccentricities, but when she began to refuse to relinquish clothing and dashed away to chew holes in the garments, we decided we couldn't tolerate that kind of behavior any longer. What if she seized a mitten or glove from someone other than a family member and then, growling and snarling, refused to return it! One rainy evening after we'd moved to the cottage for the summer, I decided to put an end to this unacceptable behavior once and for all.

Ceilidh had found one of Ron's socks lying amid the stream of clothing he'd shed along the floor on his way to the shower. When I tried to take it from her, she growled.

"That's enough, Ceil! This has to come to an end…now."

I took her by the collar and forced her out onto the doorstep in a downpour. Ceilidh loved to swim, but she hated rain. Therefore, I reasoned, putting her out into it until she willingly gave me the sock might be the answer. As I shut the door, my heart ached. The punishment seemed terribly harsh. I had to keep telling myself it was for Ceilidh's own good.

I wanted five minutes (they seemed the longest five minutes of my life) before snapping on the porch light. There, standing in the pouring rain, wet sock still hanging from her mouth, stood my bedraggled dog. My hand went to the doorknob.

"Leave her," Ron, fresh and clean, had emerged from the shower and been informed of my strategy. "She has to learn."

"But she looks so forlorn…"

"You don't want her to get into serious trouble because of some foolish fetish, do you?"

"No…"

"Then leave her."

Another agonizing five minutes passed. I returned to the window. Ceilidh, sock and all, had disappeared into the pitch blackness that is so intense in the country on a dark and stormy night.

"She's gone!" I cried. "Ceilidh's gone! She could be on the road; she might get hit by a car! I'm going to look for her!"

"Wait," Ron advised. "She won't go far in this rain. Give her a few more minutes."

This time I could only restrain myself four minutes before looking out again.

What I saw astounded me. Like some sad, bedraggled offering, the black sock lay on the doormat. Drenched and dirty, it wouldn't have been appealing to most people, but to me it was more beautiful than gold. Stepping out into the rain, I picked it up.

"Ceil!" I called. "Thank you. You can come in now."

The only reply was the relentless drumming of the rain. Suddenly she hopped up on the step beside me, soaked and dripping. Dropping to my knees, I bundled her into my arms.

"Thank you, Ceil."

She grunted. I was squeezing her too tightly.

Both of us thoroughly drenched, we went inside, where Ceilidh and Chance each got a homemade dog cookie and the former a good toweling.

That didn't entirely end Ceil's penchant for running off with clothes, but it did lessen its severity and seriousness. She no longer took clothing from strangers, and we could get our own garments back without a pitched battle, a big improvement Ron and I both agreed.

Sometimes one has to show her authority.

Quills in the Country

We once again moved to our cottage for the summer. Near river and marsh, Ceilidh came as close as we were ever to see her come to happiness. Racing across the fields behind our cottage with Chance and then plunging (alone) into the river beyond, she appeared to be in her element. We admired her as she swam around and around in the water, the long, strong, slow strokes that were her trademark making her appear tireless.

The only problem we experienced was her continuing penchant to run away for twenty-minute periods each morning, sniffing and searching. We've never let any of our dogs run about country or town on their own, and this worried us. Aside from keeping her constantly tied (we had no fence around our several acres in the country as we had around our small city lot), there was no choice but to accept her rambles whenever she managed to escape our watchful eyes.

We knew she was still searching for something. Tollers are generally non-roamers. Chance was an excellent example. From earliest puppyhood, she'd never strayed more than a few yards from us, no matter what items of interest arose elsewhere.

When Ceilidh would return, seemingly satisfied that at least at that particular instance she wasn't to be successful in her quest, she'd settle down for the rest of the day in the yard.

Although it troubled me no end—I was haunted by fears of her wandering onto a country road and being hit by a car, or getting lost in the woods and attacked by bears or coyotes—I decided I had to trust in the street smarts she frequently exhibited to keep her safe and which our pampered Chance totally lacked.

One habit of Ceilidh's we never managed to break and of which her practical cleverness hadn't made her wary was her hatred of porcupines. Perhaps, before she'd come to live with us, she'd had a run-in with them and developed a lifelong murderous obsession that neither pain nor time could erase. One old-time woodsman and dog fancier told us that once some dogs are injured by porcupines they'll attack every one they encounter in an impossible act of revenge.

"The only way to end the problem is to let the dog kill one," he said.

It wasn't a solution we'd employ.

Ceilidh's first encounter (under our guardianship, at least) occurred on August 12, 1994. We'd had company all day at the cottage. After they left, Ron and I decided to take the dogs for a well-deserved run on a deserted farm a couple of miles up the road.

It was a beautiful summer's evening, with the sun slanting through the tops of birch, spruce, and maple trees. We stopped our truck at the crest of a meadow that sloped downward toward the river and let the dogs out.

Off they raced, amber flashes crossing the freshly mown hayfield until they disappeared into a small thicket near the riverbank. Following at a leisurely pace, we assumed that the worst they could do was get into the black mud along the shore.

Not really. Outraged barking and snarling and other sounds of a major scuffle erupted from the alders. Chance emerged and headed toward us at top speed. As the sounds of feral violence continued from the trees, she reached us and paused, panting, by our side. As she looked up at us, wide-eyed with alarm, we saw quills sticking out of her chin.

"Oh, my God!" Ron exclaimed, breaking into a run toward the sounds of the altercation.

Horrified, I knelt and grasped Chance in my arms. My breath clogging in my throat, I watched Ron disappear into the cluster of trees. The yikes and screams intensified.

After what seemed like hours (but was probably no more than a minute or two) the donnybrook sounds stopped. I got to my feet in time to see Ron emerge from the thicket, dragging Ceilidh by her beautiful tail. I didn't think I would have the courage to look at her, to view the results of that terrible battle, but when they finally reached me, I had no choice.

It was horrible. Ceilidh's face and front half of her body resembled one giant overused pincushion. Quills sprouted from every inch of those parts. She had to be in terrible pain.

Still leading her by her tail (there was no other place on her body to get a safe grip) Ron took the unprotesting little dog to our truck and put her in the back. We'd never left a dog unrestrained there before, but now we had no choice. We couldn't get a collar or leash over those quills, and we couldn't put her in the front with us.

During the two-mile drive back to the cottage, we

didn't speak, lost in the dread of what we knew had to be done.

Once both dogs were inside the kitchen, Ron went to the shed for his pliers while I tried to comfort Ceilidh without touching her. Strangely she wasn't whimpering or showing any signs of discomfort. She simply stood immobile in the middle of the room, her eyes wide and quiet.

When Ron returned, he set to work on the quills in Chance's face.

"But Ceilidh has so many…" I protested.

"That's exactly right," he replied. "It'll take me hours. I can do the job on Chance in a few minutes. That way, one dog can rest easy."

He was right. Chance, however, proved unready for the operation. She squealed and leaped and screamed. It took both of us to restrain her.

When we'd finally gotten out all the quills we could find, Ron turned to a still quiet Ceilidh and lifted her onto the table. I wanted to comfort her, to make her know it was going to be all right, but all I could do for her at the moment was steady her as best I could while Ron cut and plucked the quills from her body.

The next three hours seemed unending as I held her in my arms and Ron removed what he counted to be well over three hundred quills from her snout, shoulders, and front legs. She never moved or growled or made any gesture of aggression during the entire process. I felt each pull as if the ugly barb were coming out of my own flesh. My admiration for this stoic little dog grew like bamboo after a tropical deluge.

At midnight Ron laid aside his pliers and replaced Ceilidh on the floor.

"I *think* I got them all," he said, wiping sweat from his forehead. "We'll take her to the vet tomorrow to be sure."

Sitting in the center of the kitchen, she emitted a huge sigh. Strangely, it sounded more like a lament than one of relief. Was her inner pain somehow greater than anything she could ever suffer in the flesh? I wondered as I got her a fresh bowl of water and settled her for the night on her dog bed in our bedroom.

The pain in a heart can trump the pain of the body at certain times.

One Good Roll

Ceilidh, like many gun dogs, had a penchant for attempting to disguise her scent by covering herself in another. Usually these alternatives are stinky and repulsive to humans. I think I once read that dogs respect the smelliest among their numbers most. If this is true, I'm sure at times Ceil must have rivaled royalty, in doggy terms.

Shortly after she became a member of our family, we discovered Ceilidh had a gift for ferreting out decaying matter and fresh feces with astounding regularity and, if not stopped in time, rolling in the disgusting stuff. Chance, a lady to the core, would stand back watching, one snow-white front paw raised. I think, if she could have managed, she would have held her nose. Half-sisters though they were, they nevertheless were the odd couple in many ways.

Ceilidh's penchant for stinkiness reached an all-time high one summer's evening when we took the dogs for a run a few miles up the road from our cottage. There had been Old Home Week celebrations in our little community during the previous seven days. As a result, visitors had been camping in the vicinity and we'd kept the dogs close to home during the seven-day period so they wouldn't interfere with anyone who didn't fancy canines. Now that the festivities were over, the time had come to allow them a good run.

We stopped the truck on the edge of a wide meadow and set both Tollers free. Chance burst off out of the vehicle and raced toward a spring bubbling out of a hillside. She loved to drink the cold, clear water. Ceilidh, in contrast, ran only a few yards before stopping short, sniffing, and heading into a little thicket. A moment later we heard the unmistakable sounds of her rolling in...something.

"Not again!" Ron leaned wearily against the side of the truck. "This time she definitely rides home in the back!"

Prepared for such a problem, I'd put our travel crate into the truck's cargo bed before we'd left the cottage. Ceil had rolled in unacceptable materials, leaped into the black mud of marshes, or gotten tangled in burdocks on too many previous occasions for me to travel unprepared. And, of course, there'd been the porcupine incident.

That beautiful August evening she managed her crowning achievement. When she emerged from the trees, the stench made us clutch our noses. She'd found the spot where some careless travel trailer owner had emptied his septic system. Chance, who came trotting back at that moment, skidded to a stop and backed away from her evil-smelling half-sibling.

"She's your dog." Ron and Chance clambered into the truck cab, leaving Ceilidh and me alone. "You load her."

Mentally muttering *Yuck! Yuck*! and trying to close my senses to the reality of the situation, I boosted the little stinker into the back of the truck and pushed her bodily into the crate. Dropping to my knees, I rubbed my hands on the grass with the all the vehemence of

Lady Macbeth as she cried, "Out, damned spot!"

"Don't worry, Ceil." I couldn't help pausing to reassure the reeking little critter peering out at me from behind the bars of her kennel. "We'll have you clean in no time."

Ceilidh gazed at me with those gorgeous teddy bear eyes. She didn't appear in the least concerned. Could it be she was coming to trust me?

As fast as the speed limit would allow, we drove to the nearest accessible bit of shoreline. Ron and Chance leaped out and headed for the beach, leaving me to release my odoriferous little friend.

I snapped the cage open. Water-loving Ceilidh didn't wait to be assisted from the back of the truck. Instead she made a flying leap and headed for the river. After going only a few yards, though, she skidded to a stop. Her head swiveled and her nose lifted as she sniffed the air (although how she was capable of smelling anything beyond her stinky self I don't know). Again she raced off, but this time away from the water, back toward a grove of trees to our left.

I turned to see where she was headed and glimpsed, through a small stand of birches, a blue pickup with its tailgate lowered. Seated on folding chairs beside it, a middle-aged couple enjoyed a leisurely lunch.

Oh, Lord, no!

I started to run toward the unsuspecting pair. I was too late. The man had spotted Ceilidh. Apparently a dog fancier, (although not astute at gender recognition) he called, "Hey, boy. Come here, boy!"

Ceilidh galloped toward him. I wasn't deceived. His invitation hadn't attracted her. It was the sandwich in his hand.

"Nice dog!" As Ceilidh arrived at the man's side, (downwind, I had to assume) he reached out and stroked her.

"Oh, sh—!" He jumped to his feet, holding up the hand that had touched her as if it had been burned. Ceilidh, taking advantage of his surprise, snatched the sandwich from his other hand, whirled, and raced away.

"I'm so sorry!" I tried to explain as I arrived, breathing hard, at the picnic site. "Ceilidh got into something…"

"I've told you not to play with strange dogs!" The woman ignored me as her companion grabbed a sheaf of napkins from among the lunch materials and began scrubbing at his hand. "Maybe next time you'll listen!"

"How could I possibly know…?"

"Sorry," I murmured again and hurried away from what seemed well on the way to becoming an all-out recrimination session.

I caught up with Ceilidh as she finished her sandwich on the bank above the beach. With my stomach heaving, I put a leash on her.

Unperturbed, she licked her lips and agreeably, perhaps even a trifle proudly, trotted along at my side as we headed for the river. And why shouldn't she? After all, not only was she the stinkiest dog in the universe, but she'd even gotten that lovely ham sandwich, to boot.

There are all different kinds of perfect days. This had been Ceilidh's.

A Carrot for the Digging

Ceilidh's penchant for food led to her developing many thoughtful methods of acquiring it. As the end of August arrived in her first year as a MacMillan, we began to harvest the vegetables from our garden. Ceilidh, sitting between the drills of carrots, turnips, beets, and potatoes, watched as Ron and I dug the tubers from the soft earth and shook dirt from them. She seemed satisfied to be a spectator.

Then I picked up a small, tasty-looking carrot, washed it under the spray of the nearby hose, and proceeded to eat it. Ceilidh looked up at me with renewed interest.

"Want one, Ceil?" I asked.

The bright eyes said "Yes, yes!" as eloquently as if she'd spoken the words. So I washed one for her. She snatched it from my hand, ran off a few feet, and stretched out in the warm sun to munch contentedly. Chance came up to sit in front of me as if to say, "Hey, have you forgotten someone?" So I washed one for her as well.

The next morning when Ceilidh returned from her twenty-minute AWOL search, she didn't come up onto the deck as she usually did. Instead, when I looked out into the garden, there she was, digging a fresh carrot.

She never dug willy-nilly in the garden. An economical little creature, she harvested only one vegetable at a time. Then she'd carry her treat out onto the lawn to eat it before returning for another.

She successfully digested the carrots, but when she moved into the potato field we had to put a stop to her. Prone to diarrhea, Ceilidh got violent bouts after she'd partaken of even a few small bites of *pomme de terre*. We termed her malady "potato poops."

She accepted this restriction gracefully and returned to her carrot patch as contentedly as Bugs Bunny minus Elmer Fudd. Sometimes accepting the advice of others can save a lot of discomfort.

The Natural

As autumn approached, both Ron and I were eager to test Ceilidh's prowess in the hunt. With Chance still a non-swimmer, we pinned our hopes on Ceil's ability to fetch our kill.

In late September, we loaded our canoe with scrap lumber and set off upriver from our cottage. We planned to build a blind on a prominent bit of land that jutted out into the water a couple of miles away. It would be an excellent place for an ambush and tolling. The ducks could see the dog no matter which side of the point they landed on. That vantage point combined with a well-constructed blind would give a hunter a definite advantage.

We must have made quite a sight that lovely autumn Sunday, Ron in the rear of the canoe, myself in the front, and the two Tollers perched atop the load of old boards amidships. By now both were expert canoeists and could be counted on to stay in place during the voyage. Chance remained alert, scouring the shoreline for ducks. Ceilidh, after scanning the beaches with all the intensity of a radar patrol, stretched out comfortably to snooze in the sun.

Burdened as we were, it was a slow voyage. When we arrived at the point, we let the dogs run free while we unloaded our cargo and began to build our blind.

It took time and energy, but we didn't mind. The

day illustrated autumn in northern New Brunswick at its best. The trees sported their gorgeous autumn hues of gold, red, and russet; the sun shone. A playful, little breeze kept bugs and sweatiness at bay.

Chance hung around, watching us work, but Ceilidh, once again seeking, wandered off into the tall grass up shore. "Let her go," Ron advised as I started after her. "She'll be back."

Reluctantly I watched her amble away. Ron had always been right about trusting our dogs. On the other hand, we'd never had one so obviously on a quest.

By the time we'd finished building our ambush, she hadn't returned. I think even my confident spouse began to feel a tad uneasy. He consented without argument when I suggested we walk up shore in the direction we'd last seen her. A half mile later, around a sharp bend in the shoreline, we found her.

Ceilidh waded about in the shallows, looking down into the water, perhaps watching minnows or some small marine life, with intense interest. Swimming peacefully around her were a half dozen black ducks.

Chance, who'd been meandering along behind us, caught up. Her annoyance at Ceilidh (we would never know if it was because she'd wandered off or that she'd had the audacity to toll without her) bubbling over, she made a beeline for her half-sister. The ducks burst into flight as the second little red critter landed into the water among them.

We didn't mind. Delighted by Ceilidh's impromptu luring, we had no doubt as to which Toller was going hunting on the first day of hunting season.

Demonstrating one's skills can be the key to achieving success.

An Infamous First Day

My mother once sewed my father's reversible hunting cap so that it permanently had the red side out. She was afraid he'd flip it to camouflage once out of her jurisdiction and other hunters might mistake him for some unusual type of wildlife.

As could be expected, this did little to enhance his duck-hunting success or his popularity with his waterfowling buddies. Nevertheless, he wore that glowing headpiece until it got blown away one calm November morning.

Perhaps I inherited her overprotective attitude toward hunter husbands. That first autumn after Ceilidh joined our family, when a door-to-door salesman demonstrated a unique flashlight that he claimed would be ideal for hunters, I was hooked. It not only housed a battery-operated torch and tent lamp within its slender, foot-long body, it also contained a siren and an RCMP-type blue-and-yellow emergency flasher. Any or all of these marvels could be activated at the flick of a finger. Surely, no matter how horrendous an injury (short of death) befell husband Ron, he would still have at least one digit operational and with this marvelous device could summon help.

When I showed Ron my purchase that evening, he was not greatly impressed but agreed to try it come hunting season. And try it we did two weeks later, on a most auspicious occasion known as FIRST DAY.

FIRST DAY in our household once aroused all the anticipation that the mention of Christmas does in a six-year-old. It was one of Ron's major *raisons d'etre*. It was October 1, the FIRST DAY of duck-hunting season in the province of New Brunswick.

When FIRST DAY finally arrived, we shivered our way out of bed in the dark and cold of 5:00 a.m., gathered up decoys, guns, and ammunition lying in wait near the cottage door, and slipped a collar and leash on Ceilidh.

Our blind, although easily accessible by water, had a number of logistical problems when approached by land. Cunningly concealed at the foot of a steep riverbank, the path to its inscrutable location was littered with windfalls and canopied by lofty pines that shut out any hope of light from a dawning sky. Getting to it in broad daylight was no easy feat. In near-pitch-darkness for individuals encumbered with full duck hunting paraphernalia, the trek offered all the charm of a major expedition.

Nevertheless, the pros of its location (for us, at least) eclipsed the cons. Situated on one of the best duck hunting sites for miles, it was also the only legal ambush on an extensive hundred-acre riverfront property owned by a friend. Eager to enjoy this enviable position, I threw our bag of decoys over my shoulder and waited for Ron to collect his gear.

"Let's go," Ron muttered finally, hefting guns, ammunition, and portable seat into a semblance of a balanced load.

"Wait, wait!" I stooped awkwardly to pick up our wonderful new light. "There!" Triumphantly I switched on the flashlight component. "Now we can see where we're going."

"Okay, okay," he hissed. "But keep it low. Black ducks are nobody's fool. They can spot anything suspicious a long way off."

Across the field and into the trees above the river we went, the beam of my multi-purpose light illuminating the way. I had to admit it made things a little tricky. With my left hand engaged in balancing the decoy bag steady on my shoulder, I had to link Ceilidh's leash around my wrist and trust her not to take advantage of this obvious lack of control.

Such minor inconveniences paled in the thrill of the moment. The air, crisp and clear, gave tangible hope of a great day. The tingle of excitement that once engulfed me at such moments sparkled through my veins. Ceilidh had even settled into a polite heel at my side. What could be better than this?

Then it happened. With all the shock of a spark hitting a gas-filled room, our world exploded. An early-rising squirrel burst into a vigorous fishwife scold only a few feet above Ceilidh's head.

Roaring her outrage, the little dog lunged. The leash that had been hanging about my wrist snapped tight, wrenching my fingers forward over buttons never meant to be pressed at such a moment. Light and sound burst around us—flashing lights and a screaming siren, that is.

Infuriated by the insomniac squirrel, Ceilidh leaped harder against the lead and pitched me forward into the brush. I landed with a grunt on my stomach. Decoys loosed from their bag by the impact scuttled into the underbrush like a flock of startled partridge. The flashlight, still wailing and whirling, flew from my hand into a place beneath a dense windfall. There it continued its colorful outburst while I struggled to my knees and tried to get Ceilidh under control.

The adventure did not end there.

As Ron dove to retrieve the flashlight, a figure crashed past us in the darkness. Ready to hunt illegally on our turf, a poacher had mistaken our water-fowling *faux pas* for a RCMP invasion and was making a fast exit.

Later, as we continued on to our blind, I heard Ron muttering something to the effect that any duck we'd get a shot at that morning would have to be deaf and blind. I refrained from comment.

We had a lengthy wait in our ambush that morning. Apparently all waterfowl in the vicinity had either heard and/or seen our well-announced arrival. Ceilidh, the excitement past, had curled up into a cozy little fox-like ball and settled down to sleep.

At ten a.m. a single duck finally appeared, circled our decoys, then landed. Ron jumped it into flight and fired. The duck, unscathed, flew away, quacking indignantly. Ceilidh leaped to her feet and bolted off…not toward the water to look for a possibly fallen duck but up the hill and into the woods.

Gun shy! Ceilidh, swimmer extraordinaire, for all her otherwise courageous temperament, was gun shy.

I scrambled after her. What if her terror had made her wild and directionless?

When I stumbled out of the woods and saw her pacing up and down beside the passenger door of our truck, my knees turned to Jell-O.

"Ceil!" I knelt, and gathered her into my arms.

"Oh, Ceil, I'm sorry! We didn't know you were gun shy! We should have checked before we brought you hunting!"

That ended Ceilidh's hunting career. Well, almost. Anytime Ron shot a duck near the cottage and the current wasn't running fast, he'd come and get Ceilidh to retrieve it. Without the fear of a shotgun blast, she had no hesitation in plunging into even the iciest water after fallen waterfowl. She'd swim long distances in high waves for a retrieve, her distinctive long, slow strokes making it seem she could go on forever. And she had absolutely no feather aversion. She'd carry a bird as far as necessary in her mouth.

She had one quirk that ruined anything she retrieved for photographic purposes. Before she'd pick up a fallen bird, she'd decapitate it. Then she'd proudly carry the headless bunch of feathers back to us.

Another lesson learned: Most of us have hidden fears and, if we're not alert to them, we can let the world know, often at inappropriate moments.

A Decoy Rescue

Ceilidh redeemed herself for her gun shyness in Ron's eyes one brilliantly cold November day later that same autumn. Ron had set out his decoys in the mouth of a brook a couple of miles above our cottage. Later in the day, wind and tide had made two of his best irretrievable from the shore. The only way he could get to them would be to launch our canoe and make a difficult voyage out to where they bounced over the white-capped waves.

I had an inspiration.

"Ceilidh will get them for you," I said.

"I don't know." Ron looked doubtful. "Good retrievers never touch decoys."

"Let's at least give it a try," I pressed. "It will be a lot easier than paddling the canoe upriver against the tide in this wind."

"Well, okay..." Still sounding doubtful, Ron opened the truck door and let Ceilidh scramble inside.

When we reached the brook, a flood tide was hammering at the shore high up into the marsh grass; foam-topped waves crowned the normally placid inlet. It was bitterly cold; so cold, in fact, that if it hadn't been for the cloudless blue skies, I would have been expecting snowflakes.

Suddenly I wondered at the wisdom of my suggestion. I hated to ask Ceilidh to plunge into that dark, icy water for a couple of decoys. When I saw where they jolted up and down over the wind-tossed water, I doubly disliked my idea. They had to be a good quarter mile from shore.

"Okay." I hunkered down beside Ceilidh who sat beside me and put my arm about her sturdy little shoulders. "See the decoys away out there, Ceil? Go get them, girl."

Ceilidh sneezed, looked at me in a puzzled sort of way, then padded off down the bank. As she plunged into the cold water, I flinched. (I live too much in sympathy with my dogs and judge everything they do on a human level, which I know isn't rational. Still, I can't help myself.)

I watched in agony as Ceilidh swam toward the nearest decoy with her long, strong strokes, rising and falling over the waves with all the grace of a white cap. When she reached it, she sniffed it and began to swim in circles around it.

"Fetch, Ceil!" I called, but my words were drowned out by the wind and the slap of waves against the shore.

She made a couple more circuits around the decoy, sniffing tentatively before heading back to shore.

"I knew it wouldn't work." Ron turned to go back to the truck.

"Wait!" I said. "Let me talk to her!"

Ron gave me a look of utter skepticism but paused.

After Ceilidh had swum back to shore, shook, and scrambled up the bank to rejoin us, I knelt and put my arm about her cold, wet shoulders.

"I know you're not supposed to fetch decoys, Ceil," I said. "But this is different. We need you to retrieve them this time. Try again, will you?"

She hesitated, looked at me with those wonderful brown eyes, sighed, then trotted once more back into the water. Please, please, I begged silently as I watched her head for the nearest decoy.

When she got to it, she once again sniffed and circled. I could almost feel Ron's "I told you so" expression on the back of my neck. Suddenly she seized that decoy by the neck and began to pull. With its anchor deep in the sucking mud of the brook's mouth, the imitation bird offered a formidable challenge to the forty-two-pound dog

Holding my breath, I watched as Ceilidh yanked and pulled and swam in circles until she'd managed to pull the lure free. Finally she headed for shore, the cumbersome decoy dragging its anchor in tow.

"I knew she could do it!" I cried as we watched the little dog swimming toward us. "I just knew it!"

"Pretty darn good," Ron had to admit.

After Ceilidh had fetched the second decoy, he was ready to declare her the heroine of the day.

We took her back to the cottage, dried her with towels, made sure her bed was placed near the heater so she could dry, and gave her all the treats her little heart desired. Ceilidh had demonstrated the value of showing what one can do.

The Answer

When we returned to the city later in the fall, we learned that the local kennel club was sponsoring a "fun" dog show at a local shopping mall. We decided to take Chance and Ceilidh.

Up until that point in our lives, although Ron and I had both owned dogs since we were children, we'd never formally obedience-trained any of them. They did what we expected of them and nothing more. If they were pets, they came when called, sat on command, and performed a few parlor tricks. If they were hunting companions, they retrieved, pointed, et cetera.

But after Ceilidh came to live with us, all that changed. After seeing a few dog shows on television, we'd tried her at the basic obedience commands of sit, stay, come, down, and heel. She performed them all with military precision. So when friends invited us to enter our dogs in a fun obedience trial that Saturday at the mall, we decided we'd give it a try.

Ignorant of the rules and regulations governing formal obedience trials, we led our dogs into the ring. Stacked up against a German shepherd trained by an RCMP officer, it appeared our little red critters' chances were slim to none. Indeed, poor Chance, unschooled in what was required of her, didn't have the proverbial snowball's opportunity in the devil's domain.

Ceilidh, on the other hand, easily fulfilled the requirements. She lost the top prize of the day to the German shepherd by a single point, the fault not hers but of our inept handling.

As we drove home with her paper ribbons proudly displayed on our dashboard, Ron and I knew we were hooked. We wanted more of the fun and excitement that was dog show obedience trials.

The following week we enrolled both dogs in obedience classes. Chance had a lot to learn, but Ceilidh easily led the class from day one. I think she was totally bored as she watched her classmates learning the basics of sit, stay, down, come, and heel. In fact, she was so well trained that one evening when a ten-year-old asked to take her through the routine, the child had no trouble to get the lovely little red dog to perform perfectly.

There was just one flaw in all of Ceilidh's performances. They were absolutely lackluster. She went robot-like through the commands, tail drooping, head down, and ears sagging. I felt her sadness and longed to alleviate it, but no matter how much I hugged and kissed her, no matter how much I told her she was a perfect girl at the end of each session, she continued in her automatic, expressionless manner.

When our pair graduated from Obedience School (Ceilidh with honors, Chance barely passing), we decided to try them in a CKC show that was to be held in our city in a couple of months' time. I set about rigorously training Chance, trying to bring her up to par with the near-perfection of Ceilidh's performance. Chance worked hard in spite of my inept handling and lack of experience. As the date of the trial approached, I felt a guarded optimism about her possibilities.

When we applied to enter both dogs in the show, we hit a major snag. We needed proof that we were Ceilidh's legal owners. I called Erna Nickerson and asked if she could forward her CKC registration papers to us. Never a supporter of dog shows, she reluctantly said she'd take a look for them. If she couldn't find them, she said, she didn't know what to do. Ceilidh's former owner had been a naval officer in Halifax and she was quite sure he was no longer stationed there. He would have to sign Ceilidh over to us. She said she'd already tried to contact him through the navy and been unsuccessful.

And so we waited. The due date for registrations approached. I called Erna again. This time I described Ceilidh's outstanding performance at the fun show and explained that we wouldn't be entering her in conformation competition, simply obedience trials. A week later Ceilidh's papers arrived.

"Ceilidh's former caregiver was a man named Arthur Forester," I read aloud to Ron. Looking down at Ceilidh, I had an idea.

"Ceilidh," I got her attention. "Is it Arthur you're looking for? Art?"

She jumped to her feet, her eyes looking up at me more brightly than I'd ever seen them. We had the answer to Ceilidh's quest.

I was just as quickly deeply sorry for what I'd done. I'd awakened memories and desires that couldn't possibly be realized, that could only cause Ceilidh more pain.

"Ceil, I'm so sorry." I knelt and gathered her into my arms.

As I held her close and felt her little heart beating hard and fast from the mention of his name, I envied Arthur Forester all the love and devotion this loyal little creature would give to no one but him. The piece of paper in my hand might say she was legally mine, but Ceilidh knew she still really belonged to him.

Her reaction was a lesson in the depths of loyalty and devotion.

Fated

When the days of the show finally arrived, we took both dogs to the groomers for a final spruce-up before we headed for the trials. Chance, with her white paws and chest fresh from a bath and brush, was one flashy gal. Gregarious to the core, she pranced proudly as we walked both Tollers into the arena. Ceilidh, in typical fashion, walked sedately along beside us, obedient but unenthusiastic.

Ceilidh and I were first on the agenda. She heeled, stopped, sat, heeled, walked, sat perfectly on command, and left the ring to cheers from the crowd. Typically Ceilidh showed no happiness in her reception—until I gave her a homemade cookie reward—and then it was merely a gobble.

Next came Ron's turn. As we'd been advised, I went as far from the ring as possible so as not to distract Chance. From where I stood with Ceilidh near an exit, I could see the beautiful little dog prancing along beside Ron, white paws moving with the precision of the hooves of a hackney carriage horse as she looked attentively up at him, eyes bright and eager, ready for the next command. Even to a rank amateur like myself it was obvious she was a born show dog. In obedience classes, she'd only done what was absolutely necessary, but here, with a cheering, clapping crowd, the little ham was in her element.

Had Ceilidh once danced into a show ring as proudly by Arthur Forester's side? I wondered, a sharp sting of regret pricking me. Had her eyes been bright, her tail held high, her paws prancing? I looked down at her standing at my left, and my heart hurt.

Finally all the dogs competing in that level of obedience came back into the ring for the long sit. As we lined our dogs up side by side, Chance and Ceilidh separated by a huge Rottweiler, my heart pounded. Never a fan of the big, powerful dogs, I feared he might turn on either of my girls and do them serious harm. The timed minutes that followed seemed the longest of my life.

My fears regarding the Rottweiler proved groundless. Trouble came from another, entirely unexpected, source. It arrived in the form of a rambunctious Bouvier de Flanders.

It sat only a couple of seconds before taking off around the ring like a giant black dust bunny. At the time I thought this was an acceptable part of obedience, that the other dogs were expected to ignore bad behavior on the part of their fellow participants. Now I know better. The judge should have stepped in and had a steward remove the unruly creature from the ring.

To my relief, both Chance and Ceilidh ignored the miscreant and completed that stage of the trials successfully. We felt they'd done their best. That was all we'd been hoping for, and we were happy. At the end of the first round, however, much to our surprise, Ron, Chance, Ceilidh, and I were all called back into the ring to accept the top honors.

Our good fortune and our girls' fine efforts continued throughout the two shows of that first day of the competition. Both dogs got two legs out of the three needed to attain their Companion Dog title. Delighted, we approached the following day with high hopes.

The next morning as we drove toward the arena, Ceilidh began to scratch and couldn't seem to get comfortable in any position. Her coat, much thicker than Chance's, appeared to be driving her crazy.

At first we thought she might have contracted fleas the previous day. But that didn't make sense. Chance would have been infested, too. Unable to discover the source of her discomfort, we took her into the show.

During the first trial, Ceilidh performed like the little trooper she was…right up until the heeling component. Half way through the routine requested by the judge, she sat and began to scratch violently. Of course we lost points, and of course we failed to qualify for the title on that round.

As if to compensate, Chance and Ron once again led the field and got top honors. In three consecutive performances, Chance had achieved her Companion Dog title. We were absolutely delighted. Now if only Ceilidh could finish off her title in the final afternoon show…

But that afternoon, for the long sit, Ceilidh, still taking every opportunity that she could to scratch or roll, was placed beside that ill-behaved Bouvier de Flanders. The handler had barely placed the leash behind the big, black dog and started away than it leaped to its feet and began racing around the ring.

Once again the judge failed to give the steward the signal to remove the unruly beast. After one mad trip around the obedience area, it headed for Ceilidh. A moment later he'd knocked the still sitting perfectly little Toller off her bum and onto her back. Trooper that she was, Ceilidh scrambled back into a sitting position. It proved to be too late. The judge ruled she'd broken her long sit.

Indignation rose about me in an enveloping cloud. Wasn't it enough that Ceilidh had lost the family she loved? How could life be so unjust as to cheat her out of her title? Not even Chance's stellar performances could erase the stabbing hurt I experienced for her at that moment.

As we were about to pack up and leave for home at the end of the show, Chance's Companion Dog title and High in Trial achievement in hand, a judge joined us. He patted Chance on the head.

"She's a lovely little dog," he said. "With a lot of potential. She won the show...in spite of your inexperience."

We weren't insulted. How could we be! We had the top obedience dog of the weekend and, if fate hadn't intervened in the form of a crazy Bouvier de Flanders, two Companion Dog titles.

When we arrived home, phone calls began to come from people with male dogs wanting to breed them with Chance. They'd heard of her remarkable win and were anxious to get her bloodlines intermingled with theirs. But we'd had Chance spayed, and so all those inquiries, while flattering, were in vain. We discussed the wisdom of this decision, made two years previous, as Ceilidh threw herself into a flowerbed and rolled and rolled to her heart's content.

Several days later we discovered the source of the problem. Soap. She and Chance had received a similar rinsing at the groomers but Ceilidh's thicker coat had required more water to flush the suds entirely out of her fur.

Thus I felt Ceilidh had been doubly cheated of her well-deserved title. Yet, in my heart, I knew it meant little to her. The only thing she cared about being cheated out of was the source of her continuing quest, a man named Arthur Forester.

Chance Takes the Plunge

The following summer, Chance finally became a swimmer. Ceilidh was largely responsible. The rest of the credit goes to Ron and his shrewd perception of the canine mind.

We were at the shore behind our cottage one fine July morning, throwing bumpers for Ceilidh to fetch. Chance sat on the shore, watching and waiting until Ceilidh's feet touched bottom on her return. Then she'd dash out, wrench the dummy from Ceil's mouth, and splash triumphantly to shore to present it to us.

"That's not fair," Ron muttered. "Ceilidh does all the work and Chance comes in for the big finish. It's the dog show all over again."

He bent, snapped a lead on Chance's collar, then handed another to me.

"Keep Ceil here," he said. "I have an idea."

He brought Chance into heeling position by his side.

"Forward," he commanded and strode off across the shore and into the water, the little amber dog trotting by his side.

I gasped as I watched Ron, fully dressed in sneakers, jogging pants, and T-shirt, stride out into the water, past his knees, past his thighs, up to his hips, with Chance at first trotting and then, amazingly, swimming along beside him! Concentrating on being obedient, on pleasing her caregiver, she'd failed to notice the depth of the water and had begun to swim when it became necessary.

On the shore I applauded their performance and watched in delight as Ron and his little red dog turned and headed back toward shore. A bit wide-eyed, Chance looked more than a trifle flabbergasted by her unexpected accomplishment. Her paddling was still too rapid and erratic for good form, but she no longer appeared panicked, and with each stroke she seemed to be gaining confidence.

Ceilidh apparently didn't share either Chance's surprise or my joy. She simply settled down beside me with a bored-sounding sigh.

"So she's finally swimming," she seemed to say. "Big deal!"

I knelt and gave her wet little body a big hug.

"Yes, it is a big deal, Ceil," I told her. "And you're responsible. You got us interested in obedience training. Thank you…again."

Toller Tussle

That fall Chance demonstrated a new side of her character. Shocking in its intensity and totally unexpected, that revelation occurred simply because Ceilidh happened to wander into territory Chance considered hers.

It began when Ron took Chance partridge hunting. Because of Ceilidh's gun shyness, he couldn't include her in the expedition. Their day didn't prove overly successful. They returned in the late afternoon with a single bird to their credit. Planning to dress it after supper, Ron placed it in the shed at the back of our house and came inside. Chance refused to leave what she must have considered "her bird" and remained lying beneath the shelf on which he'd put it.

Ceilidh, on the other hand, readily gave in to the siren call of supper. Only after her little belly was full did she once again wander out into the yard and across the lawn to the shed where Chance lay guarding her bird.

Involved in clearing away the dishes, I didn't take notice. After all, both dogs were in a fenced backyard. But peace wasn't to reign for long.

Just as I was placing the last of the plates into the dishwasher, snarling and screaming erupted in the crisp October twilight. Dashing out of the house together, Ron and I saw a red ball of fury spinning inside the shed. Locked in battle, Chance and Ceilidh exhibited no evidence whatsoever of sisterly love.

We ran across the yard to the shed and each seized one of the dervishes by the collar. But it was already too late. One of Ceilidh's beautiful ears was only a rag of bloody fur. A normally neutral Chance leaped against Ron's restraint, ready and willing to do the same to the rest of her half-sister's body. They'd had scuffles before, but they'd been of the type Shakespeare had described as being "full of sound and fury, signifying nothing." This had been a pitched battle, full of claws and teeth.

"Take Ceilidh back to the house," Ron instructed, keeping a firm hold on Chance. "I think I know what caused this. Chance was guarding 'her' bird in the shed, and Ceilidh wandered into her territory."

His explanation seemed logical. Chance remained the dog still most incensed. She pitched and lunged in Ron's grip, snarling and barking furiously. Ceilidh, on the other hand, bloody but unbowed, had quieted to mutters of disgust.

Once inside the kitchen, I rushed to get fresh towels and clean up the once lovely, now shredded ear. It was a mess. As usual, she remained stoic, never giving any indication of pain or suffering. After I released her, she wandered over to her dog bed in the living room, stretched out, and with a bored sigh settled to sleep.

Ron, meanwhile, cleaned the source of the trouble, put it in a plastic bag, and deposited it in our refrigerator. Only afterwards was Chance once more allowed into the house. I watched for a possible re-match between the half-sisters, but nothing happened.

Instead Chance, after a disdainful glance in Ceilidh's direction, jumped up onto the couch and settled for sleep. Ceilidh opened one eye, then closed it again. I decided to let sleeping dogs lie.

Of course, the truce between the dogs didn't fix Ceilidh's ear. The next morning, I headed for Dr. Larsen's office. Ceilidh had had lovely ears. In fact, one longtime Toller breeder had described them as perfect.

As Dr. Larsen examined the bloody tangle that had once been so soft and silky, I waited anxiously.

"Chance did quite a job on your ear, Ceil," he remarked when he'd finished. "But I think I can help." He turned to me. "You said you wanted Ceil's teeth cleaned, didn't you? Well, while I have her asleep, I can try to do a little bit of reconstructive surgery on that ear. If I leave it the way it is, it will always be ragged, catching on things and not very comfortable for her. What do you want me to do?"

"Try to fix it." I didn't pause to ask about the cost.

For the next week Ceilidh wore a swath of bandages around her head, making her look like a casualty of war. It didn't ruin her appetite or slow her down. She remained as bottomless and busy and searching as ever.

With the removal of the bandages and stitches ten days later, Ron and I were delighted with the results. Except for a bit of missing fur that would grow back, Ceilidh's ear was exactly as it had been.

Maybe trust can't always be seamlessly repaired, but apparently some physical problems can.

Into Print

The years Ron and I were privileged to share with Chance and Ceilidh I would later call a golden time. With our children grown and gone, we had the time and leisure to enjoy this remarkable pair of little red dogs. They buffered the pangs of empty nest syndrome with their eternal optimism and *joie de vivre*. They filled our lives with seemingly endless opportunities for encountering new experiences and fascinating people.

The Chance and Ceilidh years would also be a time when we had the opportunity to do numerous stories on Nova Scotia Duck Tolling Retrievers for a number of major magazines, to win a prestigious award in New York City for one of them, and to produce the first two books on this unique and amazing breed.

It began one February afternoon when Chance was about nine months old. I was finishing a story on Labs for Bob Wilbanks, editor at *Gun Dog Magazine*, and had called him to finalize a few details. In the course of our conversation, I mentioned Chance. I told him we'd never owned a Nova Scotia Duck Tolling Retriever before; that, in fact, we'd never met a living example of the breed until she came to live with us.

"Hummm." Bob paused for a moment, then continued, "How about doing a piece on your experiences with that puppy in its first year and sending it to me next February?"

"Fine," I said, always eager for any assignment that involved my dogs. I had several irons in the literary fire at the moment, but a year gave me lots of time…I thought. Anyway, he'd probably forget about the assignment. Only my submission of the story would tweak his memory, so there was no hard and fast deadline.

How I underestimated Bob Wilbanks!

Over the course of the next dozen months Chance proved no chance at all. She was a definite…definitely everything we'd hope for and much more. She was obedient, clever, funny, gregarious, an all-out joy. From time to time I scribbled notes and mapped out a very loose outline for the *Gun Dog* story.

On Valentine's Day, exactly one year to the day after Bob had first suggested the Toller article, CBC radio called with a wild idea for a live broadcast. It would involve my writing a romance novel in conjunction with two other New Brunswick writers— live on an afternoon talk show. CBC would give us a cast of characters and a basic scenario, a writer in Sussex would begin the piece, I (in Bathurst) would compose the center, and another author, in Campbellton, would conclude it. I would be given twenty minutes after the Sussex participant had finished reading her bit on the air to write my component.

What fun! I thought. A delightful challenge! Little did I know that bright, beautiful Valentine's morning how great a challenge that entire day would prove to be.

Promptly at four p.m. I was ready, paper, pen, and clipboard poised. The show started, characters and scenario were described, and the clock started ticking. The plot involved two men and two women journeying the length of New Brunswick on their way to a romantic weekend on the slopes of Sugarloaf, one of the province's most famous ski resorts.

The Sussex writer set to work. When she'd finished and had read her offering, I began to scribble on my segment.

Then the phone rang. It was Bob. Where was that story on the Toller he wanted to know?

Although my mind was racing and far from concentrated on his query, I managed to assure him I was almost finished and would have it to him by the end of the week. Then I bid him a quick (and I hope) polite goodbye, grabbed my pen, and began a frantic attempt to write the middle of that wild, improbable romance.

Only after I'd heard a replay of the program and decided I hadn't made too bad a show of myself, did the reality of what I'd promised Bob sink in. I'd assured him of a year's worth of experiences in story form by the end of the week! All I had so far were stacks of notes, a vague outline, and a few scribbled ideas.

Trying not to panic, I fed husband and dogs a hasty Valentine's supper and set to work. By Friday, I'd managed to get story and pictures (taken by Ron) in the mail (no computer or e-mail back then). *Whew! Finished.*

I had no idea it was only the beginning.

My story, with Ron's pictures illustrating it, appeared in the August/September anniversary issue of *Gun Dog* that summer. I was delighted with the layout and pleased when Bob sent us several copies. The magazines were definite keepers, Ron and I decided. We admired it, shared it with dog fancier friends, and put it away on the shelf with our other published stories.

Six months later, one cold January morning, I received a letter from the Dog Writers' Association of America. The article about Nova Scotia Duck Tolling Retrievers that had appeared in *Gun Dog* the previous summer/autumn had been nominated for an award as the Best Article in a Canine Magazine/Newspaper for that year. It had already been shortlisted to a group of three left in the running for a Maxwell Medal. Winners would be announced at the DWAA Awards Banquet in New York City on February 10, the day before the opening of the world famous Westminster Dog Show at Madison Square Garden. I was invited to attend!

I dismissed it as a hoax. A small-time freelance writer from northern New Brunswick couldn't possibly be a contender for an award in New York City. Ron, confident as ever, had no doubts.

"Call and check it out," he said indicating a telephone number. "The area code alone will give you a clue if it's legitimate."

So I called. Sure enough, I was a contender, invited to NYC for the festivities.

"That's amazing," I said, turning to Ron, overjoyed. "I wonder when they let the people who couldn't attend know who the winners are?"

"I don't know, and it doesn't matter," Ron said matter-of-factly. "Because we'll be there in person to find out."

"No, no," I cried. "We can't possibly go! It's too expensive! And…"

"And how often in our lifetimes will this opportunity come along?" Ron turned away. "That's it.

We're going."

With the idea still seeming totally outlandish and crazy to me, three weeks later we boarded a plane for New York City. I still couldn't believe it, not even on the night of the awards banquet when we stood on the curb outside our Manhattan hotel hailing a cab. Ron and Gail MacMillan, from Bathurst, New Brunswick, were in New York City on their way to join some of the most famous dog story writers in the world!

That night would get more and more incredible. As a taxi pulled up and Ron opened the door, an attractive blonde lady rushed out of the hotel behind us.

"Are you going to the DWAA awards?" she asked a trifle breathlessly. "If you are, can we share this cab?"

That woman was Betty McKinney, publisher of Alpine Blue Ribbon Books. She and her company were destined to change our lives.

An hour later I stood with the other nominees in my category as our names were called and smiled stiffly as I waited for one of the others to be declared the winner.

As if in a dream, I heard my name. Suddenly Ron was hugging me, kissing me, shoving me out into the aisle and up toward the podium. From somewhere in my state of utter disbelief, I heard fellow countrymen in the audience begin to chant, "Go, Canada, go!"

Somehow I got to the podium, and somehow, in my still stunned state, I managed to shake hands with the people who greeted me there as a beautiful Maxwell Medal was hung about my neck. Turning to go back to my seat amid lusty applause, I saw Ron, his face glowing, standing, clapping louder than all the rest.

He should have been up there with me. His pictures

had been essential to the article. Without them I couldn't have done it.

But that dazzling New York night wasn't over yet. Shortly Betty McKinney singled me out and suggested I do a book about the dogs, provided I could work with an established breeder. Buoyed by my recent success, I agreed.

Only when I got back home did the reality of the situation set in. As Chance gallivanted about in our snowy backyard, overjoyed at our return, I knelt beside Ceilidh.

"What have I done, Ceil?" I asked putting my arm around her sturdy little shoulders. "I know several breeders, but none of them would want to help write a book."

She turned those gorgeous brown eyes on me, looked up at me with that beautiful teddy bear face, and I knew I had to try. Chance had already been immortalized in print by that award-winning article. Ceil deserved no less. I had to write a book that would feature her wistful little face.

The phone rang. I gave Ceilidh a hug, stood, and hastened inside to answer.

"Hello," said a friendly voice. "My name is Alison Strang. I breed Tollers at my Westerlea Kennel in Surrey, BC. I wanted to congratulate you on your win in New York and to ask if you'd be interested in collaborating on a book about the dogs."

As I was trying to recover from my thrilled surprise, Ceilidh wandered back into the kitchen and, with a little sigh, sat down beside me. It seemed like a kind of benediction.

"There," she was saying. "Now that's settled."

****

Over the course of the next two years Alison and I worked diligently to produce the best book possible on Nova Scotia Duck Tolling Retrievers. When Betty McKinney's Alpine Publishing produced the book in 1996, it was a beauty. Hardcovered, with gold leaf inlays and a gorgeous color center insert, it was, as one reviewer said, "A book any breed would be thrilled to call its own."

Caught fetching a stick, my lovely little Harborlights Scotia Ceilidh was one of the beautiful dogs twice featured in that outstanding color section.

****

The big book, as I came to refer to *The Nova Scotia Duck Tolling Retriever* by Alison Strang and Gail MacMillan, while a marvel of production and extensive information, did not completely satisfy me. The reason was simple. The editors had seen fit to eliminate a good deal of the dog's early history in Yarmouth County. I felt the people of southwestern Nova Scotia who'd been responsible for developing the dogs and caring for them for so many years before they came to widespread notice deserved better than a few lines. The following spring I approached Nimbus Publishing in Halifax with an idea.

I wanted to write a book about the dogs' beginnings in Yarmouth County and the people who'd nurtured these amazing little red creatures for so many years. I was envisioning a small softcover book, little more than a glorified pamphlet. This wouldn't happen. Once Dorothy Blythe, the publisher/editor at Nimbus, saw a sample of my chapters and some of Ron's pictures that would be used to illustrate it, she decided to go all out.

The result was a hardcover book, complete with dust jacket so beautifully devised by Kate Westphal of Charlottetown, PEI, that it was submitted to a competition for best design of that year. It didn't win, but that was no reflection on Kate's talents. She had done a marvelous job, as had the editors at Nimbus.

Featured prominently on page after page, equally with her half-sister Chance, was Ceilidh. Chance may have been the front cover dog with her showy white chest and paws, but it was Ceilidh that was featured on the back, tolling in a vast flock of ducks for Ron to photograph.

She'd proven to be a wonderful model, patient at posing for shot after shot. We appreciated her efforts. She hadn't always been a photographer's joy. Ceilidh's gun shyness had, at first, extended to camera shots. Whenever Ron's camera would click, she'd bolt.

With patience and multiple reassurances, we'd gotten her over this problem. She went on to be our model for countless magazine articles and publicity pieces for the books. Her teddy bear face was an unfailing hit with editors and reporters.

"What a sweetheart!" and "Just look at that face!" became common comments as we publicized the book. Ceil had turned out to be a photographic star. A wistful expression can be as appealing as a joyous one, we learned.

A Springtime Surprise

Spring arrived once again. A near perfect stillness lay over the April morning as Ceilidh and I set off across the field behind the cottage. Only the crunch of my boots as they trod on the crisp fringes of snow patches broke the silence of the bright, beautiful day. Avoiding puddles thinly disguised by delicate masks of shell ice, I strode across the brown-grassed expanse. My breath formed little golden-white fog pockets in the burgeoning sunlight. If it had been autumn, I would have been enamored with the moment. In October, it would have been a perfect tolling day.

"Come on, Ceil," I called and broke into a little jog.

Obligingly she followed suit. Since Chance, always more Ron's dog than mine, had opted to stay at the cottage with him, Ceilidh and I were alone in this lovely, quiet piece of the world. I delighted in these times alone with her and saw them as bonding opportunities. I knew I'd never attain the unqualified devotion she had for her former caregiver, but I wanted at least a few crumbs of her affection.

"Go play." I gave my own version of a release command. In a flash she was off, racing ahead of me toward the shore a good quarter mile away. She, like myself, had been housebound during a good deal of the winter, and I could understand her desire to cut loose. I smiled to myself as I watched her plume of a tail vanish in the distance.

When I arrived at the top of the snow-covered bank above the river, I saw her below me on a shore crammed with ice cakes the river had muscled onto the sidelines in its bid for freedom from winter's grip. Ceilidh nosed about, sniffing, exploring, searching, as she reacquainted herself with familiar territory and, in the process, continued her endless quest.

Then I saw them. Far out on the calm, dark water, a pair of black ducks floated in leisurely circles; leisurely, that is, until they spotted Ceilidh.

Swinging like weathervanes before a sudden change in the wind, they turned toward the little red dog. Shortly they were paddling toward her so swiftly they left a wake in the still, black water.

I'd never tried tolling in the spring, but as I watched the ducks' quick response to Ceilidh, a myriad of positive aspects to the idea flooded into my mind. In spring, the ducks, untroubled by hunters as they are in autumn and unfettered by young as they are in summer, would be more relaxed and vulnerable to the dog's mysterious charms. What a magnificent photo opportunity they presented! If only Ron were here instead of asleep back in the cottage a half mile away across spongy, ice-patched fields, I fumed, my pulses racing.

The ducks approached, swimming hard, necks extended, gossiping noisily. As they drew near the ice-clogged bank where Ceilidh, ignoring them as a Toller should, continued to sniff busily, they fell silent. Drifting to within a few yards of the dog, they paused and perused her like a couple of lost tourists trying to behind some leafless dogwood bushes, I realized this was an excellent opportunity to put this bit of Toller lore to the test. This time I'd come prepared. I reached into my jacket pocket, pulled out a tennis ball, and whistled to Ceilidh.

She turned and came bounding toward us. When she arrived at our excuse for a blind, I showed her the tennis ball. Her eyes brightened like Christmas lights. (Tollers, we'd discovered early in our relationship with them, are tennis ball junkies.) I let the ball have a rolling head start down the snow-crusted bank before giving her the command to fetch.

Slipping and sliding over the crust, Ceilidh managed to grab the ball as it reached the ice piled on the shore. She seized it and dashed back to me.

Three more retrieves and the ducks once more began to move shoreward. Another toss of the ball and they were right back where they had been, in front of the boulder-sized chunks of ice that trimmed the river's edge. Beside me the shutter clicked vigorously, a roll of film advancing through the camera.

Later, as the three of us walked back across the field, my elation at our *fait accompli* inspired me to update an old saying. If a bird in the hand is worth two in the bush, then shouldn't two ducks in the camera be worth at least a dozen rising in front of a gun? Ceilidh had opened a whole new vista to us.

From that day forward, Ceilidh's gun shyness didn't matter. We were resolved to shoot ducks only with a camera. Ceilidh had shown that, even if you're lacking in one area, there are still lots of places where you can excel.

Recovery

Autumn had arrived once again, and I was back on the shore behind the cottage. The water was a deep charcoal-brown, the blue sky trimmed with fluffy-looking white clouds. A wind, cold but too light to be bone chilling, invigorated me, making me feel fully alive for the first time in weeks.

Chance and Ceilidh had rushed ahead of me to race along the shore, exuberant with the joy of renewed freedom. It had been a quiet summer for them, perhaps even a trifle disheartening if dogs, eternal optimists that they are, ever truly get disheartened. Major surgery had put me in dry dock for most of it. As a result, they had been left high and dry as well. Loyally following me about the house as I recovered, they must have longed for marsh and shore, forest and field.

I hadn't the heart or desire to order them to heel, that glorious October morning. Instead, as we crossed the field, I gave my homemade release command, "Okay, go play!" with alacrity and sincerity. I watched them go, red flashes dashing across the wide, shorn hayfield above the river, a good part of their joy rushing into my heart.

Like them, I was finally free…free of hospitals and weakness and indignities. Seeing my girls' carefree, effortless race across the sand provided the icing on the cake that was this glorious day.

As I eased down the sharp curve of the bank above the river, I saw them...three big black ducks winging upstream, necks extended, apparently intent on reaching some predetermined destination.

Suddenly the trio whirled as if they realized they'd missed a turning. Wings slanted, they veered downward toward the choppy surface of the river. They landed far out on the water and began to swim in tight circles.

The birds' abrupt about-face told me they'd spotted the dogs but were leery, far more leery than most black ducks when confronted by the Toller's subtle charms. Two weeks into duck season, these three may have been lured any number of times, may even be the sole survivors of a flock. This would take time and patience, I decided as I hunkered down in the tall, dried grass. I berated myself for choosing to wear a red plaid jacket.

Since tolling works best when the ducks get only fleeting glimpses of the dog, I whistled to my pair. Chance obeyed. Ceilidh, perhaps because of the wind but more probably because of her never-ceasing quest, continued on up the beach. Knowing it would be pointless to keep calling her, I turned my attention to Chance.

Among the seaweed I found a piece of driftwood, blanched and seasoned by the elements. The moment I picked it up, Chance, white-tipped tail flagging, one ivory front paw raised expectantly, stood poised in front of me.

"Put me in, coach!" she shouted silently.

I tossed the stick and she was off. Her fluid, bounding motion reminded me that without this animated gait she'd simply be another retriever, not the unique little creature she was. I watched, admiring.

It took only three tosses of the stick to make the ducks notice her. Interested, they swung shoreward like weathervanes before a sudden, sharp nor'easter.

By then she'd returned to the blind with the stick, tail waving, one white paw again raised in anticipation. I tossed it out toward the shore, and she flashed off in pursuit.

This time the ducks began to paddle directly toward her. With the wind at their backs to enhance their motion, they'd made their decision. I watched, delighted. Sometimes it took a goodly number of fetches to produce this result.

When Chance returned to the blind this time, I ordered her into a sit-stay. Trembling with anticipation, she obeyed. A pang of guilt hit me. With our new no-hunting resolves in place I had no way of letting Chance complete the job she loved. Today she wouldn't be able to hit the water like gangbusters in a retrieve.

I glanced back toward the river. Halfway in, the ducks had paused, a typical reaction. A single toss of the stick started them moving again. Eager for another glimpse of the mesmerizing creature, they once more swam toward my excuse for a blind. I put a hand on Chance's shivering shoulder and found her small body as taut as piano wire.

Seemingly out of nowhere, Ceilidh appeared. Ambling up the beach, sniffing at piles of seaweed, nosing around driftwood, she sauntered down to the water's edge directly in front of the incoming ducks.

A squealing mutter erupted in Chance's throat. Those were her ducks! Her ducks! Possibly remembering the partridge incident, she stood ready to defend what she considered her birds.

The ducks took no notice. They kept coming, staring, entranced. Finally they paused in the shallows no more than six feet in front of the disinterested dog. Swimming in circles, they ventured closer and closer until nearly under Ceilidh's sniffing nose.

In the tall grass, Chance and I trembled with excitement. There's nothing quite like the thrill of a successful toll. One of nature's puzzling mysteries, it won't be definitely understood until someone discovers how to decode the deductions of a duck.

Muttering and squirming as she fought to control herself, Chance was now utterly incensed by her half-sister's audacity. Knowing her high-powered personality, I strongly suspected she cursed Ceilidh's actions and appreciated her strength of character in containing her urge to rush out and throttle the brazen little hussy.

A shotgun blasted up shore. Squawking their outrage, the ducks exploded into flight. Ceilidh, gun shyness intact, whirled to run.

She didn't get far.

Beside me Chance broke. She'd had all she could take of her half-sister's shenanigans. Squealing and yelping, she tore down the bank and across the beach in hot pursuit of the fleeing dog.

There was a brief, noisy donnybrook. Ceilidh must learn to never, never, never toll, even unintentionally, on Queen Chance's territory. I could see from the outset it wasn't the blood and guts battle the partridge had caused, so I let them go to it. Better to get it out of their systems than to let it fester I'd discovered over the past few months.

Chance's attack had even had a beneficial effect

this time. It had prevented Ceilidh's running away into the bush. By the time they'd settled their score, she'd apparently forgotten that shotgun blast. I whistled to them. It was time to head home.

The memory of marsh and ducks still hot in their blood, they raced back to me, around me, dancing a Toller polka. I understood how they felt. I had to suppress the urge to race with them across the field.

It was great to be back, to be feeling alive once again! And my two beautiful girls were responsible.

I definitely felt another story coming on.

To All the Dogs I've Loved Before

Memories Are Made of This

On a recent TV talk show, the host asked a group of writers to describe a moment when they'd felt most content, most at peace with themselves and their universe. Without exception their best memories were of times of solitude when they gained an inner sense that God (or whatever being they regarded in that capacity) was in his heaven and all was, at least at the precise moment, right with their small piece of the world.

Remembering a lovely spring day when I went walking alone with Chance and Ceilidh, I realized I was no exception.

It had been one of those verdantly colored spring days that made you feel truly glad to be alive. Chance, Ceilidh, and I headed out across a meadow rich with every living shade of green under a sky as blue as sapphire.

Chance, bursting with youthful exuberance, cavorted about me, utter, sincere joy filling her expression each time she paused to glance up at me. The completeness of her happiness made my heart glad. Then I looked at Ceilidh.

When we'd first entered the field and I'd freed both Tollers from their leads, she'd galloped off beside Chance, seemingly as full of springtime happiness as her half-sister. Now she'd slowed to her typical sedate trot, quartering (moving back and forth across the path in front of us, nose to the ground, searching, always searching).

When we arrived at the top of a knoll that overlooked a little brook, I stopped and sat down amid the profusion of dandelions and daisies that decorated its crest.

The June breeze tugged playfully at my hair while a kindly sun caressed my face. Watching my beautiful red dogs running free, I experienced one of those rare moments of supreme peace and contentment. God truly must be in his heaven and, at least at this moment, in this place, all seemed to be well with the world.

Finally they returned to me, Chance prancing like a spirited Hackney, Ceilidh trotting primly along behind her.

"Come here, you gorgeous girls!" I held out my arms.

Both accepted my invitation, Chance flinging herself against me to slide down my side and onto her back, legs sticking straight up, belly exposed, dignity thrown to the winds in a display of trust and delight.

Ceilidh sat down on my other side. When I put my free arm about her and tried to draw her close, it felt as if I hugged a statue, rigid and impersonal as stone. Her head held high, she turned away to catch any new scents wafting her way. The wind ruffled the soft, amber fur on her lovely ears and neck. As I gazed at her proudly, singularly continuing her lonely quest, she looked so brave and beautiful she brought a lump to my throat. For Ceilidh, all definitely wasn't right with the world. I longed to make it as perfect for her but knew I couldn't. True love and loyalty can't be erased.

Field Trials and Errors

That summer we decided to attend retriever field trials at a site about a hundred miles from our home. We'd never gone to such an event and were eager to observe how they were conducted. We also wanted to find out if Chance and Ceilidh might be able to compete at some later date.

We arrived to a surprise. Not a single Toller was entered in any of the events.

The dogs were Labs, Chessies, Goldens...all the larger retriever breeds. Competition involved making multiple retrieves over land and water. Up to three (at this particular event) ducks were thrown, accompanied by shotgun blasts in various locations about a quarter mile away while the dog in a sit-stay stance remained by his master's side. The command was given, using the dog's name, and the competitor burst off across the field to retrieve. In doing so, the dog had to cross two small brooks and run up a steep incline to get the birds. In conclusion, he had to return them "to hand" to his handler.

Although physically challenging, I had no doubt Ceilidh, with her stubborn determination, could have mastered it...if only part of the trials hadn't included three shotgun blasts. Chance, with her smaller bone structure and more delicate movements, might have found it difficult.

When we returned to our truck, we met a different opinion. A lady reading in a lawn chair beside her trailer next to our vehicle smiled at us and pointed to Chance and Ceilidh watching the proceedings through our windshield.

"Cute as buttons," she purred. "All brushed and polished. What darlings."

I had difficulty thanking her for what she obviously believed to be an appropriate compliment. Her words seemed a patronizing, if unintentional, put-down to two remarkable little dogs.

A middle-aged man in full dog-trial gear came by. I recognized him as a columnist for one of the big national dog magazines. He had two Labs, very dirty from competition, in tow. As they passed our truck, Chance burst into a fit of high-pitched barking. Ceilidh, of course, took up the hue and cry.

"Tollers, eh?" he grunted, stopping and looking at them with ill-disguised contempt. "My neighbor breeds 'em."

"Really?" I said brightly, thinking his gruff remarks evidence of the kindly, crusty character he portrayed in his writings. "What does she use them for? Hunting, show…?"

"To annoy me," he muttered and walked away.

As I watched him slouch off with his two dirty dogs (no doubt winners) following, I determined never to read his bit of ink again.

Lesson learned: One dog breed is not every dog fancier's cup of tea.

The Case of the Missing Chocolate Bar

Later that same summer, we took both dogs to a canine show in Moncton, New Brunswick. Although we hadn't entered either dog, we'd been invited to join other Toller owners in what was called a booster—a group of Tollers and their caregivers gathered in a specific area to give the public an opportunity to learn more about the breed.

Meeting other people who delighted as much as we did in our unique little red dogs was wonderful. At this event there were no belittling remarks about cuteness or annoyances.

About half way through the show, my legs tired from standing. Ron and Chance had gone outside for some fresh air, so Ceil and I climbed into the bleachers to watch the judging of other breeds from a more comfortable vantage point. We took a place about half way up, behind a lady and her children who were watching the goings-on in the rings below with rapt attention.

I fell into their interest level. Ceil, sitting obediently at my side on a slack leash, required little supervision. Once I felt a slight stirring but didn't think much of it until that particular competition had ended and I realized Ceilidh was munching something.

"Ceil, what have you...?" I began.

An empty candy bar wrapper in the hand of the

lady sitting ahead of us caught my attention. She'd been holding it up at shoulder level as, mesmerized by the dogs in the ring, she'd enjoyed the show. All it had taken was one quick, adept move on Ceilidh's part to pull it free and make it her own.

"Where did my bar go?" The woman looked in confusion at the empty wrapper. Behind her, Ceilidh licked her lips.

"You must have eaten it, Mom," one of her children replied.

"I didn't think I did." The woman stood and began searching over and under her seat. "Well, maybe… I was pretty wrapped up in the show. Anyway, it's okay. I have another one."

She took a second bar from her purse and sat down to watch the next performance. I led a reluctant Ceilidh away from the scene of the crime. She'd gotten away with it once. Twice could be her downfall.

Sometimes crime does pay…when executed in bite-sized amounts.

A Disastrous Decision

A muggy, overcast day with intermittent drizzles of rain, August 25, 1997, marked the beginning of what was to be a traumatic period in our lives. We'd had company most of the afternoon. After they left, I decided to take Chance and Ceilidh for a run around the perimeter of our property. They'd behaved beautifully indoors for hours; they deserved an outing.

When we reached the far end of our land, both dogs dashed into the alders. Fearing another porcupine, I yelled for them to come back. When they didn't respond, I plunged into the strangely silent thicket after them. What I discovered on the far side appalled me.

Both dogs were gulping up the vilest-smelling, filthiest-looking mound of black muck imaginable. Bear feces!

Choking on the stench, I grabbed both by their collars and pulled them away from it. Somehow I managed to clamp a leash on each. With a churning stomach, I headed back to the cottage, two reluctant Tollers in tow.

The feast of filth didn't sit well with Ceilidh. Halfway across the field, she lost hers in one gigantic heave. Chance, on the other hand, appeared perfectly fine, with no regurgitating response to her revolting meal. She continued to trot at my side, head held high.

As we stepped inside the cottage, the phone rang.

Shedding my rain gear, I hurried to answer it.

Wrong number. Replacing the phone on its charger, I heard the unmistakable sounds of retching from the living room. I scrambled to get whichever of my girls was about to be sick outdoors. Too late. Chance had lost her fetid feast all over the floor.

Bear droppings in their original form are disgusting. Regurgitated ones are doubly so. The mess gave a whole new nuance to my children's favorite teenage expression, "gross."

Struggling to control the peristalsis wave threatening to overwhelm me, I began to mop up the revolting mess.

I must have become careless or over-enthusiastic in my efforts to finish my unsavory chore. As I threw the last bit of paper into the toilet and flushed, the overburdened appliance choked, refused to swallow, and belched, filling its bowl to the rim with murky charcoal water. As the first of it leaked onto the floor, Chance and Ceilidh erupted into their "someone's coming" barking.

Ron, I thought gratefully. *He'll rescue me.* After our visitors had left, he'd gone to fill our truck with gas at the corner store.

Heading for the door and seeing the dogs' stance, my heart plummeted. This wasn't their "welcome home, Ron" greeting. This was their "strangers on the property" alert.

Glancing out of the window beside the door, I was dismayed to see a neighbor couple with whom we'd recently become acquainted. Dressed in their Sunday best, they'd come for the visit we'd suggested.

I couldn't have guests, not now! Not with the toilet

threatening to flood the entire house and the stench of bear feces and dog vomit as thick as a Fundy fog filling the air.

Think, think, think! I'm a writer, I can come up with a story, I told my panicked mind as I opened the door and forced a smile.

"Nice to see you. I'd love to invite you in. Unfortunately, I'm just on my way out."

It was undoubtedly the worst tale I'd ever concocted. Standing in front of them in wet sneakers, jeans damp to the knees, and an ancient, paper-thin Ducks Unlimited T-shirt I'd pulled on to take the dogs for a run on a miserable day, I didn't appear garbed to be "just on my way out."

I noticed Janice sniffing—discreetly, but definitely sniffing—and I realized the pervasive odors from within must be wafting without. A hot blush suffused my neck and face as they said fine, they'd come back some other time. The speed with which they descended the steps told me they weren't sorry to have had the visit aborted.

Someday, I thought as I closed the door, someday when we're better acquainted I'll tell them the truth, the whole truth, and nothing but the truth. Right now I had more pressing problems.

I heard our truck turning into the drive. The sound held all the beauty of a hallelujah chorus. Ron was home! Like the little Dutch boy who'd averted catastrophe by sticking his finger in a hole in the dike, Ron would save our home from the impending flood. And he did.

Under the Barbecue

Worried about the effects any remaining traces of those awful bear droppings might have on our dog's innards, we took them back to the city the following morning to our vet.

He agreed we'd been wise to have them checked and gave them preventive treatment against possible infection. The dogs had shown no immediate ill effects, and now we felt we'd done our best to prevent future complications. But who can predict the future?

On Labor Day weekend, we returned to our cottage to discover a surprise awaiting us. As soon as we'd unpacked the truck, I let both dogs out the back door for a run in the field. Eager for freedom after several days of city living, they cleared the deck in record time and within seconds had gone racing off across the grass. I followed at a more sedate pace.

I'd only gone a few yards when Ron hailed me from the deck.

"There's something under the barbecue," he called.

"What?" Intrigued, I turned back.

"I don't know," he said, squatting down to get a better look. "I think it's a puppy."

When I joined him, all I could see were two bright little coal black eyes gleaming out from under the gas barbecue. In the cramped, shadowy six-inch high space, it was difficult to see more. It might have been a puppy...or a baby raccoon, or some other form of wildlife.

Cautiously Ron reached forward and drew the little ball of variegated black-and-tan fur out into the light. Snuggled into his hands, it didn't appear to be much more than a ball of fluff with the most intense ebony eyes I'd ever seen and a black button of a nose.

"It's a puppy," Ron concluded, looking at the black, white, and tan bib at its throat.

"But look at its face," I argued. "It's got a mask around its eyes...and there's a couple of black rings around its tail."

"It's a puppy," Ron ended the discussion decisively. "But how did it get here?" The four steps leading up to our deck appeared impossibly high for such short legs. "And who does it belong to? It couldn't have come far. I'll start checking around the neighborhood."

"No," I said. "First we give it food and water. It must have been here for quite a while, judging from the condition of the deck."

Glancing about, Ron had to agree. Apparently the tiny creature had been using it as a toilet for some time.

Chance and Ceilidh came racing back. Chance sniffed the newcomer and danced backward, inviting it to play.

Ceilidh was more circumspect. She approached gingerly and gave the newcomer a cautious sniff before sitting down to consider the situation.

"Bring it in," I said, opening the door. "I'll give it some warm milk and soft food before you try to find out where it came from." (We still hadn't checked to see if "it" was a he or a she.)

The little creature ate daintily for an animal that apparently hadn't seen food or drink in a considerable length of time. When she finished, she looked up at us, black eyes holding all the sweetness of molasses.

"She *is* cute," I said. (We'd now determined it was a she.)

"Don't get any ideas." Ron, who knew only too well my weakness for homeless critters, squelched the thoughts he'd correctly determined brewed in my mind. "I'm taking her around to the neighbors. If no one owns her, she's going to the SPCA. We have all the dogs we can handle."

I didn't say anything, but a lump congealed in my throat as I picked the tiny creature up in my arms. As I handed her to Ron, she gave a milky burp and licked my fingers.

"Take her," I said, trying not to think of the hunger, thirst, and outright terror this little darling had already endured alone for two or more days and nights alone on our deck. The darkness and rain must have been as fearful as the lack of nourishment. I wanted to hold her, to cuddle her close and tell her that it would never, never happen again.

"The little dog angel's eager bark

Will comfort his soul in the shivering dark."

The concluding words of Nora Holland's beautiful poem "The Little Dog Angel" raced across my mind, enlarging the lump in my throat.

As I watched Ron head for the truck, the small bundle in his hands, I fought back tears and tried to comfort myself with the thought that she must belong to someone…someone who *should* have been frantically searching the neighborhood for her. The "should" came unbidden and cast all sorts of doubts about her owner's commitment to the little dog.

Don't think about it. Don't. There's nothing you can do about it. She belongs to someone else. I knelt and buried my face in Ceilidh's neck.

Throughout the half hour we'd had the little foundling Ceilidh had been an attentive if passive observer. While Chance had wanted to include the newcomer in her play, Ceilidh had appeared to be seriously assessing the situation.

Now that the puppy was gone, she settled against me with a long, deep sigh that seemed to come right from the white tips of her paws.

"Ceil?" I drew her out from me and looked into her lovely face. "Did you want to keep the puppy?"

She answered with another long, deep sigh. She wasn't about to commit herself to another attachment, I guessed. Once burned, twice shy, I thought, and wished for some way to weave trust back into the little dog's soul.

An hour later Ron arrived back at the cottage, the puppy in his hands.

"No one owns her," he said, placing the tiny dog on the floor. "Some people said they'd seen her on our deck for several days and thought she belonged to us."

"But we've been gone for five days!" I couldn't believe those individuals' reasoning and/or callousness. "Why didn't they help her?"

Ron shrugged and looked down at the little dog. "Some people have no hearts," he said gruffly as she looked up at him, her eyes bright with the kind of eternal optimism and trust only a dog can exude.

"What about the SPCA?" I asked cautiously.

"Closed." He turned away. "I'll take her back in the morning. She'll have to stay the night."

"Yes!" I said and hurried off to warm more milk and make a bed for her in a laundry basket lined with a quilt.

Tonight, sweetie, I thought as I placed her into her little bed, *you won't be cold or wet or frightened or hungry. And maybe I'll be able to see to it that you never will be again.*

I'd been afraid to hope we could adopt the little dog. I wanted the decision to be unanimous and that, up until ten minutes earlier, hadn't seemed even a remote possibility. It was only then I'd recognized something in Ron's eyes and voice when he'd told me the SPCA was closed, when he'd said she'd have to stay the night. I recognized the signs. He was waffling, weakening. If I said nothing and let nature take its course, this lovable little fur ball might be ours.

"Keep your paws crossed," I whispered as I bent to give her a goodnight kiss.

When I turned away from the basket, I saw Ceilidh watching intently.

"Do you want to sleep with the puppy?" I asked her as Chance pranced around the little bed, curious and wanting to play. "I can put your bed beside it."

Ceilidh paused for a moment and looked at Chance—as always, it seemed, taking center stage as she capered around the newcomer. With a long, slow sigh she turned and plodded away.

Death of a Promise

The next morning the world would receive a horrible shock. Princess Diana had been killed in a horrendous car crash in Paris. The beautiful fairytale lady was gone.

When Ron returned from a neighbor's house with the news, I experienced that terrible sense of bereavement usually reserved for the loss of a dear friend or family member. Of course, I hadn't known Diana personally and had never actually met her. But Ron and I had been fortunate to have been included in the media entourage that had followed her tour of New Brunswick in 1983. I'd stood within a few feet of her as she met swarms of admirers at Sugarloaf Park and signed guest books in Campbellton and Dalhousie. She'd been so incredibly beautiful she'd taken my breath away.

And now that lovely young woman with the ethereal complexion, shy smile, and sun-glazed hair was gone forever. The world would be a colder, grimmer place without her.

Through my tears I looked out the window and saw Chance standing alert and ready in the September sunshine. Her white chest and feet set off her shining amber coat to perfection. Princess Diana had been like Chance—I found the strange analogy sliding across my mind—bright, beautiful, almost too good to be true.

I realized Ceilidh was standing quietly beside me. I knelt, gathered her into my arms, and wept for the loss of beauty, romance, and innocence that had been so much a part of the life of the young woman who'd been Lady Diana Spencer. A kindergarten teacher who'd loved children, her own and everyone else's, she'd married young and idealistically a husband who didn't share her values and couldn't return her love.

Ceilidh leaned stoically against me and let me air my grief. She didn't need to understand. She was simply there for me, quietly, completely. That was enough. A sorrow shared is a sorrow halved.

Barbie-Q Joins the Family

That afternoon we left the three dogs in the cottage and went to buy groceries. We didn't talk much. I think Ron, who'd photographed the Princess on that 1983 tour, was feeling much the same sense of loss that I was experiencing. But, of course, men don't express such fanciful thoughts.

We were almost back home when he finally spoke.

"The SPCA isn't open again today," he said. "I telephoned."

"Oh, really?" *Strange*, I mused, my thoughts returning to the foundling with rising hope.

"Yeah, well"—he ignored my gaze as he turned into our driveway—"looks as if we're going to have three dogs. What do you think?"

"Fine with me," I replied, fighting to sound casual when I really wanted to burst with a yell of, "Yes! Yes! Yes!"

"We'll have to take her to the vet and get her needles," I began to plan. "And we'll have to find a name for her."

"I'm going to call her Barbecue," Ron surprised me by replying promptly. Obviously he'd given the matter some thought.

"But she's a girl!" I protested.

"Well then, what would you call her?" Hurt that his choice was being rejected, he stopped the truck abruptly in front of the steps.

"Well…" I considered for a moment. "What about Barbie-Q? It's still about where we found her, but it's a girl's name."

"Okay." Ron brightened, the compromise obviously to his liking.

So Barbie-Q she became. She must somehow have always remembered who had found her under the barbecue and given her that unique name, because she became very much Ron's dog.

Changes in Chance

Shortly after we'd returned to town, three dogs in tow, Chance began to act strangely. Where once she'd cleared the jump required for a CDX title with eagerness, style, and grace, she now began to hesitate, then go over it with what appeared a struggling effort, or sometimes not at all. At night she'd climb onto our bed and pant, then dig and slap at Ron as he tried to sleep.

I should have suspected that something was seriously wrong. For some reason, our dogs have always turned to him when they felt themselves in trouble.

At that point, we both made a huge mistake. We attributed her behavior to jealousy—jealousy of the puppy Barbie-Q. I even berated her to that effect one morning when she refused to make a jump. That, of course, only served to exacerbate the situation. Tollers are sensitive animals who will do anything for praise and nothing for a harsh word or criticism. I knew better, but I so badly wanted my beautiful, outstanding girl to achieve her next title I ignored this fact and pressed on.

Ceilidh, on the other hand, seemed in top form. Although her performance was always mechanical, lacking the flair of her half-sister, she went through the required moves precisely and right on cue. No problem there, I decided, and went back to Chance's training.

But the trouble escalated. Chance lagged still more. At night her climbing into bed and slapping at Ron got so bad he finally had to put her out of the bedroom and place a baby gate across the door.

"Maybe she needs to get away from the puppy," he suggested finally. "Maybe she feels her position as alpha dog in the house is being threatened...again. Or," he continued more cautiously, "maybe she needs a break from training."

"So what do you suggest?" I asked, my tone sharpened by his last "maybe." Of course I wasn't training her too strenuously. I'd never do that.

"I'm going to the cottage this weekend to shut off the water. Why don't I take her with me? You said you couldn't go...that writers' conference you want to attend here in town, remember?"

Of course I remembered. I'd been looking forward to it for weeks.

"Well..." I hesitated. To leave a two-day gap in Chance's training with the big show only a week away seemed like courting disaster. Yet if what Ron saw as the problem truly was the reason for her lackluster performances, maybe a forty-eight-hour hiatus might be just the thing to bring her out of it.

"Okay," I agreed. "Let's give it a try."

So off they went on Friday afternoon, Chance's beautiful plume of tail waving a fond farewell as she pranced out of the house with Ron. I watched as she jumped into the passenger seat and settled herself for the ride, and I waved as they backed out of the drive. It was an image that would become indelible in my mind, Chance looking out the windshield at me, bright and happy.

I looked around for the other two dogs and found them in the backyard. Watching a squirrel high up in its branches, Ceilidh lay under an apple tree in the warm September sun. A few feet away Barbie-Q sat gazing at the older dog. During the days since the puppy had come to live with us, Barbie-Q had spent most of her waking hours with Chance or us. I don't believe it was because she disliked Ceilidh. I think the older dog's aloofness simply kept her at bay. Now, left alone with her, Barbie-Q appeared to be puzzling out what to do next.

"Come on, my girls. I'll get you each a treat," I said, feeling they'd been denied the weekend in the country Chance would be enjoying.

The invitation brought food-fetish Ceilidh to her feet. With Barbie-Q scampering at her heels, she followed me into the house.

Heartbreak

The next evening after I'd returned from my writing conference I curled up in bed to read over some of the handout material I'd received. Ceilidh was on her dog bed beside me, Barbie-Q in the spacious, quilt-lined Labrador retriever kennel by the dresser. We'd had to confine her at night. She had a habit of chewing on things when she awoke in darkness, perhaps as a result of her desperate nights alone under the barbecue. She didn't seem to mind. She could see Ceilidh sleeping outside its door. Perhaps she felt safer in there than if she'd been out wandering about the house. At least she went willingly into her little bedroom every night and snuggled down among her quilts and pillows with a contented sigh.

The phone rang. It was a call that would shatter my heart.

"Gail?" It was Ron. His voice sounded strange, incredulous. "I think Chance just died."

I was dumbfounded. I couldn't be hearing correctly.

"You think?" I finally managed to burst out. "What do you mean, you think?"

"She jumped off the couch, gave a little squeak, then fell on the floor and lost control of herself. She hasn't moved since." His voice was breaking, shaking with emotion.

"Did you call the vet?" Somehow I managed to respond pragmatically but my mind was frozen with horror. This couldn't be true. Not Chance. Not my precious, once-in-a-lifetime dog!

"Yes. I told him all about it...how it happened, how she reacted, how she looks. He says she's dead."

There was a long pause. Finally he continued, "But maybe she just had a seizure. I've put her in our bed and wrapped her in blankets. Maybe once she's warm..."

"Yes," I said woodenly. "Maybe once she's warm..."

"I'll call you if there's any change," he said. "Now I'm going to lie down with her. If she knows I'm close..."

"Yes," I said blankly. "If she knows you're close..."

I hung up and stared at the wall. I saw a cobweb in a corner, dust on a picture frame, made mental notes to do something about both. Maybe tomorrow I'd start housecleaning. Tomorrow after I knew the vet had been wrong...

I slid off the bed and gathered Ceilidh up in my arms. I held her tight, so tight I heard her grunt before I realized I might be hurting her.

"Chancey is sick, Ceil," I said. "Ron is going to lay down with her and help her get well."

I drew the little red dog into my lap and hugged her and hugged her. Desperately clinging to one Toller, I silently begged the other one not to leave us.

The following morning Ron and I had to accept the fact that Chance was gone. All night we'd exchanged phone calls. Once, in the dark, desperate hours just before dawn, Ron had called to say he thought he'd seen her eyelids flutter. In retrospect, we realized we'd only been clutching at one last, desperate straw of hope. We were forced to conclude Chance had died the instant she'd jumped off the couch.

As dawn broke on a gray, overcast September Sunday morning, I sat at our dining room picture window and looked out at the sugar maple beginning to turn to its autumn hues of red and yellow. A single leaf, amber and beautiful, drifted prematurely to the ground.

It's like Chancey, I thought, the massive lump in my throat still too hard and dry to give way to tears. Perfect in every way, dying far too soon. I remembered the beautifully fragile princess who'd died two weeks previous and wondered if some things were destined to leave us at the height of their perfection, never growing old, always remaining a perfect memory.

I felt small paws on my knee. I looked down to see Barbie-Q, black eyes round and confused, asking to be lifted onto my lap. Behind her, her lovely teddy bear face full of a softness I'd never seen before, stood Ceilidh.

I understand, she seemed to be telling me. I know how it hurts to lose someone you love. I understand and I'm here for you.

I slipped to the floor, gathered the ragamuffin puppy in one arm, Ceilidh in the other, and let the tears come.

The messages of sympathy and condolence began to pour in. Chance, through her many appearances in magazines and the Toller books, had become world famous. People from Europe to Australia wrote and called to empathize with us in our sorrow. It helped, as much as anything could in a time of such intense pain.

I recalled the message of condolence we'd received on Jet's death: "What you've cherished with your heart, you can never lose." Later, after the first excruciating pain had lessened, I would know it was true.

The most touching message came from Erna Nickerson. Although now suffering from brain cancer, she'd learned of Chance's death and insisted on phoning me.

Speaking louder than normal, she told me how very, very sorry she was, how she'd been in our position all too often in her forty years of owning Tollers, and how she understood the pain in our hearts. We talked a good half hour that rainy autumn evening, and when we hung up, I felt comforted. I also felt certain Erna was well on her way to recovery.

Sadly, I couldn't have been more wrong. Three weeks later Erna died. Another beautiful spirit had passed from this earth.

The world for me that fall was a bitterly sad place. The bleak, rainy weather seemed to fit perfectly into the desolate emptiness in my heart. I wanted to curl up in fetal position and just forget this ugly autumn had ever happened.

One morning as I sat with a cup of tea by the dining room window, I saw Ceilidh wandering about the yard, sniffing, looking, searching every nook and cranny. Ceilidh had lost her home, her entire family. Worse still, she'd been left with the cruel belief that somewhere they still existed. All she had to do was find them.

The words of the old song echoed into my mind as I watched her: "Somewhere over the rainbow, bluebirds fly. There's a land that I've heard of…once in a lullaby."

For Ceilidh that land had been her puppyhood and youth with a family she'd never be able to forget. I may have lost a wonderful companion and a dear friend, but Ceilidh had lost her entire world.

Sometimes pain just has to be borne the best that we can. There are no magic solutions.

The Road Back

For me there has always been a single-lane highway out of grief and despair. Its name is work. I returned to it, training Ceilidh for the upcoming dog show and putting the finishing touches on the Toller history manuscript entitled *A Breed Apart*. Ron and I wanted to dedicate the book to Chance's memory. The publisher agreed.

One of the hardest things I had to do was to call the dog show organizers and withdraw Harborlights Highland Chance CD's name from their catalogue of participants. Keeping my voice from cracking over the request took a huge effort, but I think I managed to do it with reasonable grace and dignity.

As the day of the show approached, I began to wonder if perhaps I should also withdraw Ceilidh's name. Whereas I'd thought there would have been the sort of transition of power implicit in the phrase, "The Queen is dead. Long live the Queen," that hadn't been the case. Ceilidh hadn't indicated any burning desire to replace her half-sister as monarch of our canine household. Instead she'd become even more subdued, retreating to her dog bed whenever she was indoors, lying passively on the patio outside, and going through her dog show routine with lagging, reluctant responses. Even the squirrels that each day grew bolder and bolder around the morose little dog couldn't bring her out of her lethargy. In spite of her frequent fights with Chance, Ceilidh must have cared for her companion more than we'd suspected. Another loss had been heaped upon an already hurting little heart. I wanted to help her, wanted to find some way to soothe her pain, but I couldn't think of a single thing.

The day of the show arrived, and off Ceilidh and I went with a friend and her German shepherd dog. Ron stayed home with Barbie-Q. Although he never put the idea into words, I'm sure memories of him and Chance in the winners' circle the previous year had made it too painful for him to attend.

From the moment we climbed out of the truck at the arena, Ceilidh dragged her paws. I led her inside and picked up my numbered armband.

To say that Ceilidh's performance that day lacked sparkle would have been a gross understatement. She failed to come to her feet from a sit when the "forward" command was given, she lagged more than the allowed distance behind when supposed to be in "heel" position, and finally left the ring entirely when a child eating a cookie leaned toward her. I knew there was no point in taking her back the following day.

I returned home feeling as tired and heavy-hearted as Ceilidh looked. She crawled onto her dog bed and, with a deep, weary sigh, closed her eyes.

Barbie-Q, who'd been waiting at the door for us, toddled slowly over to the older dog. She paused and looked down at her. With a little sigh, she climbed up onto the mattress beside her and curled up against her.

Ceilidh's only reaction was to open one eye, glance at the tiny creature sharing her bed, then appear to go back to sleep.

In the days that followed, Barbie-Q employed the dogged determination that must have sustained her during those desolate days on the deck in an effort to reawaken Ceilidh's *joie de vivre*. She remained close to Ceilidh, toddling along behind her when she walked around the yard, sitting beside her when she sat, and lying beside her when she rested. Throughout the entire process she never forced her presence on her lethargic companion. Barbie-Q always stayed at a respectful distance and never attempted any type of frivolous or playful behavior.

For several days the situation continued. I watched, and wondered what the outcome would be.

Finally it happened. One evening in early November, as Ron and I were watching TV in the family room with Ceilidh lying in front of the fire crackling in the woodstove, Barbie-Q got up from my side and walked over to the older dog. She stopped inches in front of where Ceilidh lay with her snout between her front paws, snapped into an alert little stance, and wagged her tail. Then she crouched on her front legs, tiny rear end sticking up, and barked.

Her gestures were unmistakable. She was inviting Ceilidh to play. I watched with bated breath.

Ceilidh's head came up slowly. Barbie-Q barked and jumped back. "Come on, come on!" she was saying. "It's time to play again."

Ceilidh slapped out with a paw and rolled over onto her back. In an instant Barbie-Q was all over her, wrestling, yipping, frolicking, as the older dog gently allowed her top position.

I'd never seen Ceilidh like this…playful, relaxed, abandoned of rigidity and aloofness. The throw-away puppy had done what we'd failed to do. She'd known when Ceilidh's period of mourning should end and had reached out to touch her spirit with clever little paws.

Ceilidh and I were both on the road back. Wisdom can be a silent thing that comes from deep within the heart.

Mother and Daughter

The next morning it became obvious that not only had Ceilidh decided to adopt Barbie-Q but that she was ready to embrace the position of alpha dog in our household. Trotting about the backyard, head and tail held high, the ragtag puppy bounding and barking happily at her heels, Harborlights Scotia Ceilidh had found happiness and contentment in something that was willing to be hers and hers alone.

Ceilidh also made training Barbie-Q an easy pleasure. The little dog imitated her surrogate mother in every way. By late November, when we believed she was about five months old, she was sitting, heeling, and (most times) coming when called. We were even able to walk her with Ceilidh on a leash along the streets of our subdivision without the usual puppy antics of lunging, lagging, or flipping.

One frosty early December morning as I walked my canine couple around our subdivision, a neighbor lady who was especially fond of Ceilidh came out to greet us.

"Has Ceilidh had a baby?" she asked looking skeptically at Barbie-Q.

"Barbie is Ceilidh's *adopted* baby," I replied and went on to tell the story of how we'd acquired the little one.

"She's made Ceil very happy," I concluded as my

neighbor knelt to play with both dogs.

"Oh, my!" she gasped. "What happened to her beautiful face?" She cupped Ceilidh's snout in her hands. "Just look!"

I knelt beside her and saw it for the first time…an ugly crimson rim around Ceilidh's left eye. Blood seemed ready to ooze through the skin. It hadn't been there when I'd put her collar on a half hour earlier. Dismayed, I could only stare at the painful-looking eruption. Ceilidh, in true stoic form, ignored her condition, her attention focused on Barbie-Q.

I hurried the dogs home and called our vet.

"Bring her right over," he instructed.

I loaded both dogs into the truck and headed for his office. Terrifying visions of Ceilidh losing one of her gorgeous brown eyes to some heinous infection flooded my mind.

Dr. Larsen repressed a smile when he saw the pair. We'd taken Barbie-Q for her needles, but this was the first time he'd seen mother and adopted daughter together.

"Nice baby, Ceil," he complimented as he hoisted Ceilidh onto the examining table. Ceilidh's only reply was a grunt as he deposited her onto its stainless steel surface.

"What is it?" Clutching Barbie-Q in my arms, I couldn't keep still as he examined Ceilidh's eye. "Is it serious? She won't lose her eye, will she?"

"Definitely not." He turned to me with a reassuring smile. "It's what's called an allergy hot spot, a place where an allergic reaction surfaces. I'll give you some ointment and some pills. She should be fine in a couple of days."

Weak with relief, I took both dogs home as the big, soft flakes of our first snowstorm of that winter began to fall.

The pills Dr. Larsen had given Ceilidh must have made her sleepy. When we got home she shuffled to her dog bed by the bay window and curled up for a nap. Barbie-Q watched her for a few moments. With a contented little sigh she toddled over to Ceilidh and joined her on the bed.

As the wind howled about the house, I smiled at the odd little couple curled up together safe from the elements and felt a nice, warm, fuzzy feeling slide over me. I was so very glad we'd been able to give a home to both of them. And doubly glad that, in the process, they'd found each other. Fate (or perhaps luck) does sometimes step in to make our lives better.

Years later when Ron had bypass surgery and I returned home from the hospital with his suitcase of clothing while he remained behind to recover, Barbie-Q once again showed her loyalty to the man who'd found her all those years ago. When I opened the valise on the floor to remove Ron's clothing, she immediately climbed inside and settled into a little ball. I didn't have the heart to remove her. She continued to make that valise her bed until I once again took it to the hospital to bring Ron home.

Molly

"Whoever said you can't buy happiness forgot about puppies." ~Gene Hill

While researching my second book on Nova Scotia Duck Tolling Retrievers (or, as I'd come to know them, Little River Duck Dogs), *A Breed Apart*, I'd met a remarkable gentleman from Yarmouth County named Andy Wallace. Andy had owned Little River Duck Dogs (the precursor of Nova Scotia Duck Tolling Retrievers) since he'd been twelve. When I first encountered him, he was newly retired from a career as a teacher at the Yarmouth Community College and had been breeding Little River Duck Dogs on a limited scale for over thirty years.

Andy so impressed me with his knowledge and concern for the dogs during the first conversation I had with him that I decided that if and when I decided to get another tolling dog, it would be from him. The wounds from Chance's passing were still too fresh to allow me to think of the possibility in any more than the abstract, at that point. I mentioned it casually to him around Christmas of that year and went back to my writing.

In March I received an e-mail from a friend in Yarmouth County. "Andy's dog Sadie is in heat and he's found a nice male to breed with her," she wrote.

I knew pups from Andy's bitch were in high

demand. He kept only one breeding female at a time and only bred when he felt a litter wouldn't keep her from hunting with him. I figured I wouldn't be in line for a baby from this bunch. I wasn't concerned. I wasn't ready to move on...not just yet...or so I thought.

That winter Ceilidh and Barbie-Q had formed such a close alliance that at times I felt shut out. Having found each other, they became a tight-knit couple, different physically but solidly together in every other way.

Barbie-Q emulated everything Ceilidh did. She retrieved like a Toller, pranced like a Toller, and the next summer we discovered she swam like a Toller. Some sort of imprinting had occurred, and the dog that had at first resembled a raccoon and only grew to be twenty-six pounds of long, silky, variegated brown and black fur had become a pseudo Duck Toller right down to white-tipped paws. I think she would have been shocked if she'd realized the image I tried to show her in mirrors was herself. She probably thought she looked like Ceilidh. Why wouldn't she?

On Mother's Day, I received a telephone call from Andy.

"Do you still want that puppy?" he asked.

Several weeks later, on a beautiful evening in June, Wallace's Molly MacMillan arrived to join our family. Half Little River Duck Dog (on her mom's side...Sadie by name) and half registered Nova Scotia Duck Tolling Retriever (on her dad's side...Shadowhills Copper), she was a gorgeous ball of beige fluff with tiny white toes. As she cavorted about our backyard on her first evening with us, I felt Chance would have liked her. And approved.

I'd been concerned about how Ceilidh and Barbie-Q would react to the newcomer. I'd wondered how (or, indeed if) they'd accept her into their canine hierarchy.

Barbie-Q was the first to make a move. I placed Molly on the grass and walked away. Over the years, I'd learned that it was best to leave dogs alone to introduce themselves.

Ceilidh at first remained aloof, ignoring the new arrival and going to stretch out in the last rays of evening sun beneath an apple tree. Barbie-Q, perky pup enthusiasm intact, trotted over to tiny Molly, braced into a playful stance and fluttered her curly tail in welcome.

Within seconds they were rolling about in the soft spring grass and chasing each other about the yard in happy little circles. Barbie-Q had won her way into yet another heart.

Ceilidh watched, snout between her white-tipped paws, eyes half opened. Finally Barbie-Q frolicked over to her with Molly nipping at her heels.

Barb stopped in front of the older dog, her newfound friend colliding with her rear end. For a couple of seconds they stood like two small statues. Ceilidh raised her head, looked at them, and got slowly to her feet, yawning and stretching.

As if this was some sort of signal, both little dogs danced up to her. Molly actually had the audacity to nip playfully at the older dog. Ceilidh gave her a look that put that sort of shenanigans at bay, then ambled across the lawn, both pups cavorting behind her.

That was that. Ceilidh was the Queen, the mother, and the alpha dog. And she was comfortable with her position.

Molly's arrival barely made a dent in the bond between Ceilidh and Barb. Theirs was a meeting of spirits, of two souls that had been forced to leave what they'd once called home and been placed into a strange and alien world. They knew about loss and the miracle of finding a kindred soul. That knowledge held them together as no physical bond ever could.

I was glad for two reasons. First and most obviously, because Ceilidh and Barbie-Q needed each other and, second, because it left Molly free to bond with me.

And bond she did. Tumbling along behind me on short puppy legs, she devoted herself to me. From time to time, she frolicked with the other dogs. But when the fun and games were over, she returned to me while Barb and Ceil remained together, unfailing in their loyalty to each other.

A Last Kiss

Later that summer we noticed Ceilidh was slowing down. The playing and retrieving she'd always loved were becoming an effort for her. We decided to consult Dr. Larsen. He did tests, sent them off to the veterinary clinic on Prince Edward Island, and brought back the verdict. Ceilidh had a heart condition.

The good news was that with diet and medication she could be made much more comfortable and her life prolonged indefinitely.

So Ceilidh began a new way of life with reduced fat intake and a series of little white pills. For the next few years, she was back to her old self.

We rejoiced.

In the late summer of 2001, while we were still living at the cottage, Ceilidh suddenly stopped eating. She tried, but any food or water she managed to get into her mouth fell back out. I put in a call to Dr. Larsen.

"Has she been digging up carrots again?" he asked, by now well aware of most of Ceilidh's foibles.

"She could have been," I replied. With three dogs in the big field and extensive gardens behind the cottage, I had to admit I didn't know exactly what each was doing at every minute.

"If she's eaten any of the parts where the roots join the top, she could be in trouble," he said. "When can you bring her in?"

"First thing tomorrow morning," I said.

Later that afternoon I took all three dogs in the truck to the beach for a swim. Ceilidh had become too weak to walk more than a few yards.

For the first few minutes she simply sat on the shore, aloof and solitary as she watched "her" puppies frolic in the water.

Finally she stood and walked with great dignity and purpose into the river. Shortly she was swimming straight out toward the channel. As she neared the choppy, fast-moving flow, fear rose in my heart. Weakened from lack of nourishment, Ceilidh might not be strong enough to handle the current.

"Ceilidh!" I shouted into the wind. "Ceilidh, come back!"

I don't know whether she heard me or suddenly decided to change direction, but she swung to her left, heading upriver parallel to the shore, battling wind and an outgoing tide. Her little red head rising and falling with the swell, she plodded along with the slow, strong strokes that had been her lifelong trademark.

"Ceilidh, come!" I shouted running up the shore in an effort to keep abreast of her, the two young dogs racing at my heels.

It was to no avail. She kept right on. I realized I was in the water up to my hips, calling her, begging her to come back to me.

Then she did. Turning as abruptly as a weather vane in a sudden change of wind, she swung to her left, toward the shore...and me.

The moment she got near enough I caught her up in my arms and staggered back to shore. She didn't appear exhausted, but her small heart was beating a ragged tattoo against her ribs. She'd swum nearly a half-mile.

I bundled her into the truck and took her back to the cottage. As I dried her with a towel and placed her on her dog bed by the kitchen heater, I pondered her strange performance. Ceilidh had never done such a thing before. What could have possessed her to take that sudden long, solitary swim?

The next day we took Ceilidh to see Dr. Larsen. I expected him to give her one of the laxatives he'd given her on other occasions when she'd ingested unhealthy matter.

After examining her, he turned to me and hesitated. An instant hard, cold, painfulness closed in around my heart. I'd seen that same look on his face thirteen years earlier when he'd told me there was no hope for Brandy.

But it couldn't be this time. Not with Ceil. She was only twelve. She'd only eaten carrot tops, hadn't she? He could do something for her. He had to. Ceilidh had to live, to come to know how much I loved her before…

"Gail, I'm sorry," he said finally, slowly. "Ceilidh has severe liver disease. There's nothing I can do for her."

I put my arms around her as she sat, weak and dejected, on the examining table, and I hugged her and hugged her. I wanted all the love I had for this beautiful little dog to flow out of my heart and soul and into every inch of her proud little body and spirit. In these last moments she had to know. Tears streamed down my cheeks.

She raised her face to mine and began to lick away my tears with the first and last kisses she would ever give me.

Suddenly I understood that strange, long, solitary swim. Ceilidh had known it would be her last.

Finding Her Family

We buried Ceilidh beside Chance in the field behind the cottage and planted another white rosebush beside the one we'd placed for her half-sister. The two young dogs stood beside us, their playful antics stilled. They knew, I know they knew, they'd lost their friend, their mentor, their surrogate mother. Like the two little orphans they'd become, they recognized their loss and, unlike the brave little dog in the grave before them, they accepted it. There was no point in searching or hoping, as she'd done all the days of her life with us. They knew Ceilidh had passed over the rainbow bridge.

I can't describe my pain, my sense of loss. The only comfort I could find was in the remembrance of those final kisses. While Ceilidh might never have loved me as the people she'd looked for all of her years with us, she had, in the end, told me she cared, understood my affection for her. That was the best I could ever have expected from her.

When I could manage to speak Ceilidh's name again without choking over it, I e-mailed Helen Matheson, my contact at Nimbus Publishing where so many of Ceilidh's pictures had found their way into *A Breed Apart*. Helen, a devoted dog fancier like myself, shared my grief and comforted me. Later she told me a copy of *A Breed Apart* had been placed on the counter at the publishing house that day, opened to the last page, which featured a large colored image of Ceilidh.

As winter closed in and we moved back to the city, I knew I had two things yet to do for Ceilidh: I had to write the story of her life, and I had to complete her quest. I had to find the person for whom she'd searched for nine years. I had to find Arthur Forester.

I had no idea how I'd manage to do it. Erna Nickerson had told me she'd tried to locate him unsuccessfully several times, and now Erna herself was gone.

I had a sudden inspiration. I could utilize a new search device. In the past year, I'd gained access to the Internet via my computer.

One foggy November evening, I logged onto Canada 411 and submitted the name Arthur Forester. It would be truly a miracle if I found him this easily, I thought as I waited for the machine to search.

Eight matches popped up from across Canada. Prepared to call each and every one until I found Ceilidh's Art, I didn't have to. Two names seemed enhanced in bold type. Art and Kim Forester.

I dialed their number, unsure of what kind of reception I'd receive from the man and/or his family after all these years. Erna had said he'd appeared truly sad to part with Ceilidh, that he'd even had her immunization updated before he'd brought her back to Harborlights. Surely a man who'd apparently done his best for her, had had only her interests at heart, would like to know what had become of his little red dog.

A lady answered the phone. When I asked if her family had ever owned a dog named Harborlights Scotia Ceilidh, she hesitated, then slowly replied in the affirmative. My call must have been like a bolt out of the blue.

I hurried to explain who I was and why I was calling. Kim listened, then replied, "We always wondered… Art will be so glad to learn she had a good life. He still keeps her picture by our bed."

In that instant it all became crystal clear. The love and loyalty Ceilidh had felt for Arthur Forester had been mutual. He hadn't forgotten her any more than she'd forgotten him.

I didn't get to talk to Art on that occasion, but shortly afterwards I received an e-mail from him. It brought a sense of closure for both of us…answered all those nagging questions about the wonderful little dog I'd called my Ceil. And for both Art and me, both of us who'd believed we'd somehow failed her, our meeting gave us each the best feeling of peace we'd ever have where Harborlights Scotia Ceilidh was concerned.

To All the Dogs I've Loved Before

Art's Story

After I found Art and Kim, Art agreed to tell the story of their years with Ceilidh and send along pictures of those times. Art's kindness filled in the gaps and gave closure to the life of a kindly little dog whose middle name should have been Fido (fidelity). Thank you, Art and Kim. Ceilidh and her memory can now rest in peace.

In his own words:

Kim and I married at CFB Cornwallis (NS) in May, 1988. We were both in the military. Kim was an army physiotherapist and I the dashing naval officer. After many years at sea, I was happy to settle down and well, (gulp) raise a family. So, we thought it best to start with a dog. Another couple on the base had a Little River Duck Dog. It was a beautifully gentle dog. So, being a proud Canadian and always looking for the "unique" we (I) decided on a Duck Toller.

I cannot remember how/why we heard of Avery Nickerson, but we were told that his breed of the dog was the best. So we paid a visit to Yarmouth and fell in love with the dogs. Avery and his wife Erna were very kind to us. I think Avery and I bonded as he was a WWII naval vet. They were a wonderful couple. Ceilidh was supposed to go to a hunter in California, but something went wrong—fortunately for us—and she became available to us.

Shortly after our first visit we got a call from the Nickersons and we hurried to Yarmouth to pick up the feisty eight-week-old pup. Right from the start she was beautiful, mischievous, energetic (very), fearless, and all fuzz.

We named her Ceilidh because we loved that Celtic term for celebration. And that is exactly what she was to us...a beautiful, fun-loving dog. We were and still are in love with the Maritimes and its culture. (I'm Irish and Scotch.) Harborlights was, of course, the kennel name. I think the Scotia was added for CKC purposes.

Like new parents, we read all the books on raising a dog. We studied the techniques of those Monks in New England. But, still, we weren't truly prepared for a Duck Toller puppy. We quickly began to think those Monks must have had too much time on their hands! Nevertheless we loved every minute with Ceilidh and her antics.

She soon proved amazingly easy to train. Or maybe I should say she trained us. She was great in the house...apart from occasionally drawing blood from our ankles. And she appeared inexhaustible. Retrieving came naturally to her, and although I was not a hunter, I tried to exercise her in a manner appropriate to her breed. We spent a lot of time on and in the Bay of Fundy, running and hiking. And together we'd jog around the base. I would go fast because during our first base jog Ceilidh insisted on pooping in front of the base commander's office. (I didn't have a bag.) I'm sorry to say (to hunters and breeders) that she had a great propensity for chasing and catching Frisbees and golf balls. She would catch the former at very amazing verticals. I am an amateur golfer who practiced driving off a rise on the Bay. Ceilidh would get the balls for me. The recruits at Cornwallis thought it was pretty neat. As a company commander at the recruit school, I would take Ceilidh down for evening inspections. Once again, the recruits loved her, despite her scratching their nicely waxed floors.

So it was a great life. I stayed at home for three years. Kim and I loved Ceilidh dearly. My two ladies did tend to struggle from time to time, however. I think Ceilidh wasn't happy as being number three in the pack! She displayed this lack of contentment with various amusing(?) acts of defiance against Kim. The most notorious and embarrassing was her appetite of Kim's bras. Our neighbor (we shared a military duplex) came to the door one Saturday morning and politely suggested that we might want to watch Ceilidh's diet. Sure enough, a pooper scoop of our yard revealed bra straps mixed with the feces.

Our time in the Annapolis Valley ended in 1991. It was time for me to go back to sea. As is the fashion for the navy, it came at the worst time…Kim was pregnant with our first daughter, Eryn. I would spend the next nine years at sea (give or take the odd month). We had a second daughter, Katherine, and life became very busy at home. Kim continued to work and struggled to look after our girls and Ceilidh while I was gone. As you can imagine, Ceilidh became number five in the pack and was not overly thrilled. To make matters worse, she was getting very little exercise—she was bored and aggravated.

As my sea time was not about to end, I decided that it was not fair to either Kim or Ceilidh to let the situation continue. Kim wanted to try, but we both feared the situation could only get worse. Ceilidh needed a better life and a family who could look after her.

Reluctantly I called Erna Nickerson. She assured me she could find a good home for Ceilidh if that was what I wanted. She also informed me that her husband Avery had died recently.

My trip to Yarmouth with Ceilidh was probably one of the worst days of my life. Mrs. Nickerson greeted us warmly, but I couldn't stay to chat. Leaving Ceilidh hurt too much. I had to get away…quickly.

My memories of Ceilidh are mixed with love and guilt. We have two lovely dogs now, but they haven't replaced her in my heart. As a boy, I never had a dog. It was my dream to have my own Ceilidh. And then I failed her.

Your love for Ceilidh has made me feel much better about that hard decision I had to make over a dozen years ago. From the pictures you sent, I am certain she was very happy with your family. Thank you for providing her with the life she loved!

Art

Ceilidh's Legacy

Ceilidh left Ron and me a wonderful legacy in the two young dogs she'd so generously adopted and taught to behave. Molly and Barbie-Q went on to be model canine citizens, lovely testimonies to Ceilidh's proud, beautiful, and unquenchable spirit.

As Molly matured, she took over Ceilidh's role as alpha dog in our home. She fetched the newspapers as she'd watched Ceilidh do each morning and became adept at bringing up canned food from our basement.

Barbie-Q, too, accepted her loss with grace and dignity. After a period of mourning, she turned to Molly for companionship and found it. Although there was never to be the intense bond she'd shared with Ceilidh, Barbie-Q adapted to the situation and moved on, a little quieter, a little more reserved, but still our own sweet little foundling.

As a result of her association with Ceilidh, she became an excellent obedience dog, and although we could never show her because of her multi-breed mix (which, at that time made her ineligible), she did serve as a fine example of what could be accomplished with most dogs. Highlighting the plight of abandoned pets, she was featured in *Dogs in Canada Annual* and invited to appear on national television. Only the fact that the show taped in Vancouver, a full Canada away, prevented her becoming a television celebrity coast to coast. At age five, she garnered the caption "Christmas Cutie" in a provincial daily newspaper that had asked for the most appealing pet photos.

Barbie-Q's obedience only suffered lapses when we moved to the cottage for the summer. Loving the freedom our rural property afforded, she often refused to come inside when summoned…by me. If Ron called her, she obeyed. They'd apparently formed a special bond the day he'd found her on the deck, and it would remain a lifelong attachment.

If Ron wasn't available to call her and I went to physically fetch her, she had several tricks to foil my attempts. First, she'd fall on her back, stick four short legs up in the air, and play dead…except for black eyes rolling to watch my every move. When I'd attempt to pick her up, she'd do what I came to call her bag-of-milk imitation. She'd slump all her weight first one way and then another as I tried to carry her. Getting her back into the cottage in this condition was a balancing act.

Then came the day this lack of obedience to me almost got both of us killed…or at the very least, seriously injured.

Ron was away. I'd been walking Molly and Barbie-Q near the back of our property when I saw a strange cloud formation moving toward us. The sky darkened suddenly. I didn't need a meteorologist to tell me a major storm was afoot.

Breaking into a run, I headed for the cottage, the dogs at my heels. We'd barely gotten inside when, through the kitchen window, I saw a wall of rain bearing down on us, a roaring wind accompanying it. The three eighty-foot poplar trees in front of the cottage groaned and bent before its fury. The one directly in front of the cottage gave a gigantic ripping sound. I knew what that meant. Yelling to the dogs to follow, I ran for the back door. Molly obeyed and raced outside with me.

Not my disobedient little Barb. No. She'd hidden somewhere inside.

The wind roared. The tree cracked and bent. I rushed back into the cottage to find her half-hidden under the bed. I grabbed at her hind legs to pull her out, but it was too late. With a mighty crash the tree smashed down on our little cottage.

For a moment I could only lie where I'd flattened myself beside the bed, Barb's legs in my hands. Relief washing over me, I realized the roof was still over our head. I dragged her out and surveyed the damage. The front door had been bashed in by tree limbs, the windows on the upper side of the building obscured by dense branches, but in the main the old place was still standing.

By the time we'd joined Molly outside, the storm had passed as suddenly as it had arrived. I looked about at the carnage...the huge fallen tree, uprooted out of the ground, my broken clothesline, the ruined deck...and realized how lucky Barbie-Q and I had been.

"Look what you almost did to us!" I held Barbie-Q in my arms and spoke sharply to her. "You almost got us both killed!"

She looked up at me, little black eyes bright, and planted a kiss on my nose. I couldn't stay angry at her any longer. I kissed her back as Molly cavorted around us.

The Pug That Came to Dinner

One fine summer's day the year after Ceilidh's passing, when I opened the cottage door to call Molly and Barbie-Q to dinner I was greeted with a new canine. I recognized him. I'd seen him playing on the deck of the cottage across the road. New neighbors had moved in two days earlier. The Pug was part of their family. He looked up at me, big brown eyes round and appealing above the black mask that covered his snout, and wriggled his curly pig-tail.

"Hello," I greeted him as Barb and Molly trotted up the steps and into the cottage.

Beside me Molly paused and looked up. I knew that expression. I glanced over at the neighbors' cottage. No one around. Maybe they'd gone for a walk or swim.

"Okay," I answered Molly's silent request. I looked down at the Pug. "Would you like to stay for dinner?"

He wriggled his tail again, pranced up the steps, and passed me to follow Barb and a now-contented Molly toward the kitchen.

Poor, innocent Molly! How unsuspecting she (or any of us, in fact) was of how this seemingly innocuous-looking, affable Pug that came to dinner would ultimately alter all our lives.

An appreciative guest, his enjoyment of our doggy cuisine became obvious as he burrowed his little black mouth deep into gravy-laced kibble. He even gave a lusty burp and licked his chops with gusto when he'd finished.

"Bruiser! Bruiser, where are you?"

Someone was calling her dog, but surely the Pug couldn't be... I looked down at the eighteen-pound amber-fawn-and-black critter at my feet. He cocked his head to one side, then trotted to the full-length screen door and looked out, tail wiggling. His reaction left no doubt. He was Bruiser.

I opened the door for him and followed him onto the deck.

"He's over here," I called to the young woman in shorts and tank top across the lane. "He stayed to dinner."

"Thanks." She jogged across the road as Bruiser rushed to greet her.

"Unusual name for a Pug," I said as she caught his wiggling body up in her arms.

"I named him after the dog in the movie *Legally Blonde*." She grinned.

"Oh, right," I replied, remembering the charming Chihuahua in the film. "Cute. We enjoyed having him."

"Hope he wasn't any trouble." She waved and headed back across the road carrying the Pug, who seemed intent on licking clear through her epidermis.

"Any time," I called.

The trouble started soon afterwards—the next morning, in fact—when Molly dashed out as usual to fetch the morning paper at the end of the drive. At the corner of our cedar hedge where the carrier normally tossed it, she stopped short. No paper. She lowered her nose and began a serious investigation of the area.

After a few minutes of watching my dog's unsuccessful attempts to find the daily news, I scuffled into my moccasins and went to help her.

Neither of us met with success. I returned to the cottage convinced that our faithful carrier had made her first faux pas or that the paper had not gone to press on time. Molly, a retriever of the never-give-up-on-a-fetch variety, remained on site, rooting around in the shrubbery.

As I reached to open the front door, I saw my new neighbor running across the road in slippers and PJs. She waved something in a blue plastic sleeve. Under her left arm Bruiser hung in an ignominious grip.

"Sorry," she said breathlessly as she ran up the steps. "Bruiser's been watching your dog fetch the paper for the last couple of days. He must have thought it was a good idea, so he brought your paper to us."

"No problem," I replied taking the paper and giving Bruiser a little head-pat. "Shows initiative, right, guy?"

He licked my hand, snuffled a Pug sound, and wriggled his tail. I couldn't help grinning at him.

It's been said you can't outfox a fox, and this soon proved to be the case. As an NSDTR, Molly's legendary roots supposedly (if genetically impossible) come from the red fox. The fact remains that Nova Scotia Duck Tolling Retrievers have been bred to resemble red foxes both in brains and body. So bright and early the next morning, like the rabbit at the cabbage patch, Molly posted herself on the front step.

The Pug would prove a worthy opponent. As I glanced out the front window, I saw a small black-masked snout peering out from the hedge.

I got my coffee and drew up a chair. This was going to be interesting.

A few minutes later the carrier's car appeared over the crest of the knoll. Molly sprang to her feet, alert and ready. In the hedge a small beige-and-black body also braced to attention.

The car slowed at the end of our drive, an arm appeared through its open driver's window, and the morning news flew through the air.

Simultaneously (or so it appeared) both dogs lunged.

The collision occurred at the corner of the hedge. A yelp, a squeal, and a Pug went flying through the air.

Molly paused a moment, shook herself to regain her dignity, then picked up the paper precisely in its middle and triumphantly trotted back to the cottage, the obvious winner in this war for words.

Bruiser scrambled to his paws. He, too, shook vigorously, paused a moment (I assume to make sure he was still intact), then proceeded to prance behind Molly toward the cottage. Definitely no hard feelings on his part.

When I opened the screen door for Molly and accepted the paper she presented "to hand," Bruiser, his *joie de vivre* unabashed, trotted inside behind her, the corners of his mouth curled up in a good-natured grin. He looked up at me, eyes bright, tail wagging, an irresistible little paper pirate.

When Molly received her customary reward for paper delivery, he got one, too. It seemed only the neighborly thing to do.

The following morning it bucketed rain, and Molly opted to watch for the paper from the front window.

She may have speculated the Pug wouldn't come out in such inclement weather for a fetch he now knew he couldn't possibly achieve.

Molly would soon learn never to underestimate the tenacity of a Pug.

I'd gone back into the kitchen when I heard the carrier's car approaching and Molly's excited whines.

"No rush, girl," I assured her as I headed toward the front door to let the now yelping, prancing dog out.

I saw the reason for her distress. Bruiser had darted out of the hedge and lifted his leg. His aim perfect, he peed on her precious blue-sleeved paper.

Molly trotted slowly through the rain toward the bundle. Normally on such a day she'd have been super fast, but on this occasion I understood her reluctance.

When she arrived at the paper she paused. She was waiting for the rain to wash her coveted fetch.

Finally she picked it up, giving poignant illustration of the adverb "gingerly." When I opened the door to let her in, instead of her usual neat "to hand" delivery she spat the blue bundle on the floor at my feet. When I offered her the dog biscuit reward, she dropped it on the floor. Flicking her tongue disgustedly in and out of her mouth, she proceeded to the kitchen to flush away the taste with a long drink of water.

A little exhale that sounded like a sigh drew my attention back to the door. Standing on the step, a drenched Pug looked in at me, tightly curled tail quivering.

"What did you do?" I asked, trying to sound severe. "You should be ashamed."

For a split second two little black ears and curly tail drooped. But it was only for a moment. Then they sprang back into position, pert and alert, even though rain was coursing down his mask. Again the knot that was a tail jiggled. This time the corners of his mask quirked up in a grin.

"Oh, okay, come on in." I shoved open the door. He trotted briskly inside, scooped up the biscuit Molly had rejected, and followed her into the kitchen, munching contentedly.

Five minutes later I found all three dogs curled up on the couch, warm and content. Apparently rivalry began and ended with the paper.

Two weeks later Nancy, Bruiser's mom, crossed the road to ask a favor. She and her partner were going to visit non-dog-fancying relatives for a couple of weeks. Could we keep Bruiser?

No problem, husband Ron and I readily agreed. By then, Bruiser had become a frequent and welcome visitor. Barbie-Q and Molly enjoyed him and so did we. So the Pug that came to dinner gathered up his collar, leash, and bowl and moved in.

"He's housebroken and doesn't chew things," Nancy said as she placed him on the kitchen floor. Looking down at him, she hesitated. "There are only a couple of *tiny* problems," she continued finally, a bit apprehensively. "He steals, and he loves parties."

"Oh?" we replied in surprised unison. The former came as no surprise after the newspaper incidents. But as for partying... A Pug? Really!

"Not to worry," I assured her. "He'll be fine."

The first couple of days nothing untoward occurred. The three dogs played happily on the deck, in the yard, and at the beach. On the third morning, things changed.

When I went to call the dogs in after their morning ablutions, I found a pair of pink plastic flowers, a few of their fake petals missing, on the deck. Remembering having seen them on a neighbor's lawn, I looked at Bruiser sitting beside them, a grin plastered across his pushed-up little face.

"Did you take those?" I asked pointing at the posies. "No, no! Bad boy!"

The black ears dropped—for a moment—before he blinked an eye at me and wiggled his tail.

An hour later, when our neighbor went grocery shopping, I furtively stuck the two worse-for-wear flowers back in her garden.

That was easy, I thought as I trotted home. And now that he knew better, our houseguest wouldn't do it again. He'd looked so contrite.

Hadn't I learned anything from the persistence of his paper pirate days? I wondered later that week as each morning our deck sported new booty. A tennis ball, a toy truck, a plastic shovel, a baseball cap, a deflated beachball (I refused to reflect on how it had gotten into that condition), and, most alarmingly, what looked like a doll's amputated arm.

Worse still, we soon noticed, he'd drawn Barbie-Q into his highwayman antics. She began accompanying him on his raids and started coming home with other dogs' bones and miscellaneous other purloined items.

Then came the day her following the Pug's lead almost got both her and me killed. It happened one Sunday afternoon. Bruiser had decided to go across the road, most likely on yet another scavenging mission. He raced safely across the width of chip seal, Barbie with her shorter legs and less speed at some distance behind.

I spotted them from the front window of the cottage. "Bruiser, no!" I ran out in a vain effort to call him back. Just then I saw a truck coming down the road. Barb was in the center.

"Barbie, no, come back!" I raced after her.

Seeing me, she did her disobedience trick. In the middle of the road, she threw herself on her back and stuck her legs in the air. She looked for all the world like a dead raccoon.

Waving my arms frantically and hoping the driver would see me, I ran to snatch her up.

Fortunately he did, and the truck eased to a stop.

"Did someone hit your dog?" He looked at the prone creature I was trying to gather up from mid road.

"No, no." Struggling to get Barb upright as she went into her milk bag imitation, I staggered to my feet. "She just plays dead sometimes."

"Bad spot for that." He grinned as he eased his truck back into motion and drove past us. Yet another tale for the locals to enjoy about the lady with the dogs.

Bruiser arrived back at the cottage a few minutes later, for once empty-mouthed. By that time we'd more or less given up the struggle to return the ill-gotten gains of this couple of canine culprits. Instead we decided to spread out all of their purloined trinkets on our front lawn as a sort of motley lost-and-found display—your belongings returned, no questions asked.

But then the shoe appeared on the deck. Obviously new, obviously expensive.

"Oh, Bruiser!" I breathed turning the slender, high-heeled strappy sandal over in my hands. "What have you done now!" There could be no doubt about the thief. Barb never took anything but food items.

For a moment my tone of voice made his ears droop and his tail straighten. For a moment he looked almost ashamed. Almost. And only for a moment. Then his tail re-knotted, his ears went up, and his wide mouth widened in that now-familiar roguish grin.

Ron joined me on the deck.

"There's only one thing to do," he said.

He took the shoe from my hand and, like the Prince in Cinderella, set off down the road to find someone with its mate.

Lady Luck, like the summer sun, must have shone on him that day. Two cottages away he spotted a similar shoe on a front porch. Possibly someone returning late from a party had opted to shed their elegant footwear before going inside. Since no one yet appeared to be stirring, Ron was able to replace the footwear unobserved.

"That's it." Ron picked up the Pug on his return and looked him squarely in the eyes. "No more stealing, understand?"

For a moment black ears drooped, tail unknotted, and the broad mouth sagged. For a moment one could almost believe he was truly sorry. Almost.

The moment Ron replaced the canine culprit on the deck, his entire body flashed back to perky exuberance. He turned on his partner in crime, who'd been dozing in the sun, and began racing around her, barking and daring her to play.

At first she ignored him, but when he dove in to pull her tail, she leaped to her feet and took off after him. Tucking his tail between his legs—he'd learned Barbie-Q could often get close enough to seize him by it when it curled over his back—he dashed away. As they made circuit after circuit of the cottage, barking and yelping, Ron asked, "When did Nancy say she'd be back?"

That evening marked the beginning of a long weekend in New Brunswick. Shortly after six p.m. the air became rich with the smell of barbecuing beef and pork from our neighbor's barbecues. All three dogs lying on the deck, bellies full of supper, sniffed deeply. Leaving them to savor the aroma, I went inside to clear away our dishes.

When I returned to the deck twenty minutes later, Bruiser was missing. I wasn't overly concerned. Mr. Congeniality, as we'd nicknamed him, usually took a little trot among the neighbors' cottages each evening. He was popular and well-liked.

But when nine p.m. arrived and he hadn't returned, I set out to look for him. Yes, most of our neighbors informed me, he'd visited, but he wasn't around now.

As darkness and mosquitoes gathered around me, I headed home. I hoped to find him on the deck. No such luck.

When the rest of our household settled to sleep— "He'll be along," Ron said confidently as he headed off to bed—I curled up to wait on the couch with a book. The situation brought back memories of when I'd waited up anxiously for three teenagers.

I awoke with a start. Paws on the deck. I stumbled to my feet and switched on the outdoor light. There he stood, a big T-bone thick with meat and barbecue sauce clamped in his jaws. He looked completely spent.

"*Where* have you been?" I scolded opening the door for him.

He glanced up at me a trifle disdainfully, then

stumbled up the steps and past me into the cottage, still clutching his booty. He reeked of meat fat and barbecue sauce.

He looked up at me again and gave a weary sigh before continuing toward the kitchen. With a grunt, he climbed up onto the couch that had become his bed at our house. With what appeared to be the last of his energy, he buried his booty under a pillow before settling to rest. The task completed, with another sigh, he sank down on top of it and closed his eyes. His belly, bloated with the results of foraging from party to party, stuck out from beneath him.

I should have been annoyed. Instead I found a chuckle bubbling in my throat. Bruiser gave literal meaning to the phrase Party Animal.

Nancy arrived home several days later. With big news. And a request. She'd decided to join the armed forces. Could we keep Bruiser while she was away at boot camp and basic training?

Ron and I exchanged glances and looked down at the most affable little rogue we'd ever known. He needed a home, and we had room both in our house and in our hearts. We'd gotten three children through their teen and university years. Surely we could handle one small dog for a few weeks or months or…

"Okay," we agreed.

For some reason Molly chose that moment to demonstrate a trick I'd been trying to teach her for several days. She lay down on the deck and covered both eyes with her paws.

Bruiser, sitting beside her, grinned.

Molly, Mist and Me

Eventually Nancy admitted that she couldn't care for Bruiser while she was a member of the armed forces and allowed us to adopt him permanently. Ron and I were back to having a trio of dogs. For a number of years we were a happy group. This small pack consisted of a balance of dogs, easy to manage in any circumstance. A lot of this was Ceilidh's legacy.

Things changed when I took Molly for her yearly checkup the spring she turned twelve. The vet assured me she was in excellent health, but when we moved to the cottage in May, Ron mentioned that Molly wasn't quite herself. I should have listened to him. Ron has always been an excellent barometer when it comes to our dogs' health. I simply couldn't face the possibility that Molly might be ill. We'd been through so many canine losses. I didn't think I could bear another one.

Here, I admit, I fell short of being a good caregiver. Traumatized by the passing of other beloved canine companions, I refused to admit anything was wrong. I'd resigned from my position as an executive assistant in the local school district ten years earlier to be with my husband and dogs and to write, thus allowing all three dogs to become my almost constant companions, especially Molly. While Barbie-Q tended to think of Ron as her person and Bruiser saw both of them as his boon companions, Molly and I had bonded completely.

We snowshoed together in winter and took long, solitary rambles on the beach and marsh in spring, summer, and fall. One of our favorite activities was walking through the tall marsh grass on an isolated shoreline on foggy mornings. The vision of Molly's beautiful red tail waving ahead of me in the mist will always be one of my most cherished memories of emotional peace. The silence, the feeling that there were only she and I in this mysterious, gossamer world often brought the words, "Molly, Mist, and Me" to mind as story title…a story I would not write until now.

In late May, with a tingle of fear starting around my heart, I began to admit Ron might be correct. Molly was making mistakes, forgetting which way I threw a stick, running back to shore with it only to gaze about in confusion as she tried to find me. Sometimes she refused to give up a fetch, clinging to it for dear life, something she'd never done, even as an untrained pup.

Then came the dreadful morning in late June when she started out of the cottage for her morning ablutions and fell down the steps. Struggling to her feet at the bottom, she looked up at me, beautiful amber eyes registering fear and confusion.

"She slipped in the dew," I told myself. "There's nothing wrong."

But the next day her disorientation worsened. She stumbled into a chair in the cottage and stared about, seemingly unable to focus. Still I wouldn't admit she had a serious problem. I couldn't bear to lose her, my soul mate, my Molly of the Mist.

The next day we were invited to go sailing by a neighbor. I hesitated. Molly seemed fine, sleeping in the air-conditioned cottage with lots of water provided and the companionship of Barbie-Q and Bruiser. The others were insistent. She'd be fine, they claimed. And so off I went on a voyage I would forever view as one of the worst mistakes of my life.

When we got back that evening, Molly was staggering about, completely disoriented. When I helped her outside to relieve herself, I practically had to carry her down the steps. Once on the ground, she stumbled and began circling aimlessly.

"We have to go to the vet," Ron said.

I knew, with my heart plummeting, that he was right.

The next morning we took her to our vet and received the dreadful news. Molly had an untreatable brain tumor. There was only one fair decision to make.

And so I lost my beautiful Molly of the Mist. I will never forgive myself for being persuaded to take that sailing adventure on the second last day of her life. I should have followed my heart and stayed with my best friend.

Now, on mornings when the air is thick with fog and silence shrouds the marsh, I believe I can still see her beautiful tail flagging ahead of me and know my Molly of the Mist is not so very far away and that she's forgiven me as she forgave all my shortcomings during her dozen years with me. A lesson in the largeness of the canine heart.

Fancy

For several years prior to Molly's passing, I'd been corresponding by e-mail with a British Columbia lady named Joan Trask. She and her husband Harold owned a cattle ranch at Pink Mountain. She'd purchased my Toller books when she bought her first Toller from my friends Jim and Deanna Jeffery and thus we "met" and became friends.

Once Joan discovered I was an avid equine fancier, she began to send me photos and information about the beautiful horses on her ranch. When one especially beautiful foal was born, she allowed me to name her. I chose Fancy from the old Oak Ridge Boys song "I'm Setting Fancy Free."

Fancy grew to be a beautiful charcoal-colored filly with a silver mane and tail. Joan kept me informed about her. She and her photos and news of Fancy became an important part of my enjoyment of life.

Fancy was not like the other horses on the ranch, Joan wrote. She'd been conceived when the ranch stallion got at Harold's favorite mare in an unauthorized visit. After she was born, a bit later than the other foals, she bonded more with the dogs in the dooryard than the horse herd on the mountain.

A beautiful if somewhat shy girl, she finally found a friend among the ranch horses and headed out on the range to take her place in the herd. I looked forward to

Joan's letters describing the maturing, uniquely beautiful Fancy.

Suddenly Joan's e-mails stopped. Puzzled, I thought perhaps she'd decided to end our internet friendship. It had happened with other e-mail correspondents, but losing Joan would be a sad day indeed for me. We'd formed a special horse-dog fancier relationship.

Finally Joan's e-mail arrived, but it was not until the second paragraph that she found the courage to tell me the reason for the hiatus in her correspondence. Fancy had been killed in a terrible accident on the ranch, struck by a truck, along with a companion horse.

I couldn't believe it. The beautiful little filly I'd come to know so well through Joan's photos and e-mails was gone. She'd been like my own horse, my very own, very special horse. The computer screen blurred as tears filled my eyes. Fancy was gone.

The following summer, Molly was gone, too. Suffering the pain of her loss, Ron declared, "No more dogs." Like my father, he'd had all the pain he could take. As for myself, I felt certain there'd never be another dog I would bond with like I had with Molly. And so the summer passed. Bruiser and Barbie-Q mourned her loss, then returned to the intimacy of their companionship.

Two months to the day after Molly's passing, I received a call from Andy Wallace. He first expressed his sympathy at our loss, then cautiously mentioned he had a red female pup that had been born on Labor Day weekend to his bitch Sox. Maybe it was too soon, he said, but...

When I finished the call, I went out into the

backyard to tell Ron.

"No." His reply was emphatic. We were too old to get involved with a pup. And furthermore...

I went back inside, picked up the phone, and called Andy.

"We're taking the pup," I informed him. "Her name will be Fancy."

Eight weeks later, my friends Roberta and Keith MacKenzie went to Yarmouth to pick up a pup they named Fawna, a half-sister to Fancy. They brought both pups back to New Brunswick.

During the nearly two months I'd waited for Fancy to become old enough to leave her mother, Ron never once mentioned the pup. His disapproval was evident in every move he made, every word he didn't speak.

On the evening Fancy arrived at our house, Ron came up from his basement den while the family was exclaiming over her cuteness. He looked at her for a few moments, then reached out for her.

"Give me the little dog," he said. He took her and carried her gently back downstairs. When I found them a few minutes later, Fancy was fast asleep, curled up against his sock feet.

Fancy arrived at our home the Sunday before Halloween. In the process of her socialization, we decided to have Ron sit in the living room with the puppy on his knee while he handed out treats to our costumed visitors.

All went well, with children and puppy equally delighted with each other, until a two-year-old toddled into the room dressed as a lion. He made his way over to Ron and the treats, opened his sack, and ordered, "Put puppy in bag."

"No, no." Startled by the child's misunderstanding, Ron tried to be gentle in his refusal. "The puppy isn't a treat."

"Put puppy in bag!" This time the words weren't a request, they were an order.

"No, no, honey, they're not giving away puppies." His mother came into the room to collect her determined son, but when she tried to take his hand to lead him away, he yanked free and screamed, "Put puppy in bag!!!"

The last we saw, they were going up the street, the mother carrying a screeching, kicking toddler who still demanded a puppy in his bag.

Misunderstandings can come from the most innocuous events.

A Heart Too Large

Shortly after Molly's passing, Barbie-Q developed a disturbing cough. We took her to the vet, and she was given a prescription. It helped for a while, but then the cough worsened. Over the winter the vet tried various treatments, suggested our woodstove and carpets might be causing allergic reactions. But by spring the cough had developed into such a retching, painful-sounding thing the vet decided x-rays and more tests were in order. We agreed.

When we returned several hours later to pick Barb up, the vet summoned me into her examining room to show me the x-rays.

"Look," she said, pointing. "Look at how badly enlarged her heart is. It's huge for such a small dog."

I stared at the mound on the screen as the thought flashed through my mind that we'd always said she had to have a big heart to be capable of so much love. Now, ironically, a large heart was killing her.

She was put on strong doses of barbiturates, and for over eighteen months she struggled along. Then the bouts of coughing became one after another, the gagging retches at the end of each making my heart ache. She never gave in to self-pity or lay around listlessly. She went to the park with Bruiser on short walks that seemed to relieve her cough. Her dark, bright eyes greeted me each morning at six a.m. when, after the first coughing bout of the day, she seemed to know she needed the small ball of meat that contained her pill.

Finally she was so weakened she could barely stand. On a fine Sunday in July we took her, Bruiser, and Fancy to a quiet beach. For a short time she seemed to revive, even going for a swim.

But the next day her struggles became too great. We took her to the vet, who said there were no more medications that would help. We'd seen that look on a vet's face too many times not to know what had to be.

We buried Barbie-Q with her friends Chance, Ceilidh, and Molly. As I stood by her grave, I recalled the words of a lady I'd met once when walking Barb as a nondescript puppy. Beside Ceidilh, her beautiful surrogate parent, Barbie-Q appeared a ragtag little creature.

"She's not as pretty as her mom," I remarked as the lady knelt to look at her.

"Love will make her beautiful," she said softly, stroking the little brown head.

I never again encountered that lady. Perhaps she was a good angel sent to confer a benediction onto the foundling. Whatever the reason, Barbie-Q grew into a truly lovely-looking little dog, so pretty, in fact, people often stopped us on our walks to ask where we'd gotten her and if there were any more like her available.

The little dog's angel had indeed watched over our girl and blessed her with beauty and a heart filled with love. We'd always regard her as a most special gift that love had indeed made beautiful.

Into the Future

Fancy, still more or less a puppy, moved on with life after Barb's passing, but not Bruiser. He became despondent, refused to play. He'd never return to the beach where he'd spent so many happy hours playing in the water with her. Instead, when we'd go to the shore, he'd sit down dejectedly by the front tire of our Jeep and remain there until we'd had our swim and returned. We'd jokingly nicknamed him Mr. Congeniality because of his affability with all living creatures. Now Mr. Congeniality had lost his glow, his *joie de vivre*. Even Fancy's playful antics couldn't revive him. It was the story of Jet and Brandy all over again, the story of one dog mourning another. We knew there was no easy solution. We'd just have to wait and hope he'd recover.

It took nearly a year. He moped and appeared to lack energy for anything other than eating and sleeping. But finally, the following spring, one beautiful June day when I drove him and Fancy to the beach near our cottage, he came out of his slump.

Feeling confident that he'd remain by the Jeep, I headed off with Fancy through the burgeoning marsh grass. Fancy was on her third water retrieve when my peripheral vision caught something white moving into place beside me.

Glancing down, I saw Bruiser looking up at me. His round eyes told the story. He was back.

I threw another tennis ball, and he leaped into the water. In under a minute, he was back with it clamped in his jaws, tail wagging. It wasn't flogging wildly as it would have been if Barb had been by his side, but still it was curled over his back and moving.

Recovery doesn't happen in a single day and is seldom complete.

These days Fancy and Bruiser companion me. I call Fancy my sunshine, since she's the reason I get up bright and early each morning and head for the park. Bruiser takes his airing later, ambling along the walking paths, greeting each and every one of his friends in his old Mr. Congeniality fashion. Perhaps there's a little less skip in his trot and a little less mischievous gleam in his eye, and perhaps without his Bonnie by his side his thieving Clyde days are over, but there's still a lot of spunk in the old guy.

Epilogue

When Bruiser turned nine, his health became a problem. He developed a lump on his eyelid that had to be removed, and his crooked Pug teeth caused so many problems a number had to be extracted. The winter he turned ten, the vet made the comment that she'd never seen a Pug survive beyond a decade. This turned into a dire prediction. Shortly he began to bleed from his anal glands. It took three surgeries to repair the damage. Then he developed diabetes. We set him up on a regime of insulin and diabetic food, but as spring turned to summer it was obvious the disease was gaining an upper hand. He became lethargic and no longer wanted to go to the park to play with his dog friends.

Growing thinner and thinner in spite of regular visits to the vet for evaluation, he began to lose his eyesight. Those bright, round eyes that had glistened with mischief and the happiness of life grew dim and clouded. Fearful of his new, rapidly darkening world, he'd stand in the center of a room, a small statue, and frequently lost control of his bladder. By the time Hurricane Arthur struck our area in early July, Bruiser was totally blind, and the storm terrified him. Trembling in my arms, his emaciated little body rigid with terror, he told me the time had come. Five days later Bruiser crossed the rainbow bridge to be with his friend Barbie-Q.

Bruiser left behind wonderful memories and a glowing example of what happens when you see only the best in others. He met everyone who entered his life with a wide grin and a wiggling tail. Outgoing and happy-go-lucky, he greeted each new person and animal with the expectation of liking them and of their liking him. His approach never failed. In all the years he shared our lives, he was never disappointed in his optimistic outlook.

He taught me to expect and look for only the best in others. If the entire world would adopt the philosophy of this happy little bandit, what a truly wonderful place it would be.

Thank you, Bruiser boy. You may have travelled in and out my door...sometimes even with a T-bone steak dangling from your jaws...but you, like all those wonderful canines who've gone before you, will never exit my heart.

From all these wonderful, beloved creatures, most importantly, I've learned I was right when I told my father all those years ago that it wasn't the pain of loss that should overwhelm us with each passing but the memory of all the love that had gone before.

A word about the author...

Gail MacMillan is the award-winning author of over thirty published books, with numerous articles published in magazines throughout North America and Western Europe.
Visit her at:
macgail@nbnet.nb.ca

~*~
Other Books by Gail MacMillan available from The Wild Rose Press, Inc.
Non-Fiction:
How My Heart Finds Christmas
Historical Romance:
Highland Harry
Heather for a Highlander
Shadows of Love
Caledonian Privateer
Lady and the Beast
Contemporary Romance:
Cowboy and the Crusader
Counterfeit Cowboy
Rogue's Revenge
Holding Off for a Hero
Ghost of Winters Past
Contemporary Suspense:
Phantom and the Fugitive

Thank you for purchasing
this publication of The Wild Rose Press, Inc.

If you enjoyed the story, we would appreciate your
letting others know by leaving a review.

For other wonderful stories,
please visit our on-line bookstore at
www.thewildrosepress.com.

For questions or more information
contact us at
info@thewildrosepress.com.

The Wild Rose Press, Inc.
www.thewildrosepress.com

Stay current with The Wild Rose Press, Inc.

Like us on Facebook

https://www.facebook.com/TheWildRosePress

And Follow us on Twitter
https://twitter.com/WildRosePress